OPEN YOUR EYES

TO 2012 AND BEYOND

Drew R. Maras

authorHOUSE®

AuthorHouse™
1663 Liberty Drive
Bloomington, IN 47403
www.authorhouse.com
Phone: 1-800-839-8640

First published by AuthorHouse 7/9/2010

ISBN: 978-1-4389-8246-5 (e)
ISBN: 978-1-4389-8244-1 (sc)
ISBN: 978-1-4389-8245-8 (hc)

Printed in the United States of America
Bloomington, Indiana

This book is printed on acid-free paper.

The following book deals with controversial subjects. The theories, opinions, and beliefs expressed are not the only possible interpretation. Readers are invited to make a judgment based on all available information.

TABLE OF CONTENTS

Preface...vii

Introduction..xi

CHAPTER 1: Established Prophecies of Dire Warning.....................1

CHAPTER 2: Alien Intervention with Past Civilizations 19

CHAPTER 3: What the Government Doesn't Want You to
　　　　　　Know 41

CHAPTER 4: The Biggest Catch in the Sea...............................123

CHAPTER 5: Our Untamed Galactic Backyard 155

CHAPTER 6: The World as We Don't See it................................163

CHAPTER 7: What We do in Life Echoes in Eternity.................171

CHAPTER 8: The Tangled Knot From Hell Left by the Bush
　　　　　　Administration...191

CHAPTER 9: America, The Confused..235

CHAPTER 10: Prepare for the End of Life as We Know It 245

PREFACE

The Apocalypse, Armageddon, Judgment Day, Doomsday, the End of Days. This book is the key. This book is the light. This book is your guide and roadmap to navigating the revelation, and most importantly, this book is the Rosetta Stone to deciphering a once-every-25,800-year galactic alignment set to occur next on December 21, 2012. *Open Your Eyes: To 2012 and Beyond* will lay a foundation and build a framework around 2012 to help ascertain the answers to a question synonymous with ambiguity. When will the world as we know it end? What I don't understand is how so many individuals draw conclusions to things they know nothing about, or come to foregone conclusions on subjects that we don't have all the information on yet. Unexplored subjects where each and every day brings forth new discoveries not known the day before. "December 21, 2012 is just a Y2K paranoid theory where nothing is going to happen," "aliens aren't real," "we are alone in the universe," and "there was no conspiracy to kill JFK" are the shortsighted mentalities that *Open Your Eyes* will polish and spit shine by the book's end. These types of stale ideologies are equivalent to the "Earth is flat" statement from past scientists who were proven wrong when Earth was discovered to be round. *Open Your Eyes* will release us from our programmed minds in order to shed light and truth on provocative subjects bound together far from coincidence.

In order to incorporate a revamped mentality, *Open Your Eyes: To 2012 and Beyond* will act as a Marine Corps drill instructor. Subconsciously, our brains have been programmed with a certain ideology absorbed from our past and present surrounding environments. We all know old habits are hard to break. The only way to learn a new concept is through repetition and reiteration, which is exactly why drill instructors are so effective in shaping new mentalities from old molds. Think of a dog when learning a new trick or unlearning a bad habit; it's the same principle for us humans. It can take a while to re-program a set-in-stone stubborn mentality and takes constant effort in order to succeed. Well ladies and gentlemen, December 21, 2012 is right around the corner, so the speed at which we must unlearn our bad habits is paramount, to say the least.

My brain has sponged vital information throughout my life that I'd really like to share with you. Trust me, if I could sing or play a guitar I would give you my message through lyrics and a song instead of a book. However, that vocal shoe does not fit as I can't sing, but I can and am blessed to write the book inside of me. I'd like my book, *Open Your Eyes: To 2012 and Beyond*, to act as an air raid or tornado siren to get not only your attention, but to raise the flag of awareness. It's not only what I've been through, but it's my perception of the world and how I see it from behind my eyes that I'm honored and privileged to share with you. Unorthodox thinking is my platform and launch pad for exploration into literally opening your eyes. I am so intrigued by the hot topics I'm about to share with you that I have information percolating through my brain and can't type fast enough to relay my thoughts to paper, not to mention the fact that I had three cups of Columbian coffee and am all hopped up trying to type 1,000 words per minute...just kidding. I've traded my past Marine Corps uniform and infantry weapons for a pen to set us free from being programmed slaves and reveal the truth about December 21, 2012. We will be covering ground on topics including: prophecies from the Bible, Torah, and Koran, the Maya, Nostradamus, the Web Bot Oracle, St. Malachi, the great Egyptian pyramids, the Incas, the Hopi Indians, the I Ching Oracle, Merlin, NASA and Planet X (a.k.a., Nibiru), the "ancient astronaut theory," flying machines and vimanas, polar shift, Albert Einstein, the invention of the airplane in 1903 by the Wright Brothers, UFOs seen by astronauts, pilots, and military officials, the UFO fabric (i.e., cattle mutilations, crop circles, alien encounters and abductions), Roswell, the mass UFO sightings over Washington D.C. and the Capitol Building in 1952, USOs and deep sea alien life, the Lost City of Atlantis, Area 51, the Dulce Base in New Mexico, reverse and back-engineering of UFOs, "The Phoenix Lights" spectacle on March 13, 1997, the Midway and Chicago O'Hare International Airport UFO sightings of 2006, the Tinley Park, Illinois mass UFO sightings of 2004, energy vortexes (i.e., Stonehenge, Easter Island, Chile, Machu Picchu, Peru, the ancient pyramids of Egypt, Sedona, Arizona, the Bermuda Triangle, the Dragon's Triangle), Puma Punku, Bolivia, the Nazca Lines in Peru, black holes, gamma-ray bursts, super-volcanoes (i.e., Yellowstone National Park, Wyoming and Mammoth Mountain, California), the universe, organized religion, the Bush Legacy, 9/11, the art of misdirection, John McCain vs. Barack Obama 2008, Iraq and Afghanistan, the 2000 Presidential recount of Bush vs. Gore, the JFK assassination, NASA and space exploration, Vietnam, black/covert operations, the U.S. military-industrial complex, collateral damage, love and relationships, the business of college, and made-up holidays are all topics of exploration. However, the bulk—meat and potatoes—of *Open Your Eyes* is to address how many of these "top secret" and "classified" topics correlate and work synergistically, culminating in a doomsday event foreseen to commence on the winter solstice of 2012. Keep in mind that many of these topics are highly debated and ridiculed, most not indoctrinated into mainstream science. And, since the government can easily cover up and discredit one story as a hoax, my book provides a plethora of credible sources and cited documents to open your eyes to a sobering realization.

Each chapter provides you with a synopsis on each subject and a piece of the, as they say in the movie, *JFK*, "mystery wrapped in a riddle inside an enigma." Together we will captain our ship and navigate through the rough seas to find clarity and discover the treasure of truth. So, let us embark on this journey into the depths of *Open Your Eyes: To 2012 and Beyond.*

INTRODUCTION

December 21, 2012, is the end of time as we know it. It's the beginning of the end, a prelude to the End of Days. In *Open Your Eyes,* the answers to how, why, what, when, and where will all be addressed in due time. We must keep in mind this is not some lone prophet's predicted date and not some fallible Y2K theory that MIGHT happen. This is a date predicted thousands of years apart by the Maya, Incas, NASA, ancient Egyptians, Bible Code, the Hopi Indians, Black Elk of the Sioux Indians, I Ching Oracle (i.e., Book of Changes), Merlin, Nostradamus, St. Malachi, the Web Bot Oracle, and not to mention the man who figured out $E=MC^2$, the one and only Albert Einstein. The great galactic alignment that is about to occur within the next four years is bigger than me, it's bigger than you, it's bigger than all of us, yet it will greatly affect how we live on planet Earth and will directly affect you, me, and all of us that call Earth home. With so much brilliance and discovery that came before us, why haven't we listened to their advice and their warning of events to come? It's like these prophets left us their field manuals and the pieces to the grand puzzle—clues, if you will—and we just threw them away without even trying to put the pieces together and understand the puzzle. No, it's more likely that these pieces are just being hidden from the public to avoid panic because the last thing the government wants is pandemonium. They want order, they want structure, and most of all they want CONTROL. Even if the media received word on some of these issues, the subject would wither away and die long before making print. Press is regulated, period, and there's always someone who can be gotten to. Whether they are gotten to through a bribe of being paid off not to leak information, an editor who's on some corrupt agency's payroll, through fear of being fired, or even beaten and killed, there's always a way to keep a high profile story with a war zone amount of flak silent. There's a strong chance that control could morph into chaos and the world as we know it, end, beginning December 21, 2012. Unfortunately, our poisoned American capitalistic and narcissistic culture and media care more about the whereabouts of Paris Hilton, Britney Spears, and Lindsay Lohan than discussing a species-endangering issue, and the endangered species is US. Now, common sense goes a long way and tells me that these life threatening issues SHOULD be headlining all the major news channels and newspapers. However, this is not the case since the government regulating agencies want control, structure, order, and obedience, even if it means silencing and concealing the truth. This is unacceptable, people! Instead, these pages rectify the dire issues at hand, act as a crowbar to pry open a vaulted door that has remained shut for far too long, and most importantly, to start a chain reaction of critical mass.

Greed Can Precede the Downfall of a Civilization

Our problems start at the beginning, which is why our excessive greed must be addressed. What's your mentality when you open your eyes in the morning? Is it more of the same old, same old ideology or is it a world of possibilities, unknown adventure, and spontaneity that awaits you each day? After reading this book, hopefully the next time you literally open your eyes you will see an entirely different realm of the truth in an entirely new light with an overhauled perspective. First, which is really the biggest step towards enlightenment and opening your eyes, we all must learn to release ourselves from the self-centered narcissistic propaganda and poison that a majority of our population currently subscribes to. We MUST detach ourselves from self-interests, our obsession with worldly things, the conquest for material wealth and the never-ending cycle of impulse buys that we're convinced we NEED to have. Only after we've lost everything can we be free to do anything and then, and only then, can we have a rebirth, attain enlightenment and free our spiritual selves lost within. "Happy are those conscious of their spiritual need" (Matthew 5:3). True happiness can only be found if we take steps to fill our greatest need—our hunger for spiritual truth about God and his purpose for us. For millions of people across the globe, truth and salvation are found in the Bible, the Koran, the Torah, and many other pure sources of belief. Truth can help us discern what is really important and what is not.

In our 2010 world, obsessive self-interests and narcissistic behavior create a roadblock and hinder many from reaching true spiritual enlightenment, nirvana, and Zen. We must detach ourselves from this destructive way of life. When the number one cause for murder is money we know that the dark side of the force is strong, and that the Devil is recruiting his army of darkness. Many have unknowingly pushed God aside and forfeited that relationship to follow a path of greed and sin derived from the Devil. From a Christian point of view, "allowing Bible truth to guide our decisions and actions leads to a more meaningful life" (Luke 11:28) because once our eyes have been opened we will see that the best jewel in this life is the reward of helping and giving. We need to be asking ourselves how we can help one another instead of hurting each other. We have to stop being so shortsighted and start experiencing all the colors of the spectrum and not just the ones we're seeing now. We all must open our eyes and start thinking on another level where black is white and white is black. Too seldom do we unchain ourselves from the binding shackles of our everyday hustle and bustle to look up and gaze at the stars in the night sky or the clouds taking shape before a storm. We need to pause for a moment in order to rediscover our lost innocence, to reinvent ourselves and our lost, childlike imaginations. We need to open our eyes and ears to see and listen to the unspoken beauty behind Mother Earth's elements and feel the beauty of God's architecture. Too seldom do we open our eyes to honor true enlightenment through the naturally created tryst found within God's pristine wilderness. We must rediscover ourselves, our imaginations, and be the orchestrators of our lives in their entireties, compose our own music and reopen our eyes to a world of cerebral nirvana. This is an unorthodox book crafted for believers and nonbelievers alike. A book made to circumvent the system and designed to challenge our hardwired, programmed-since-we-were-born way of thinking. It is a book entailing an outside-of-the-box style of thinking, a book of metaphors, innuendos, onomatopoeias and euphemisms, a book of "what ifs" and possibilities, right or wrong, to challenge our human minds to explore further than we've ever been. In a nutshell, this is the epitome of everything we're never taught in school regarding the matters that NEVER make the front page of the papers or headline news but somehow dictate our country's every action and direction. This book is tailored to address the things that don't exist—but do. Some may ask "how can something not exist but exist?" That's a great question and after reading *Open Your Eyes: To 2012 and Beyond* you will understand. This precocious knowledge may not be conducive to everyone's particular beliefs and tastes, but the point of *Open Your Eyes* is to have us break on through to the other side intellectually, and most importantly to provide us with a master, universal key so that we can open cranial doors that were locked before in order to see what lies behind. Some of *Open Your Eyes: To 2012 and Beyond* may come across as hard to believe with your current ideology, but throughout the course, and especially after completion of the book, there will be no denying how many of these subjects integrate and blossom in the year 2012, a year of great change that we all need to accustom ourselves with.

The Clock is Ticking

Like anything in life, change is inevitable, but this time it's not going to leave us in a better place—or will it? The compelling question of "when will the world end?" passed down from generation to generation, is about to be answered in our lifetimes, and within the next four years. By then it will be too late for many and the "I wish I would've, I wish I could've" saying will become the greatest cliché of all time. Most people in this world are living in their comfort zone, their complacency bubble, where everything is safe and routine, mundane and predictable. However, our merry-go-round ride is about to end so we all need to wake up and open your eyes to an event that's stirring in the cosmos and the heavens above us, a power and force greater than all of us. If you knew that your life and the world as you knew it would change forever, how would you live your life differently? Would you start to believe in God? Would you become a better person or worse? Would you start healing or start stealing? The old cliché, "live everyday as if it were your last" may actually become a trend. The reason being the apocalyptic date lurking around the corner. Tick, tock, tick, tock, tick, tock...the sand in our hourglass of time is reaching the end of days yet we still haven't opened our eyes to see what's ahead—and it's already 2010.

Through collective prophecies we know what's to come in the future chapters of OUR human book, but still we act as if we do not know. Maybe it's that deep down inside we don't want to read and acknowledge the final chapter on the demise of our human race. Well, fate is closing in as we are coming up on the final chapter of our book of existence, the Book of Revelations is starting to bear fruit and we need to raise the level of global awareness ASAP. Our blindness to acknowledge what's to come is, at the moment, our biggest flaw and downfall as a human species. The biggest threat that mankind faces is ourselves with our current monotonous way of thinking. Just as the dinosaurs were the dominant species of our planet billions of years ago, so are we as of recent times, AND just as the dinosaurs were guests on planet Earth so are we. 95 percent of Earth's past habitants have gone extinct so why do so many think the human species will endure forever? Most are shortsighted and naive and cannot possibly fathom the idea that we are just fragile guests inhabiting a planet that harbors so much life and diversity, yet that's exactly what we are—temporary and fragile guests. A billion years from now, if our sun is still shining bright, another intelligent species may manifest itself on Earth, dig up our remains, and study our past to understand the footprint left by humans left on Earth.

I am a dreamer and hope to see the day where we not only understand the Biblical principle that "all men are created equal," but we actually live and breathe it. A world where we don't discriminate according to the color of one's skin, race, creed, or country. Could we ever unite under one flag? Imagine a coalescent world with no Russian flag, no Chinese flag, no British flag, no American flag, no North Korean flag, no Iranian flag, no French flag, no German flag. Just one flag—an Earth flag—united as one, working together in harmony. It seems like it would take an event of epic proportion to open our eyes, a global event or catastrophe, possibly December 21, 2012, to bring human beings back to where we need to be, which is to be caring, loving, and helping human beings, not narcissistic, capitalistic money hungry monsters segregated according to wealth. Ronald Regan, the Great Communicator, hit the nail on the head when he stated to the Forty-Second United Nations General Assembly on September 21, 1987, "In our obsession with antagonisms of the moment, we often forget how much unites all the members of humanity. Perhaps we need some outside, universal threat to make us recognize this common bond. I occasionally think how quickly our differences worldwide would vanish if we were facing an alien threat from outside of this world. And yet—I ask—is not an alien force already among us?" (http://www.presidentialufo.com/reagan_ufo_story.htm)

President Regan, a witness to UFO activity, helped unveil the secrecy curtain from the discussion and ridicule of UFOs and specifically requested that the alien invasion piece be added to his speech to the United Nations. After Regan's presidential term, which the UFO security handlers had survived, the next president George (Herbert Walker) Bush, former CIA Director, brought disclosure to the subject. JFK, a man of fortitude, also hit the nail on the head when he spoke June 10th, 1963, at the American University in Washington when he passionately advocated,

"I have therefore, chosen this time and this place to discuss a topic on which ignorance too often abounds and the truth is too rarely perceived—yet it is the most important topic on Earth: world peace. What kind of peace do I mean? What kind of peace do we seek? Not a Pax Americana enforced on the world by American weapons of war. Not the peace of the grave or the security of the slave. I am talking about genuine peace, the kind of peace that makes life on earth worth living, the kind that enables men and nations to grow and to hope and to build a better life for their children—not merely peace for Americans but peace for all men and women—not merely peace in our time but peace for all time. I speak of peace because of a new face of war. Total war makes no sense in an age when great powers can maintain large and relatively invulnerable nuclear forces and refuse to surrender without resort to those forces. It makes no sense in an age when a single nuclear weapon contains almost ten times the explosive force delivered by eleven of the Allied air forces in the Second World War. It makes no sense in an age when the deadly poisons produced by a nuclear exchange would be carried by wind and water and soil and seed to the far corners on the globe and to generations yet unborn. Today the expenditure of billions of dollars every year on weapons acquired for the purpose of making sure we never need to use them is essential to keeping the peace. But surely the acquisition of such idle stockpiles—which can only destroy and never create—is not the only, much less the most efficient, means of assuring peace. I speak of peace, therefore, as the necessary rational end to rational men. I realize that the pursuit of peace is not as dramatic as the pursuit of war—and frequently the words of the pursuer fall on deaf ears. But we have no more urgent task. Some say that it is useless to speak of world peace or world law or world disarmament—and that it will be useless until the leaders of the Soviet Union adopt a more enlightened attitude. I hope they do. I believe we can help them do it. But I also believe that we must reexamine our own attitude—as individuals and as a nation—for our attitude is as essential as theirs. And every graduate of this school, every thoughtful citizen who despairs of war and wishes to bring peace, should begin by looking inward—by examining his own attitude toward the possibilities of peace, toward the Soviet Union, toward the course of the cold war and toward freedom and peace here at home. Let us examine our attitude toward peace itself. Too many think it is impossible. Too many think it unreal. But that is a dangerous, defeatist belief. It leads to the conclusion that war is inevitable—that mankind is doomed—that we are gripped by the forces we cannot control. We need not accept that view. Our problems are man-made—therefore, they can be solved by man. And man can be as big as he wants. No problem of human destiny is beyond human beings. Man's reason and spirit have often solved the unsolvable— and we believe they can do it again." (www.ratical.org/co-globalize/ JFK061063.html)

We must take JFK and Ronald Regan's words to heart; not just hear their words but absorb, sponge and incorporate their knowledge into our daily lives. We must study the past and listen to sage individuals like JFK and Ronald Regan to unify the human race for the security of our own vitality. Know that the organizing principle of any society is for war, which is exactly why the UFO topic is deemed untouchable because of national security interests. The black operations world is thinking too small, too petty, and too wrapped up in a fight for power and new technologies in the global chess games of the U.S.A. vs. Russia vs. China, or Iran, or North Korea, etc. The black world is selfish in wanting to solve jargoned alien technology by themselves. How can 100 brilliant minds working together to solve a problem be better than 1,000,000 brilliant minds collaborating to solve a problem? A juggernaut of high IQs have a greater chance and probability of solving a crisis. The black operations world must open up their eyes and open the ufology topic to the world so we can all begin to prepare for December 21, 2012. Or in the end, only an elite few will survive.

CHAPTER 1: ESTABLISHED PROPHECIES OF DIRE WARNING

2012 DRAWS NEAR

The time is soon approaching, yet nothing changes. The curable symptoms are everywhere, yet the condition worsens. The end as we know it is barreling down on us, yet we don't move to respond. December 21, 2012, is not a lone wolf prophecy. It is not a Y2K event. This is an event foreseen by many brilliant and gifted minds, each predicting the same vision at different and random times throughout history, all of whom foresaw December 21, 2012, to be the beginning of the end. We MUST learn from the past to survive the future. Even NASA is predicting a catastrophic event, possibly of Biblical proportions, to occur. Solar flares from the sun and/or polar shift (polar reversal) would severely alter the life that we take so casually for granted. Every 25,800 years, our Earth, sun, solar system, and Milky Way line up. Although this great cosmic alignment is unarguable, what happens and stems from the alignment is highly debated. We must remember that everything runs on a cycle like our weather patterns and seasons. This alignment happens every 25,800 years and will precisely align on the winter solstice of 2012, a date that most of us will live to see.

This date is real, as are the consequences of not acting now. We should live our lives in a different light and with a greater respect for the small things in life that we take for granted. We must open our eyes to see that everything as we know it could be over in the snap of a finger. Nevertheless, many individuals are too caught up in their everyday lives and don't want to comprehend just how fragile our way of life is. Some may think it to be cynical, pessimistic, or opinionated and just don't care to hear it, but a realist knows that with the good comes the bad, with the positive comes the negative. It's not just one-sided. The sweet can never be as sweet without the sour.

THE MAYA

The Maya calendar began in 3113 BC and is set to end on December 21, 2012. To this day, we still have a lot of questions regarding the ancient, yet extremely sophisticated Maya cyclical calendar, also known as "The Tzolkin," or Maya Sacred Calendar.

The Tzolk'in is the Maya version of the 260-day Mesoamerican calendar, in widespread use throughout the pre-Columbian region. This calendar is also called the Aztec sun stone.

This was their instrument for interpreting the date, time, and celestial events in the night sky with astonishing precision. To get the Maya prophetic Long Count Calender, the Maya communities combined their 365-day solar calendar, or Haab, with their 260-day Tzolkin calender to form a synchronized cycle lasting for 52 Haabs, called the Calendar Round. Their solar calendar, the Haab, was ten times more accurate than our current calendar which is something that's hard to fathom from a supposedly primitive culture. In 2010, our common calendar system is called the Gregorian Calendar and consists of 365.25 days in a year, which is the amount of time it takes our Earth to orbit the sun. Each year obviously breaks down into 12 months of approximately 30 days each. The Tzolkin consists of 13 months of approximately 20 days each, and more importantly, counted the cycles of Earth revolving around the sun with respect to the sun's galactic orbital cycles. Their prophetic calendar, which last renewed itself approximately 5,125-years-ago, is due to end again, with catastrophic consequences on the winter solstice of December 21, 2012. "The Maya civilization flourished in what is now Central America and Mexico from 300-900 AD and actually had an understanding of 17 total calendars, some of which charted time accurately over the past 10 million years." (http://skepdic.com/maya.html) The sacred and radically advanced "Maya calendar was so accepted that it was adopted by other Mesoamerican nations like the Aztecs." (www.webexhibits. org/calendars/calendar-mayan.html)

Using their three different dating systems in parallel, the Long Count, the Tzolkin (divine calendar), and the Haab (civil calendar), the Maya believed and predicted a disastrous convergence to occur at the end of the Mayan calendar cycle—December 21, 2012. The Maya were so meticulous and obsessed with keeping time that their calendar's precision was calibrated enough to predict lunar eclipses and galactic activity ACCURATELY thousands of years in the future. Yet, their calendar mysteriously ends on the day of December 21, 2012, and when the cycle ends the apocalypse and End of Days will be upon us. The Maya left their prophecies in codices, many of which were burned and destroyed in 1519 when Hernando Cortez arrived with the Spanish conquistadors and their fleet of eleven Spanish galleons. There are four remaining codices which can be seen and studied in libraries across Europe. If it weren't for sympathetic Spanish priests there wouldn't have been any message to be passed along and studied from generation to generation. The best Mayan codex was purchased in Vienna in 1733 and is known as the Vienna-Dresden Codex. This codex was deciphered by Mayan scholars to show destruction of the Earth by flood.

The Maya were gurus and masters of the dynamics of astronomy and astrology, so much so that their temples were built to mirror the constellations in the night sky. Their temples and stone formations were set up to mimic our planetary alignment and, from a bird's eye view, replicate the orbit of the planets in our solar system. They knew that the sun was the center of our solar system hundreds of years before Western astronomers discovered that truth. The Maya pyramids were also built as three-dimensional calendars, an architectural marvel and feat. Many find it hard to believe that a primitive civilization could not only conceive of, but construct and build such things without alien intervention. The Pyramid of Kukulkan at Chichen Itza was used as a calender comprised of four stairways, each with 91 steps and a platform at the top, making a total of 365, equivalent to the number of days in a calendar year.

The Mayan Temple of Kukulcan, in the archeological city of Chichén-Itzá, in the state of Yucatán, present day Mexico. Often referred to as "El Castillo" (the castle), this step pyramid has a ground plan of square terraces with stairways up each of the four sides to the temple on top. On the Spring and Autumn equinox, at the rising and setting of the sun, the corner of the structure casts a shadow in the shape of a plumed serpent - Kukulcan, or Quetzalcoatl - along the west side of the north staircase. On these two annual occasions, the shadows from the corner tiers slither down the northern side of the pyramid with the sun's movement to the serpent's head at the base.

The Maya are best known for their prophetic calendar that ends on December 21, 2012, but they should be known for their elongated skulls as well, another valuable clue linking the Maya with alien intervention. The unnatural, elongated skulls found near the Pyramid ruins of Kukulkan from the Kukulkan God that the Mayans worshiped have scientists and archaeologists utterly baffled. These types of unnatural, elongated skulls were also found in the ancient Egyptian pyramids. The Maya were so devoted to their Kukulkan God that they spilled their own blood with human sacrifices, and the possibility that they spilled their own blood for an extraterrestrial God is more likely a reality than a possibility. Have you seen Indiana Jones and the *Kingdom of the Crystal Skull*, or The Coneheads on

"Saturday Night Live"? Well, just like many of these other supposedly science-fiction movies like *Star Wars, the Abyss, the Alien Trilogy, the Terminator Trilogy, the Lord of the Rings Trilogy,* and *Stargate,* these flicks may not be too far off from historical fact. The real question is: Did someone get abducted by aliens only to get a glimpse of another species from another world and use that knowledge to write a book or movie about their experience?

You might be thinking it is impossible, but after reading this book and dismantling the UFO fabric you might just reconsider that notion to be very plausible. It's called the "ancient astronaut theory" and suggests that mankind has been visited and helped since the beginning of time from intelligent species that traveled to Earth from another planetary system, or even our own solar system. Some scholars speculate the elongated skulls to be alien-human hybrids. Debunker groups and even some historians claim the elongated skulls to be a deformity caused by inbreeding. What do you think?

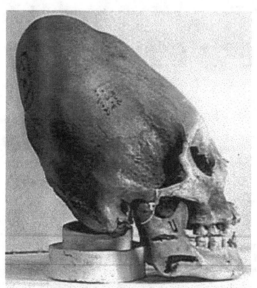

An elongated skull from the exhibit at Museo Regional de Ica. This is from a being known as Nephilim, Nephilium, Annanuki, or Alien hybrids-many of which have been discovered in Peru, Egypt, Bolivia,

China and India. Fossils, like the skull photographed above, tell a story that is being kept sheltered from the mass public. This crucial knowledge that is being withheld and covered up is crippling our understanding of ourselves and the origin of our species.

If these elongated skulls were indeed caused by deformity from inbreeding then why are so many of these pictures hidden from the mass public only to be found in the Library of Congress in Washington? (http://www.burlingtonnews.net/skulls.html) And furthermore, if these debunker groups are correct then why haven't we seen this elongated skull deformity in 2010? Many believe that these huge elongated skulls are solid evidence of beings from another world as well as their attempt to create a hybrid offspring containing large craniums that provided them with superior intelligence, thus adding validity to the ancient astronaut theory of alien intervention with humans.

The Maya obviously knew something that we still do not know to this day. Many believe that knowledge was shared with them from an alien species on how to live, how to build 3D monolithic temples mirroring the constellations in the sky, and more importantly, many believe the alien species warned the Maya of events to come and to prepare for them. Now, if doomsday was anchored to their understanding of their calendar cycle, and with every prior cycle ending in disaster, shouldn't we be a little concerned and heed to their warning of events to come? The Mayan civilization and their prophecies are just one piece of many to the End of Days puzzle that will be assembled by this book's end.

THE WEB BOT PROJECT

The Web Bot Project is yet another valuable and intriguing piece to the grand 2012 puzzle. The Web Bot Project, which is a non-human oracle, was created in the late 1990s to pick and decipher possible stock market trends. They use independent mini-programs called spiders or agents to comb the Internet for hints and patterns of behavior for future financial news. These massive scans of language reveal a direct connection to the collective unconscious, and a gateway to the future. The Web Bot Project has an incredibly impressive record which includes the foretelling of the Anthrax attacks in Washington DC in 2001, the World Trade Center and Pentagon terrorist attacks on September 11, 2001, the massive East coast power outage of 2003, the Tsunami in 2004 that killed 200,000+ people, and Hurricane Katrina in 2005, but it's the future predictions of the Web Bot oracle that strike a similar chord to other oracles' End of Days predictions.

Back in 2006, the Web Bot remarkably made a series of predictions about the coming events of late 2008 through mid-2010, which we see to be occurring in today's day. Some of these predictions include the following: "In October of 2008, a global emotional release event begins—largely economic. The rest of the world will begin to seriously question the stability and reliability of the US dollar." The prophecies of the Web Bot claimed that a catastrophic collapse of the dollar bill was possible and foresaw consumer confidence collapsing by mid-November 2008. This could be a direct result of the recent government bailouts and failures of several large financial institutions in the U.S., along with the devalued U.S. dollar and the increased cost of living. The Web Bot oracle also claimed that a global economic collapse was possible in the Fall of 2008, cascading off the country's woes. Think of the U.S. economy as a lit fuse that was lit over the early part of 2008. The rest of the world has no choice but to react to the declining US dollar and the enormous debt that the US has accumulated and put upon itself. It may be a global replay of the 1932 bond crash in the Great Depression.

The Web Bot oracle states that tensions will build in cities and scarcity will run abound. As the cost of food, fuel, and other necessities of life continues to rise so does people's levels of stress, and as the holiday season approaches, individuals find themselves taking extreme actions that they would've never considered in the past (and we've seen these hardships covered in the news lately). The Web Bot says the mood of the population will improve as people have a renewed sense of optimism that the corporate elite can and will be replaced in the elections, but the "us against them" mentality grows. This appears to be directly related to the recent presidential elections of Senator John McCain vs. Senator Barack Obama. People will briefly experience a renewed optimism and confidence in the promises made by the new president, but the mood will be quickly changed when they realize it's business as usual in Washington. The Web Bot oracle also foretells of a West Coast/Vancouver area large-scale earthquake around the 2010 time frame. Many have seen warning signs of this disastrous episode and it may not be the "Big One" but it will prove to be significant enough to be devastating to the area. It predicts that there will be a 2010 winter/spring natural disaster, which will cause people to become angry about government response. With the dramatic increase in natural disasters, such as, earthquakes, hurricanes, and floods, the government's inability to respond to the immediate needs of the people will prove to be devastating for many.

The Web Bot foretells of a global coastal event likely in early to mid-2010, where it sees a permanent loss of low-lying territory globally and foresees that one continent in particular will get hit badly, but it does not specify which one. Places to avoid would be any destinations at sea level (i.e., Miami, Florida). And reaching the pinnacle of insightful predictions, the Web Bot project has predicted a life-changing event of epic proportion to occur in December of 2012, so we must prepare ourselves for what is coming. The Web Bot tells us that bad will only precipitate to get worse. (www.december212012. com/articles/news/Web_Bot_Predictions_for_2008_2009.htm) The 2012 event of polar shift will trigger a domino effect. Polar shift is not to be taken lightly, especially when our country's right and left flanks are surrounded by massive oceans that could rise up from triggered deep sea earthquakes and flood our seaboard states and cities. Once that happens, economic collapse and WWIII will become reality.

THE HOPI INDIANS

Another spoke on the 2012 wheel are the Hopi Indians of the southwestern U.S. The Hopi Indians claim that the world has been created and destroyed four times already and that we're on the verge of a fifth transition set to start on December 21, 2012. The Hopi Indians believe the first time the world was destroyed by volcanism, the second was by polar shift, the third world was destroyed by flooding (hence Noah's Ark), and the fourth destruction of the world was by fire— all natural and extremely powerful forces of the Earth. The Hopi Indians, "Hopi" meaning "peaceful people," now number less than 10,000 and inhabit the four corners area of Arizona, Colorado, Utah, and New Mexico. (www.travelpod.com/travel-blog-entries/erriuc/ aroundtheworld/1184959140/tpod.html)

They called this area "Turtle Island" and it can be viewed as a macrocosm of the entire planet. Each Hopi clan performed a unique ceremony and the ceremonies together maintained the balance of natural forces of sunlight, rain, winds, and reaffirmed the Hopi respect for life and trust in the Great Spirit. (http://actionsbyt.blogspot. com/2008/07/hpoi-indian-prophecies-more.html) An ancient Hopi Indian tribe prophecy states that, "When the Blue Star Kachina makes its appearance in the heavens, the fifth world will emerge." This will be the Day of Purification according to the Hopi and holds a similar proclamation to the Maya doomsday prophecy. Their calendar too ends with a once-every-25,800-year celestial alignment. The Hopi believed that "Turtle Island could be turned over two or three times and the oceans could join hands and meet the sky," which appears to be a prophecy indicative of polar shift. Polar shift would reverse our current North and South poles, throwing the Earth off tilt and is a rare event that Mother Earth has endured since the days of Pangaea when the Earth and her seven continents were interconnected. Our Earth habitually wobbles to a different axis after completing a once-every-25,800-year procession.

The Hopi Indians called this imminent condition "Koyaanisqatsi," which means "world out of balance...a state of life that calls for another way," which many believe will occur December 21, 2012. In addition, the Hopi also predicted that there would be three world-shaking events before Koyaanisqatsi occurred. The first two world-shaking events are believed to be WWI and WWII with the third shaking of polar shift and WWIII unfolding within present times around 2012. The third shaking of the Earth is believed to trigger around the time when the sun rises to the center of the dark rift in our Milky Way on December 21, 2012. Or if you prefer Hopi lingo, "When the Saquahuh (Blue Star) Kachina dances in the plaza and removes his mask, the time of great trial will be here."

We should open our ears and listen as the Hopi have urged and warned us "to be alert of the omens" that will come about to give us courage and strength to stand on our beliefs. Blood will flow. Our hair and our clothing will be scattered upon the Earth. Nature will speak to us with its mighty breath of wind. There will be earthquakes and floods causing great disasters, changes in the seasons and in the weather, disappearance of wildlife, and famine in different forms. There will be gradual corruption and confusion among the leaders and people all over the world, and wars will come about with powerful winds. All of this has been planned since the beginning of creation. It's 2010 now and the clock is quickly closing the gap towards December 21, 2012, so we, not as a nation but as a world, must put aside our petty differences, open our eyes and heed all of the prophecies that converge on 2012. If we don't acknowledge their advice then we're the epitome of stupid for not even trying to rectify the cataclysmic situation at hand. On the precipice of defeat we must always remain hopeful and proactive. If we truly are endangered as a species, and if the surface of planet Earth is going to be inhospitable, we need to pull together and start building underground life-sustaining bases across the globe. If we're not able to live on the surface of planet Earth then we'll have to live underground like ants.

NOSTRADAMUS AND THE 2012 DOOMSDAY PROPHECY

A name pretty familiar in households around the world, Nostradamus was a 16th Century prophet whose maverick gift of foresight brought him posthumous fame and popularity. His predictions included the naming of the first two Anti-Christs being Napoleon Bonaparte and Adolf Hitler, as well as World War I and II, the JFK assassination, the Apollo Moon landing, the September 11 2001 attacks on the World Trade Centers in New York City, the deadly Tsunami of 2004, and yes, doomsday in 2012. With that said, we must pause for a moment to ponder what vital insight Nostradamus brought to the table. In some of his 942 recorded predictions, or quatrains, Nostradamus points to climaxing catastrophes reaching critical mass in 2012, with economic deterioration and WWIII stemming from the aftermath of the natural disasters and fallout from polar shift. Dr. Michael Rathford, who has studied the quatrains of Nostradamus for over 30 years, has used traditional analysis techniques alongside new, state of the art data mining algorithms to bring about significant, eye-opening discoveries. In his new book *The Nostradamus Code* he writes, "A very bright, previously unknown comet (possibly referring to Nibiru/Planet X) will appear and coincide with the time of great geological trouble, with earthquakes and volcanoes erupting and disrupting weather systems. This will cause widespread famines, droughts, and social upheavals in unexpected places. Nations that are considered prosperous and powerful, particularly western nations, will be weakened. They will be torn with civil strife and rioting and people migrate to areas that have water and can support crop-growing. The social upheaval and weakening of political structures will help the Anti-Christ come to power. The United States in particular will be subject to serious natural disasters, particularly earthquakes and flooding, flattening the nation from end to end, causing enormous conflict, despair, and misery. The U.S. will be bankrupted attempting to deal with the disasters. Three other great nations will send aid to help the citizens survive." (www.nostradamusonline.com/sample_chapter. php) Polar shift from the once-every-25,800-year galactic alignment is the spark that will trigger the catastrophic natural disasters and lead the chaotic world to WWIII.

As far as the U.S.A. is concerned, we have taken our neighboring oceans' kindness for granted for far too long. The U.S.A. has always trusted the Atlantic and Pacific Oceans to guard her and provide her with protection from our adversaries. Unfortunately, in the end our vulnerable coastlines will be inundated by the oceans rising up against us in the form of towering tsunamis spawned from deep sea rupturing earthquakes. The U.S.A. also harbors some of the world's largest super-volcanoes, like underneath Yellowstone National Park, Wyoming, and Mammoth Mountain ski resort in California. Dr. Rathford's book makes a great point saying the U.S.A. will be bankrupted coping with the natural disasters, a foreseeable Hurricane Katrina and FEMA-like nightmare for the future, especially with our current 2010 economic recession and declining dollar value around the world. Dr. Rathford states in *The Nostradamus Code*, "Earth changes will take place that will help the Anti-Christ's drive for world conquest. In central Europe, southern Europe, and in the Middle East, around the eastern end of the Mediterranean, there will be severe floods. As a result of the disruption to local governments by the natural disasters, the Anti-Christ will move his troops in under the guise of helping people restore civil order, but really use this as a device to take over countries, and to use the populations like slaves. Serious economic problems will persist along with great social unrest, contributing to the ease with which the Anti-Christ can seize power. The frightened and hopeful populace will be vulnerable to his rhetoric. The Anti-Christ will use the disasters as opportunities to overthrow governments and sneak spies into countries. Martial law will be declared in many areas to stop rioting and looting. The Middle East, the source of his power, will not be as devastated as the rest of the world. He offers assistance to other countries trying to recover but he will eventually stab them in the back." (www.nostradamusonline.com/sample_chapter.php) We must listen to Nostradamus' prediction of the coming of the Anti-Christ and we must not be blinded by the deception that the Anti-Christ will bring forth in the coming years. We all must open our eyes and remember that Satan's henchmen and emissaries have been trained under "The Great Deceiver" whose greatest trick was convincing mankind that he didn't exist. We all must help one another because only the mentally strong will be able to see through the Anti-Christ's treachery.

Deemed one of mankind's "Great Seers," Nostradamus' predictions are legendary for being accurate and for being able to see future events before they happened. The recently uncovered *Lost Book of Nostradamus*, along with his quatrains, describe a great galactic alignment that occurs once every 25,800 years. In his quatrains, Nostradamus predicts the galactic alignment will also coincide with peak solar activity, thus changing the Earth's atmosphere. This drastic, apocalyptic change that Nostradamus foresaw brings a worldwide domino effect collapsing humans to the brink of starvation and cannibalism. Referred by Nostradamus as the "Time of Troubles," this period after the galactic alignment of 2012 is full of war, despair, and evil bringing mankind to its knees during WWIII. (www.nostradamusonline.com/?a=110)

There's a good reason why Nostradamus is known as one of the most accurate prophets that ever lived. Nonetheless, many skeptics cannot reach an accord on his quatrains and see the prophecies as too cumbersome to live life any different. If it were just Nostradamus claiming 2012 to be the year of great change then there'd be room for debate, but that's not the case. It's more than just one or two individuals proclaiming 2012 to be the end of days as we know it. An overwhelming number of prophecies that have provided us with clues from different periods throughout history that are bound together far from coincidence. We must not only listen to their advice but we must prepare ourselves for the worst.

ST. MALACHI AND THE ANTI-CHRIST

The list of clues goes on to lead us to St. Malachi. St. Malachi (1094-1148AD), was a 12 Century Irish bishop, who at his death in 1148 AD was found to have left behind a prophetic list naming all the future popes beginning with Pope Celestine II, whose papacy began in 1143 AD. St. Malachi miraculously predicted the names of all the popes from his own day until the end of the Catholic Church—all 112 of them. The 111th pope since Pope Celestine II is serving now, and is supposed to be the "false prophet" according to St. Malachi. To top it off, St. Malachi included a single line in Latin identifying a characteristic of each pope, which historians say have been amazingly accurate. Now, to the average John Q. Citizen on the street, the ability to foresee the names of all the popes in chronological order is impossible; it cannot be done. According to Malachi's unfathomable predictions, Pope John Paul II, whose papacy ended with his death in April of 2005, was the third-from-last pope. The newly-elected Pope Benedict XVI is the next to last according to Malachi's predictions and the pope following him will be the final pope who will oversee the destruction of the Church. For the current pope, Malachi saw the name "Gloria Olivae," (i.e., the Glory of the Olive) and predicted that he would be a member of the Benedictine order. Intriguingly enough, "Gloria Olivae" is supposedly the one known in John's Revelations as 'the great deceiver' and the one who paves the way for the Antichrist, the final destroyer of the Roman Church. The Antichrist, according to St. Malachi, is the next pope, who, like the first pope, will be named Peter. The 112 prophecy says, "In the final persecution of the Holy Roman Church there will reign Petrus Romanus (Peter the Roman), who will feed his flock amid many tribulations, after which the seven-hilled city (Rome) will be destroyed and the dreadful Judge will judge the people." Strangely enough, even in Rome within the Vatican portrait gallery, there is only room for one more pope's portrait, so the Vatican also appears to be well aware of the December 21, 2012, Armageddon date and future events to come. (www.rense.

com/general64/newp.htm & http://archive.newsmax.com/archives/
ic/2005/4/3/180901.shtml)

Once again, if it were just one individual proclaiming 2012 to
be the end as we know it then it really wouldn't garnish too much
attention, BUT unfortunately that's not the case. We can see 2012
around the bend and now St. Malachi's legendary visions coincide with
the Maya, the Web Bot Project, the Hopi Indians, and Nostradamus.
We must open our eyes as a world community and unite through
action, instead of alienating ourselves from one another through
differences and imperfections. We all need to pull together as ONE
and be strong enough to banish and resist the Anti-Christ's siren song.
We must be ready for Satan's mortal emissary to be sent to Earth. We
must be ready. Or is he already here and recruiting upon us?

ALBERT EINSTEIN AND 2012

What we don't know and understand CAN alter our very existence,
especially if we're too blind to heed the advice that's been laid out for
us by past prophets. How could Einstein, NASA, Nostradamus, the
Maya, the ancient Egyptians, the I Ching Oracle, the Incas, the
Bible Prophecy, Merlin, the Web Bot, and the Hopi Indians, all at
different times throughout history, predict the same cataclysmic date
of December 21, 2012? How and why did all these various sources
foresee 2012 as being a time of great change? Could this be just
coincidence? Hardly. Most of the subjects and names listed above entail
foreign knowledge not known or heard of by much of the mainstream
world, and because of that it's easier for many individuals to dismiss
the claims and shrug off any "end of the world" predictions.

However, if there was ever a man's advice we wouldn't want to
shrug off, it would be Albert Einstein's. This man, for a large portion
of his life after the death of his second wife Elsa, wore the same
ensemble every day. After Elsa passed away, Einstein spent his last
20 years as a professor emeritus at Princeton methodically wearing
khakis and a white shirt everyday so that he didn't have to waste

valuable time thinking about what to wear. (www.answerology.com and www.einsteinatoz.com/faq.shtml) These proclivities, specifically regarding his clothing, were the genius' way to completely focus and hone in on his work, free from petty materialistic distractions. Albert Einstein solved the E=MC^2 equation, the basis for atomic power, and established himself as a Jedi Master of mathematics, physics, and alchemy. E=MC^2, part of Einstein's theory of relativity, is the atom-splitting method for creating nuclear energy. This famous equation laid the foundation for nuclear energy, and the nuclear age that we currently live in where power and weapons are produced using the atomic process for creating energy. Albert Einstein harnessed a deep knowledge of algorithms and quantum physics that's unfathomable to basically everyone.

He was also one of the few individuals in the world capable of seeing patterns or messages encrypted within a matrix of numbers. What Einstein deciphered from this encrypted matrix was a pattern where science and religion emerged as one in the same. This vision was a dynamic gift that 99.9 percent of us are not born with. If we did have this rare gift we'd be working for the NSA (National Security Agency) as code breakers or have some classified intelligence job along those lines. Have you ever seen the movie *A Beautiful Mind* with Russell Crowe or *Good Will Hunting* with Matt Damon? These movies depict the rare gift of unparalleled brilliance similar to that of Albert Einstein's intellectual capacity. Long story short, Einstein believed polar shift would occur around December 21, 2012. Albert Einstein is just another spoke on the 2012 wheel, just one of many credible sources that all point to 2012 as the End of Days as we know it.

CHAPTER 2: ALIEN INTERVENTION WITH PAST CIVILIZATIONS

THE NAZCA LINES

The Nazca coast of Peru had a rich culture long before the Maya and Aztecs came into history's limelight. Peru is a South American country located above Chile along the Pacific Ocean and it is absolutely shrouded in mystery. It is home to the famous gigantic geoglyphs scattered across the landscape of the inhospitable Nazca Desert, a high arid plateau that stretches 53 miles between the towns of Nazca and Palpa on the Pampas de Jumana. In the Nazca Desert, dubbed "the greatest scratch pad on Earth," strange, massive pictures discovered alongside airfields and runways are visible from the air, but barely noticeable from the ground. Of the geoglyphs found, some of the figures are larger than a football field and can easily be spotted from a mile away in an airplane. Some archeo-astronomers calculate that the Nazca ground figures mirror star constellations two thousand years ago. The plethora of images and ancient airfields are said to have been made by scraping and clearing away miles and miles of dirt, stones, and rubble to produce a subtle, two-tone picture on the Earth's surface. The hundreds of geoglyphs, range in complexity from simple lines to a intricately detailed hummingbird, bird, fish, insect, spider, monkey, lizard, and a human being.

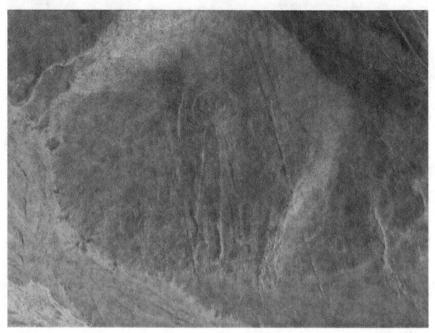

The Nazca Lines astronaut geoglyph seen from an aerial perspective. The many unprecedented Nazca Lines prove to be invaluable pieces to validating the ancient astronaut theory.

For whom were these huge pictures and airfields made since they were crafted between the years of 200BC to 600AD, long before the airplane was invented in 1903? Interestingly enough, similar geoglyphs detailing a shark and fish, among others, have been found sculpted into the massive sand dunes of Bimini, an island off the eastern coast of Miami, Florida, located in the middle of the Bermuda Triangle, a known energy vortex and UFO hotspot. Coincidence? Not likely.

Since the geoglyphs don't look like much on the surface and can only really be recognized as coherent symbols from an aerial view, common sense would guide any rational thinking individual to believe that the Nazca and Bimini lines were designed as a guide and roadmap for intelligent beings with flying machines—UFOs.

Furthermore, the ancient airfields, equipped with dozens of obvious runways, were found by celebrated German author and researcher Erich Von Daniken to have unknown white debris on them. Von Daniken had the unknown white substance tested and results ascertained that the substance was crystalline glass. Von Daniken was lucky to have been able to take samples of the crystalline glass because no digging or tampering with the earth around the sacred Nazca lines is permitted today. Adding further validity to the ancient astronaut theory, the Nazca ancient airfields and runways were located at the apex, the highest pinnacle of the surrounding mountains. Yet, at the apex of these particular mountains there is no apex. It has been completely leveled and cleared off without a trace of rock debris at the foot or valleys below the mountains. All the surrounding mountains around the ancient airfields have peaks and are not leveled off. Why were these particular peaks in the Nazca desert leveled off at their apexes to create runways? Where did all the rock debris go from this construction process? Also, and most intriguing, there's a reason why the Nazca desert is an ideal hub for studying the Earth. According to researcher and author Georgio Tsoukalos, these ancient astronauts were drawn to the "abundant raw materials in Nazca which provided them with Cliff's Notes for planet Earth." From A to Z on the periodic table of the elements, the Earth's blueprint can be found in the Nazca desert.

These concepts adhering together add weight and validation to the ancient astronaut theory that a growing number of theorists subscribe to. Remember that, according to our current Western philosophies and science, nothing flew before the Wright Brothers invented the airplane in 1903. What I have to say about that is, "it is often wiser to unlearn than to learn." Because once the hypothesis of the ancient astronaut theory is no longer a theory, and it is accepted that Earth has been visited by UFOs in the past, it will immediately broaden our understanding of Earth, our solar system, the universe, world religions, and most importantly ourselves. (http://www. cloudriderbooks.net/2012AndTheOldEquator.pdf)

MACHU PICCHU

Peru is not only home to the world renowned Nazca Lines, but is also home to the Peruvian City of Cusco, known as the Cradle of the Incas, the Incan Citadel of Machu Picchu, and the Crystal City in the Clouds.

The view of Machu Picchu, Peru from a short way above the site, hiking towards the Dawn Gate. This New Seven Wonders of the World site, which was somehow built mostly of quartz located on an energy vortex in the most inhospitable mountainous terrain, was supposedly constructed by a primitive civilization.

Machu Picchu, like Easter Island, Stonehenge, Sedona, and the ancient Egyptian pyramids, was miraculously built on an energy vortex that has many scientists baffled. How, without any sophisticated measuring instruments or devices, did these ancient builders know to build directly on top of an invisible energy vortex? Described as a tourist "must see," people claim that a visit to this remote area will change your life indefinitely and is the one spot in the world that epitomizes true peace and serenity. Many have described a fairy-tale-like experience, enchanting with a magical aura—and some even report an accelerated physical therapy while in its presence. Tourists claim that Machu Picchu naturally heals and some have speculated the white granite stones composed of 40 percent quartz crystal to be the reason. Visiting tourists with crippling back, knee, and joint aches and pains have reported an alleviation of their pains while in the presence of the energy vortex and quartz crystal of Machu Picchu, so much so that they've been able to climb up the steps to the top of the temples, a feat not usually possible with the medical conditions that usually kept them from such physical and strenuous activities. The same subtle and rejuvenating metaphysical changes of the mind, body, and soul have been described at Cathedral Rock in Sedona, Arizona when in close proximity to the converging energy lines.

However, the enigmas of Peru and Machu Picchu do not end there. Not only was the Inca Citadel built on an invisible energy vortex, but it was also built in an extremely hazardous mountainous area prone to earthquakes, yet the structures still stand and remains intact today. Furthermore, the megalithic stones that were used to create Machu Picchu range anywhere from 20-120 tons. 120 tons! Bear in mind that this civilization was supposedly one step out of the Stone Age, yet they could move 240,000 pound megalithic blocks into position into the most inhospitable rugged terrain WITHOUT heavy machinery? To put this into a 2010 perspective, a Caterpillar steamroller (that paves our roads and highways) weighs approximately 20,000 pounds or 10 tons. So, if alien intervention was not involved in this unfathomable construction process then one would have to conclude that this primitive civilization was supposedly moving around stone blocks that would be equivalent to the weight of 12 Caterpillar steamrollers, which is ludicrous.

Furthermore, the unparalleled craftsmanship and the fact that a single piece of paper can't fit inside the seams of the interlocking blocks is beyond comprehension for architects today, which leads us to believe that alien intervention was involved in the Incans' advancements. (www.divatribe.com/content/view/454/115/)

The Incan civilization may have assisted in the construction project of Machu Picchu, but at a low level. The Incans did not harness the superior intellectual knowledge that these visiting extraterrestrial architects, general contractors, and project engineers wielded—which is exactly why this ET species was in charge of building the Crystal City in the Clouds. This marveled architectural wonder is more than just a clue, it's a solid piece of tangible evidence left as a testament that we have been visited in the past. Many people want proof that ancient astronauts and ET intervention are the real deal. Well, ladies and gentlemen, please book your next vacation to Machu Picchu, Peru to literally open your eyes to a whole new reality of what is possible. One of the top ten things you have to do before you die is to watch a sunset and sunrise at Machu Picchu, Peru. You'll never be the same after the experience.

EASTER ISLAND

Easter Island, also known by its inhabitants as "the navel of the world," is without a doubt one of the most fascinating and intriguing places on the face of the Earth. It is one of the most remote islands in the world, without any links to the outside world, located in the southern Pacific Ocean 2,300 miles off the coast of Chile and 2,500 miles southeast of Tahiti. It's a relatively small island, only measuring 15-miles-long and 10-miles-wide, and was discovered on Easter in 1722 by a Dutch captain. When exploring the island, normal was not in the cards as hundreds of giant statues were found, each weighing several tons.

A tourist dwarfed in size next to Moai Statues at Rano Raraku, Easter Island (Chile). Could you imagine discovering this island and venturing inland only to find the most bizarre surroundings where logic is defied? Easter Island is exactly that kind of place, which is strangely enough also located on top of an energy vortex.

These huge stone figures are called "Moai," and were supposedly crafted from island rock. They have been found strewn across the island and its coastline in different sizes, shapes, and stages of completion. Some of the Moai, which sit on platforms or ceremonial shrines called "Ahu," face the sea while some face inland to watch over the villages. When studied further, the Moai are found to have been situated with absolute astronomical precision, especially at the sacred celestial observatory and sanctuary of Ahu Akivi. Far inland, the seven Moai statues found at the religious site of Ahu Akivi look directly to the point where the sun sets during the equinox, which also aligns with the moon.

The Easter Island sacred celestial observatory and sanctuary of Ahu Akivi. Its seven massive, several-ton Moai statues look towards the point where the sun sets during the equinox.

The Ahu Akivi carvings each stand about 16-feet-high and weigh approximately 18 tons, with the average Moai between 12 and 20 feet tall. Of the 887 discovered statues, the tallest Moai on Easter Island exceeds 30-feet in height with the occasional miniature Moai measuring over six-feet. Some of the largest Moai figures have been estimated to weigh as much as 80 to 90 tons, or 180,000 pounds! How was it feasible for the Easter Island inhabitants to create precise celestial alignments and move 90-ton statues into position without heavy machinery?

As a realist and an avid researcher, I believe that an alien species, or ancient astronauts, intervened in this construction process and were able to move these massive structures into position with their radically advanced anti-gravity and levitation technologies, just like at Machu Picchu. When you break it down and cut through all the misdirection, misinformation, conspiracy, and propaganda, these Moai structures had to not only be crafted but moved into position from miles away,

AND THEN lifted and hoisted atop of their ceremonial platform shrines, or Ahu. How could the inhabitants of the remote island, located on an energy vortex, with no links to the outside world and NO heavy machinery, have accomplished these feats?

If we study the past we know that UFOs and USOs are apparently drawn to Earth's energy vortexes located across the globe. In addition, at these energy vortex locations we find unfathomable architectural wonders that were built in a primitive era just out of the Stone Age. Our savvy ET visitors supplied the building blueprint, technology, and machinery to construct these architectural marvels, while the indigenous people provided the human labor force. In working together harmoniously with these advanced and superior races, it catapulted the wisdom of the inferior human civilizations exponentially. Remember, our galactic neighbors' planes, their UFOs, have the ability to create crop circles as well as displace water and create water impressions. We also know that their otherworldly technologies allow them to make objects levitate, which is exactly the advanced technology advances that moved the Moai structures into position from miles away.

When trying to fathom this concept we must not think about our own human technology because we're in the Stone Age compared to these other species. Even though we have been breaking down the barriers between science-fiction and non-fiction, our rules may not be their rules and may not apply here, and vice versa. What may be impossible to us may be very possible for them. We should heed the Adidas slogan that "Impossible is Nothing" because it's more than true, and not just for the world of sports. From a scientific standpoint it's more than possible; it's just that our human technological capabilities haven't reached that milestone yet. We as a human species, however, are quickly getting up to speed on what we've been missing, moving our human species technologically closer to the level of our cosmic visitors. These superior aliens, or ancient astronauts, left us a template of benchmarks that we are definitely trying to learn from and emulate. Many of our own human technological leaps have alien knowledge to thank. In the last 100 years we've made more technological leaps and bounds than in the last 5,000 years combined and we should be thankful for the template that our visiting galactic neighbors provided. At the rate and direction that our human species is headed we need all the help we can get. Let's get back to Easter Island...

The devout worshipers of Easter Island praised these gods, or ancient astronauts, for bringing them gifts of civilization, including, plants, agriculture, and the teachings of writings, sciences, medicine and the arts. Once their ordered society had been established on the island, the gods were said to have left with the promise to return around December 21, 2012. Followers claim that "people from the planet Nibiru (Planet X) came to Earth almost half a million years ago and did many of the things about which we read in the Bible. They traveled from their planet to Earth and splashed down in the Persian Gulf. The Sumerians had immense knowledge and were proficient in mathematics, astronomy, writing, and in many respects, their knowledge surpassed modern times." (www.greatdreams.com/ufos/long-ears.htm) These ancient astronaut gods coming from Nibiru and elsewhere were the ones who supposedly created mankind. Is it possible that God was a divine ancient astronaut who brought mankind from another part of the universe or galaxy to inhabit planet Earth? There are obviously hard-nosed skeptics who believe in Darwin's Theory of Evolution, that mankind evolved from apes, gorillas, and monkeys. What do you believe?

THE ANCIENT EGYPTIAN PYRAMIDS AND 2012

As the 2012 wheel rotates, it brings us to our next eye-opening chapter concerning the great, ancient pyramids in Egypt.

The great Egyptian pyramids perfectly align to celestial and galactic bodies. Shown in the picture above are some of 138 pyramids discovered in Egypt as of 2008. The great Egyptian pyramids were ALSO built on top of an energy vortex. Where we find energy vortexes we find unfathomable architectural wonders built in a primitive, Stone Age era with simple tools and without heavy machinery.

The ancient Egyptians also saw 2012 as a year of great change that would bring about the End of Days. Just like with Puma Punku, Machu Picchu, Easter Island, and Stonehenge, the great Egyptian pyramids were also built on an energy vortex. While studying these pyramids, scholars, architects, scientists, and many, many others have been blown away and humbled by their quality, craftsmanship and how these great pyramids could have been erected. With the unknown around every corner, and with new excavations revealing new clues every day, many theories have been brought forth about how and why these astonishing landmarks were built. Even more perplexing than the pyramids' creation is how the pinnacles of the Egyptian pyramids were built to align with the ecliptic plane of our galaxy. The alignments mirror the celestial and galactic bodies in the night sky, just like Stonehenge, Puma Punku, Machu Picchu, and the Maya Temples.

Tourists are humbled by the massive monolithic blocks of Stonehenge, England. And do you know what, that's right you guessed it, the marvel of Stonehenge was also built on top of an energy vortex.

Were these built by humans on an energy vortex to mimic galactic alignment by chance? Doubtful. The fact that modern human beings don't understand the raw power of these energy vortexes and highly magnetized areas is testament that another intelligent species DOES understand this mysterious energy and are drawn to build atop these highly magnetized areas. In addition to the ambiguous questions of how and why these great pyramids were built, they were also somehow constructed with complete synchronization to the azimuth of the sunrise and sunset on the horizons. The sun's rise and fall throughout the day follows the angled slopes of the pyramids with exact precision, and at noon each day the sun aligns to the apex or pinnacle of the pyramids.

Furthermore, these massive, ancient Egyptian pyramids are thousands of years old and thought to be built and engineered between 2589-2566 BC. Remember, that was 2,500 years BEFORE the birth of Christ and only basic tools were available. Yet, the megalithic blocks of the great pyramids weigh between 2.5-61 tons. To wield the weight of 61 tons at this time in history without an armada of heavy machinery would've been impossible. From an engineering and architectural standpoint, it's an inconceivable feat to not only pull this amount of weight but to actually lift and position the megalithic blocks with exact calibration. A ton weighs 2,000 pounds and the heaviest blocks of the pyramids weighed 61 tons, and these blocks were supposedly moved from rock quarries several miles away. That's equivalent to 122,000 pounds for the largest stones, which would not have been feasible even with an army of slaves. Even more intriguing is that many of the blocks were intricately cut flush, as if by laser, further validating the ancient astronaut theory. The fact that these megalithic blocks were aligned and stacked together without imperfections in some of the most inhospitable locations on Earth point the finger to the divine intervention of supreme beings. These supreme beings, interfacing with past human civilizations, made it possible to build these architectural marvels atop energy vortexes—forces of energy that our primitive human species still see as enigmatic. In addition, the pyramid blocks were assembled so that even today you can't even fit a razor blade or thin piece of paper through any of the seams. These structures have perfectly interlocking and mortarless blocks where no adhesive binds the megalithic blocks together.

There's a reason why archaeologists, scholars, and architects don't have all the answers to this unparalleled craftsmanship, because there was, without a doubt, extraterrestrial intervention. The answers they're trying to ascertain aren't derived from this world. Yet, many debunker communities don't want to acknowledge the giant elephant in the room and want to believe that primitive man created these miraculous structures on their own. However, I implore all of us to open our eyes, think outside the box and decipher fact from fiction to understand that mankind was not capable of making these radically advanced innovations at this point in time. Nonetheless, this is a fact that debunker communities and nonbelievers will habitually argue as these revelations are much too cumbersome for them to stomach. In turn, it becomes a battle of who's right and who's wrong with both sides advocating their principles and doctrines. Methodical misinformation campaigns do a stellar job of blanketing the truth with their destructive tactics. This only injures our cause, our movement, and shuts people's eyes instead of opening them. It's up to us to bring the real truth into the limelight.

Now, the ancient Egyptian pyramids were built with such sophisticated precision that they line up with the Orion star constellation, Sirius, as well as with the sun and other stars at certain times of each day and year. We must open our eyes and embrace the unequivocal fact that we as a species have definitely been helped in the past and that we assisted the real directors of these progressive construction projects, our alien neighbors. We have learned through past history that lower, primitive species tend to emulate the more sophisticated and advanced species. Look closely at all the pharaohs, the Sphinx, and all the Egyptian wardrobe of tassels, gold, and pizzazz. Where do you think this primitive, ancient Egyptian civilization learned to dress with such otherworldly pizzazz? KNOW that they picked up that trend, that fashion from their project engineers, the extraterrestrials. These galactic visitors were years beyond our time. Lucky for us, these aliens gave us a glimpse of what their worlds may look like without any of us actually having to travel to their star systems or planets. Fortunately, they brought and left a building template with our species. Maybe these otherworldly visitors build pyramid subdivisions.

Unfortunately, we're still too technologically inept to reach the stars and meet our neighbors. We know we're reverse-engineering crashed UFOs, i.e., the other species' planes, but we need to be able to get in the game sometime soon. We're so far behind technologically that we're like the third string water boy sitting on the bench without any hope of getting into the game. We haven't even walked on Mars yet and we haven't been back to the Moon since the NASA Apollo Missions of the late 1960s and early 1970s. We need to start harnessing gravity like our ET friends and get away from the same old, same old look of our modern airplanes. Obviously, we as a species have learned a considerable amount in the last 100 years as we now have planes like the SR-71 Blackbird, the B-2 Stealth Bomber, the F-117 Stealth Fighters, the F-22 Raptor and F-35 JSF (Joint Strike Fighter), and the now classified "Aurora project." (http://en.wikipedia.org/wiki/Aurora_aircraft)

The B-2 Spirit stealth bomber blueprint was ascertained through the reverse engineering of otherworldly UFO craft. Notice the drastic difference between the B-2 Spirit and conventional looking KC-10 Extender. If history has taught us anything, it has clearly shown that the less advanced civilization tends to emulate the more advanced culture. In this case, the human race is the less advanced species trying to learn from a more sophisticated species. It's monkey see, monkey do and our species is the monkey that is reverse engineering a superior race's radically advanced technology.

Littleton, Colorado's Lockheed Martin's F-117 Nighthawk stealth fighters fly in formation. The debut of this stealth craft in the Persian Gulf War, or Gulf War, proved and solidified the use of stealth technology.

We need to advance ourselves forward to the point where our commercial airplanes in the civilian world are getting a major face lift. A face lift to the point where we would not recognize the fleet as conventional planes but as something foreign, a spaceship-UFO-looking craft with an overhauled shape and propulsion system. We need to start harnessing the other forms of gravity which will enable mankind to get in the game and see our neighbors in the galaxy and throughout the universe. Once harnessed, these new propulsion systems will expedite passengers from New York City to Los Angeles in 45 minutes. Our revamped armada of traveling vehicles and vessels will be able to travel and penetrate the mediums of space and water with immunity, emulating the secrets of our extraterrestrial neighbors. The reality is that WE ARE the primitive species trying to follow in the footsteps of our advanced extraterrestrial visitors, and sooner or later our planes are going to look very similar to the ideal UFO streamline saucer shape that our black project engineers are currently trying to replicate. Once accomplished, George Lucas' *Star Wars* movies may not be as fictional as many may think. All you *Star Wars* fans out there who subscribe to the motto "In a galaxy far,

far away," I'm with you. We're getting closer to reaching the stars and beyond.

PUMA PUNKU

As discussed in previous chapters, and to continue laying the groundwork integrating 2012, UFOs, and religion, these cosmic extraterrestrial visitors acted as decorated project engineers and built some of Earth's greatest architectural enigmas, many of which still bewilder mainstream science. If you thought the bizarre couldn't get any stranger, visit Puma Punku in Tiahuanaco, Bolivia. Puma Punku is a region in Bolivia of a pre-Incan culture that is not well known outside of the archaeological and ufology communities. To keep Puma Punku off the public's radar, and to retain secrecy, media and news coverage on the subject have been extremely quiet. Yet, Puma Punku is the crème de la crème of extraterrestrial intervention and deserves to be put in the media limelight. This 17,000-year-old, four-part, truly massive and now collapsed building is said to have no comparison.

The detail of granite (diorite) stone at Puma Punku, Bolivia, with precisely cut straight line with equidistant drilling and laser-equivalent leveling, an inconceivable feat for a primitive civilization. Why would a simple culture with basic tools choose one of the most impenetrable stones to build with? And how in God's name was this astonishing feat erected on a highly magnetized energy vortex?

The largest blocks of the Egyptian Pyramids, the largest stones at Stonehenge, the largest Moai at Easter Island are said by author and researcher, Georgio Tsoukalos, to be mere "child's play" compared to Puma Punku in Bolivia where "logic does not exist... There are 440-ton megalithic blocks located at this site, which is the equivalent weight to nearly 600 full-size cars, and that's a conservative figure." Some claim the largest blocks weigh 800 tons or 1.6-million-pounds. To put this weight into perspective, the weight of one 800-ton block at Puma Punku equates to the total combined weight of four blue whales. Do you really believe it possible for primitive man to be moving around megalithic blocks that weighed the same as four blue whales? Even better, according to Fox Sports, the new Jumbotron screen at the new Dallas Cowboys Football Stadium, has fans stunned by its 1.2 million pound weight The Jumbotron screen weighs 600-tons, yet it is still 200-tons lighter than the largest blocks found at Puma Punku, Bolivia. How, 17,000-years-ago, without any heavy machinery, was this inconceivable feat possible without alien intervention? With the largest confirmed construction blocks at 440 tons, or 880,000 pounds, these blocks were supposedly hauled to an elevation of 13,000 feet above sea level from the rock quarry 10 miles away on the western shore of Titicaca. The Andean people who lived at Puma Punku around 500 AD were still using simple tools and reed boats and could not have physically moved these monstrous blocks that defy logic and reason.

Even more astonishing than the weight of the blocks, these several-hundred-ton blocks displayed six millimeter wide, 1millimeter deep, precision-made grooves containing equidistant drilled holes, not one millimeter off from edge to edge. This feat of craftsmanship would be impossible to construct with the Andean people's primitive use of stone and copper tools. Forget about the fact that these were 100-800 ton megalithic blocks; forget that the blocks were supposedly moved uphill into position from a rock quarry 10 miles away; forget that these blocks were precision cut aligning perfectly like interlocking building blocks not one millimeter off from edge to edge; forget the fact that the structures at Puma Punku were aligned astronomically to mimic our planetary alignment and celestial events. What we need to UNDERSTAND is that these megalithic block stones were constructed from the hardest granite on planet Earth, granite diorite, AND CAN ONLY BE CUT WITH A DIAMOND OR LASER. So, why would a primitive civilization with only the use of stone and copper tools decide to use granite diorite blocks for construction? Even today, with all the modern advances in engineering and mathematics, we could not fashion or transport such a structure. (http://go.webassistant.com/wa/cont_pub_view_item.lhtml?-Token. Id=25025&-Token.cId=100530&-Nothing)

The notion of alien intervention, or ancient astronauts, from outer space assisting earlier human civilizations may seem trivial and highly unorthodox to many but that's only because it's what we thought we knew to be the truth, until now. With new breakthroughs as of 2010, where each and every day opens more doors and sheds more light on the world of science, many people are taking another look at the facts and re-examining their own beliefs. Many subjects that we've been programmed to learn and much of what we've been taught throughout the schooling process has had the real truth, the inconvenient truth, withheld. In addition, without the REAL exact truth being taught on subjects like Puma Punku, as provocative as it may seem, those fallacies will only hinder our species from reaching new heights intellectually. We need to knock down those learning walls and open our eyes to a 2010 understanding of what's at stake. There's no room for error with 2012 right around the corner and there are already too many obstacles to avoid and maneuver around to find the truth. Disinformation campaigns born of clandestine government agencies are not only crafty at misdirection and propaganda, but are experts in the art of covering up their tracks. The agencies that are angling for power against the people and our adversaries will deny, deny, deny, and be mum about what is really going on with subjects like Puma Punku, but they'll be vocal and quick to denounce any claims of alien intervention once the finger is pointed at them regarding a cover-up. But we must not surrender because the closer we get to the truth the more vocal they get in dismissing our allegations as hoaxes—which is a terrible bluff and a dead give-away for a cover up. As a former US Marine, I know and have seen these "dark side of the force" agencies work and let me tell you, they are masters of their black craft. These agencies have been programmed with specific protocol to lie and cover up anything infringing upon their idea of what constitutes national security; it's what they do. To all of a sudden reveal the truth to the public is certainly out of the question. If they ever revealed the real truth about alien intervention and ancient astronauts then they know the general public would never trust or believe them ever again. This is why we must ask ourselves, not our government, what we believe.

CHAPTER 3: WHAT THE GOVERNMENT DOESN'T WANT YOU TO KNOW

1903

When will we look to the past to understand that UFOs are old news? According to our current Western beliefs, the Wright Brothers, Wilbur and Orville, were the first men to invent and fly an aircraft. The Wright Brothers accomplished this celebrated airborne feat on December 17, 1903, with the invention of their (now primitive) Wright Flyer. Western world teachings would have us believe that before 1903 nothing motorized flew, period. The indelible mark left by this chapter of *Open Your Eyes: To 2012 and Beyond* will prove without a doubt that UFOs have been gracing Earth's skies long before Wilbur and Orville invented the airplane in 1903. So, it really doesn't matter if the UFOs flying around in 2010 are human or an alien creations. Are these UFOs the military's latest top secret stealth craft or are they alien and otherworldly? It doesn't matter. All that matters is that if something was flying around in Earth's skies before 1903, which *Open Your Eyes* intends to prove, then that epiphany will reveal the biggest cover up of all time. In 2010, we take our traveling pretty much for granted and hop on a plane to visit friends and family, or to travel from one destination to the next. But remember, human planes have only graced our skies for approximately 106 years. Furthermore, there have been documented reports for thousands of years of intelligent vehicles moving around in our skies. Use your common sense instead of listening to the government lie about the subject. If nothing flew before 1903, then what would be flying around in our skies before that date? It's alright; you can say it—UFOs.

The Wright Flyer's historic flight on December 17 1903. Were they really the 'first in flight'?

We as a human species have been watched and observed for thousands of years by these UFOs and USOs. Hieroglyphics entailing visitations from intelligent vehicles moving around in our skies have been found on cave walls from ancient civilizations. There have also been detailed inscriptions found on ancient Egyptian pyramid walls like the "images of vimanas (flying machines) on the ceiling beams of a 2000-year-old New Kingdom Temple, located several hundred miles south of Cairo, Egypt and the Giza Plateau, at Abydos.

The revelatory hieroglyphic inscriptions found inside the 2,000-year-old New Kingdom Temple of Osiris at Abydos in Giza have sparked heated controversy in debate arenas across the world, and for justifiable reason. If a picture is worth a thousand words then this image screams out truth on the ancient astronaut theory and past visitations by a supreme race of beings. This eye opening discovery has become very difficult to debunk for any hard nose skeptic and critic.

A vimana is a mythological flying machine, described in the ancient mythology of India. References to these ancient flying machines are commonplace in ancient Indian texts, even describing their use in warfare. The vimana knowledge is commonplace and well accepted throughout India, so much that I'd be out of a job over there. As well as being able to fly within Earth's atmosphere, vimanas were also said to be able to travel into space and travel submerged underwater. Sanskrit texts are filled with references to gods who fought battles in the sky using vimanas equipped with weapons as deadly as any we can deploy in these more enlightened times." (http://www.crystalinks.com/vimanas.html) Remember, no airplane flew before 1903, yet sightings have been reported since the beginning of time. Christopher Columbus, Alexander the Great, and Moses all reported UFO and USO sightings centuries ago, long before any plane flew in the sky. Evidence of UFOs is everywhere, even from Biblical times with Jesus, the Virgin Mary, and Moses. The famous painting, "The Madonna with Saint Giovannino," painted in the 15 Century by either Jacobo del Sallaio, Sebastiano

Mainardi, or Domenico Ghirlandaio, has long been proof of UFOs gracing our skies.

"The Madonna with Saint Giovannino" painting. What do you see in the background? Remember, this is a period in time according to Western beliefs where nothing flew in the skies.

A man and his dog gaze directly towards the UFO craft in the background of "The Madonna with Saint Giovannino" painting. We must all reprogram our minds to understand that 'UFO' does not necessarily mean 'little green men.' For all we know God and his divine Angels, or another race similar to us humans, use these craft like we use airplanes to get from point A to point B and so forth. What if these craft are as simple to them as airplanes are to us? What if this is just their means of transportation and in their eyes it's the norm and 'no big deal'?

This famous painting is on display in the Sala d'Ercole in Palazzo Vecchio, the Town Hall of Florence, and has been celebrated and discussed among ufologists as tangible proof of UFO activity, long before the Wright Brothers took flight in 1903. In the painting you can clearly see, behind the Virgin Mary's shoulder, an individual in the background, along with his dog, who is holding his hand up to his forehead to block the glare off an apparition hovering in the sky. The man's dog is even gazing towards the strange object lurking in the sky. Animals have the best credibility of detecting an unknown anomaly with their equipped, built-in sixth sense. With that said, a dog and his master wouldn't just be staring up at the sun only to burn their retinas.

Notice the man keeping a hand to his forehead to block the sun's glare while looking towards an apparition in the sky. With the man is his dog, who also looks curiously at the unidentified flying object. Common sense guides us to never look directly into the sun, and a dog would never just stare into the sun out of natural instinct. Paintings such as this one are tangible proof of past visitations which have been captured and preserved in paint.

The next eye-opening painting where UFO truth is preserved in paint is kept at the Earls D'Oltremond, Belgium depicting Moses with "flaming horns," receiving the Ten Commandments from God atop Mount Sinai, Saudi Arabia with a squadron of several UFOs seen in the background.

Moses receiving the Ten Commandments tablet from God with a squadron of UFOs seen in the distance. UFO intervention with Biblical figures is plausible and could explain many miracles cited within religious books such as the Bible, Torah, and Koran. One must learn to read between the lines, and to look deeper, to see the true encrypted message encoded within the scripture.

Could God be a divine ancient astronaut? Could UFOs just be radically advanced airplanes capable of traveling through different mediums (i.e., water, air, space, etc.)? Could Heaven be a planet or a star system in the universe where God and Jesus came from? The answer could very well be YES. If you're religious and bound by faith then you know the story of Moses, as well as the parting of the Red Sea to escape the Egyptian pharaoh's wrath. How do you think Moses parted the Red Sea? God himself or one of his affiliate angels helped Moses displace the Red Sea for the Israelites to escape. "And Moses stretched out his hand over the sea; and the LORD caused the sea to go back by a strong east wind all that night, and made the sea dry land, and the waters were divided" (Exodus 14:21). If you truly believe that the Bible is the word of God then learn to read between the lines. UFOs and USOs have the unique ability to make crop circles on land just as they are able to displace water, which you're aware of from earlier chapters in my book. How do you think these higher feats of technology were performed? It's not fantasy, it's reality and there's proof of the drowned Egyptian army with Egyptian chariot wheels, and human and animal skeletons found at the bottom of the Red Sea, 3,500 years after the event is said to have taken place. "And the waters returned, and covered the chariots, and the horsemen, and all the host of Pharaoh that came into the sea after them; there remained not so much as one of them" (Exodus 14:28).

After two diving trips to the Gulf of Aqaba, Peter Elmer tells WorldNetDaily, "I am 99.9 percent sure I picked up a chariot wheel." Several authorities have confirmed Peter Elmer's discovery to be a chariot wheel dating back to the time of Exodus. "I believe I actually sat in an ancient chariot cab," Elmer said, referring to his time exploring a submerged item in what he describes as an underwater scrap yard. "Without question, it is most definitely the remains of the Egyptian army." Peter Elmer's unbelievable discovery in the 1970s has led the Egyptian government to close the door on allowing artifacts to be removed from the area. This is a problem for current day explorers and scientists. However, and thankfully for Elmer's discovery before the Egyptian government's exploration ban, "the hub had the remains of eight spokes radiating outward and was examined by Nassif Mohammed Hassan, director of Antiquities in Cairo. Hassan declared it to be from the 18th Dynasty of ancient Egypt, explaining the eight-spoked wheel was used ONLY during that dynasty around 1400 BC." (www.worldnetdaily.com/news/article. asp?ARTICLE_ID=33168) However, and not surprising at all, the eight-spoked wheel has disappeared. Obviously, governments don't believe that their people can handle the truth, which is exactly why when a piece to the grand puzzle is found it is immediately taken away, confiscated, and hidden forever. When these devious actions occur and the tangible evidence disappears we know that we are close—close to unraveling the truth that government agencies will go to the ends of the Earth to keep secret.

"The Crucifixion" was painted by an unknown artist in 1350. It is currently located above the altar at the Visoki Decani Monastery in Kosovo, Yugoslavia and clearly shows links to Christ, God, UFOs, and ancient astronauts. This one painting alone debunks the 1903 Wright Brothers date that claimed them to be the first in flight. This painting speaks volumes and CLEARLY depicts two UFOs, easily noticeable in the top left and top right corners, flying by Christ's crucifixion. These crafts need no explanation as you can obviously see a pilot in the fuselage working the controls. Yet debunker groups claim the images to be that of the sun and moon. Does this painting depict the sun and moon to you?

"The Crucifixion" painting with two hard to miss UFOs clearly seen in the background. Why were these types of craft being painted if this technology supposedly hadn't been conceived of yet?

A close up of the UFO craft in the upper left-hand corner of "The Crucifixion."

A zoom in of the UFO vehicle in the upper right-hand corner of "The Crucifixion."

"The Baptism of Christ," by Flemish artist Aert de Gelder, can be located at the Fitzwilliam Museum in Cambridge, UK. This oil painting is a true relic conveying UFO history within the preserved painting. In the painting you see a classic disc-shaped UFO casting beams of light down upon John the Baptist and the holy infant Jesus, proof of angelic UFO intervention at Jesus Christ's birth.

"The Baptism of Christ" painting with a saucer shaped UFO obviously intervening in the Baptism process of Christ. The relationship between God, Jesus Christ, ancient astronauts, religion, Biblical miracles, and UFOs is closer than many have been led to believe.

"The Miracle of the Snow," created by Masolino Da Panicale from Florence, Italy, can be found in the Church of Santa Maria Maggiore. The image portrayed illustrates a 13th Century legend regarding a 4th Century supernatural event where miraculous snow manifested on a warm August day over a small area in Rome. The painting shows Jesus and Mary orchestrating and directing a squadron of flying discs, as well as the gathered citizens below who are gazing up attentively.

"The Miracle of the Snow" painting with a fleet of UFOs in the background hovering above the buildings and mountains. Did Jesus travel from Heaven to Earth on what we would call a UFO? Could Heaven be another star system or planetary system where similar beings to ourselves reside?

"The Life of Mary" and "The Magnificent" are both 15ᵗʰ Century tapestries illustrating the life of Mary on display in the French Basillica, Notre-Dame, in Burgandy. What do you see in the background on both tapestries? Flying saucers—which are ironically the same shape then as witnesses describe today. If nothing flew before 1903, then what motivated these painters to include the same classic-looking UFO discs in their paintings? Debunker communities have claimed them to be distant islands. What do you think? Now, I'm not a rocket scientist or astrophysicist but I've never seen or heard of islands floating over buildings parked in the sky. Have you? You see what I'm getting at? In my opinion, only a shortsighted, inside-of-the-box thinker could possibly concede that the tapestries of the Virgin Mary also contain flying islands. However, many people are dangerously misinformed and obviously must have a low threshold for gullibility to even consider that a valid explanation.

"The Magnificent" is hard to brush aside and ignore. If nothing flew at this point in time, then what is hovering in the background of this tapestry? UFOs have been here since the beginning of time and evidence of this is preserved in paint. It's not just one or two paintings either, it's a myriad of palpable evidence that once revealed to the light will set us free.

"The Life of Mary" shows a UFO monitoring the situation seen in the background above the buildings in the classic disk 'hat-like' shape. Since there weren't any video cameras or iPhones to film these craft paintings were the way of capturing the moment to preserve the moment in time to pass on to later generations. Proof is in the paint.

Hopefully these paintings have assisted in opening your eyes. Believe me, there's a plethora, a giant pool of paintings and further evidence just like the examples I've provided, all valuable pieces to the puzzle and all part of the UFO and ancient astronaut theory fabric. Debunker communities love to play their games, calling this topic science-fiction, but after reading *Open Your Eyes* in its entirety and seeing such an overwhelming amount of evidence, you might just consider that outlook to be a narrow dogmatic viewpoint. Just as Jesus prayed for those who condemned and crucified him, we must pray for those who've condemned and crucified us for our beliefs.

These paintings have preserved the UFO truth in paint and, in my opinion, solidify the UFO existence since the beginning of time. The proof-in-paint doesn't end there, and once again I am only providing the tip of the iceberg on these subjects. There is more proof than one could possibly fathom so I have provided you with a sliver of plausible evidence for what I believe is necessary in order for you to open your eyes. These ancient painted UFOs are the same shape that witnesses describe in today's day of 2010, so don't let yourself be deceived or even listen to the government and its affiliates' hilarious lies and explanations about what these objects are. They've insulted our intelligence time and time again, and are masters of the black arts, reverse psychology, and misdirection, which is exactly why this subject is up to the civilian world to unveil. Why do we keep asking the government to release files on the UFO phenomenon? If you want doctored files that have been fabricated with every other line blackened-out, then be my guest, but if we think for a minute that these governmental agencies are going to reveal anything substantial in their released, declassified files, then we're really blind and haven't learned a thing from our past mistakes. It's up to us to read between the lines and to piece the puzzle together. We all must open our eyes to see that there weren't any handy video cameras that one could pick up at their local Target or Wal-Mart to capture the moment, which obviously would've preserved the moment in time forever. No, instead the detailed inscriptions, paintings, and hieroglyphics were the cameras and video cameras of ancient times. What they preserved in time for us on cave walls, pyramid walls, and canvas, is certifiably tangible, plausible evidence.

Vimanas and Ancient Flying Machines

Golden Vimanas unearthed in pre-Colombian tombs. Their remarkable resemblance to modern aircraft is uncanny.

Unearthed, deep in the jungles of Columbia were airplane figures made entirely of gold. These ancient airplane artifacts, made to honor the extraterrestrial gods' flying machines, were discovered in pre-Columbian tombs dating back to 800-600BC. The graves that housed these golden artifacts, were from the Muisca, Calima, Tairona, and Tolima Indians of modern day Columbia. The *UFO Hunters* provided a special for their audience when the History Channel aired an aerial spectacle based upon what was discovered in the tombs. The unearthed golden airplane artifacts, or vimanas, were made to exact model scale and proved to be aerodynamically sound, that is without imperfections or flaws. How in this period of time of 800-600BC, before Christ and thousands of years before the Wright Brothers invented the conventional aircraft in 1903, were aerodynamically sound airplane models being conceived? How did they even know about flying machines at this point in history? It's quite simple actually. Our earlier ancestors witnessed a superior technology that they wanted to emulate. We can all have our eyes opened by watching the replicated model test flight on the History Channel's *UFO Hunters*, as well as witness the once entombed ancient golden airplanes video on YouTube. (www.youtube.com/watch?v=F1HEo2E70kg&NR=1)

Regardless of how taboo the concept of planes before 1903 is to scientists, this is real and we have a solid template of evidence to base our claims on. Why can't we embrace this anomaly and move toward a world acceptance on extraterrestrial life? After all, just because we can't see something doesn't mean it doesn't exist. Belief is a funny thing; take religion, for example. It has been thousands of years since Jesus or Mohammed walked this Earth, yet religiously bound people embrace God and put him on a pedestal, even though we can't touch or see him in the physical form. After thousands of years truth fades in the sands of time as story becomes legend and legend becomes myth, yet many still passionately believe in and pray to a God that they cannot touch or see. We must open our eyes to realize that UFOs have been seen and observed since the beginning of human existence and will continue to be seen by witnesses across the globe.

NASA has known since the beginning, so have all the astronauts from the various Apollo, Gemini, Viking, Mercury, and Challenger missions. Every time the astronauts witnessed something extraordinary, such as a UFO, the code phrase homeward bound to Houston to disguise the paranormal was "Santa Claus." In the agency's infant stages, NASA and its astronauts quickly learned to never broadcast the word "UFO" over open radio, which in turn could be intercepted by anyone in the public tuned in to their frequency. From that point forward, non-disclosure of the word 'UFO' became NASA protocol and in their eyes was absolutely paramount to not jeopardize the integrity of the ongoing space missions. Keep in mind that the government funds the National Aeronautics and Space Administration, hence www.nasa.gov, so the organization is kept under a zero tolerance, "hush-hush" policy and members are not, under any circumstances, allowed to leak top-secret information to the public or press. NASA goes about its business under airtight surveillance and scrutiny and only reveals information, pictures, and videos to the mainstream public on a need-to-know basis. They provide the public just enough to keep the majority of the population satisfied with pictures of awe-inspiring star constellations and nebulas. However, a secret of this magnitude is bound to get out sooner or later, and already seems to be the case with several retired NASA pilots and astronauts. As they near the end of their lives, many of these space pioneers and heroes, who were sworn to secrecy, are now speaking and revealing the priceless information buried inside of their brains' vaults. Take for example the Apollo 14 astronaut and sixth man to ever walk on the moon, Edgar 'Ed' Mitchell. A trusted astronaut who has not only been to space but who actually walked on the moon DESERVES to be heard, because if the government trained and trusted him with top-secret missions and security clearance, we should take his word seriously.

Dr. Edgar Dean 'Ed' Mitchell Apollo 14 Astronaut & 6th man to walk on the Moon. What astronauts and pilots say counts and should be taken seriously.

"Such a journey in space changes everything. When I landed on the moon I had an overwhelming feeling that even the universe itself is a conscious being. This means that all life forms, whether on Earth or somewhere else, are part of a whole. I have no doubt that extraterrestrials visited our planet. Governments possess thousands of documents about UFO sightings. As a scientist, it is for me logical that a few of these eyewitness reports are about extraterrestrial flying objects. Due to my training, the military was ready to talk with me rather than with people that could have been called crazy. And what they tell me leaves no doubts: The Earth was already visited by extraterrestrials. The astronomer Copernicus was convicted as a heretic about 500-years-ago because he believed that the Earth was not the center of the universe. And today the majority of us still believe that mankind is the biological center of the universe. We still do not believe that intelligent life outside the Earth exists until we meet an alien during shopping." (http://images.google.com/imgres?imgurl=http://www.pacal.de/goldplanes.jpg&imgrefurl=http://www.pacal.de/startseite_en.htm&usg=__FpjiZZUBsmj_JmedMaK3iyFDR0w=&h=260&w=188&sz=16&hl=en&start=87&sig2=8CZ2gFPobc1gBDT5L52Evw&um=1&tbnid=sOaBTK81rxkwhM:&tbnh=112&tbnw=81&prev=/images%3Fq%3Dvimana%2Bflying%2Bmachine%2Bpictures%26ndsp%3D18%26hl%3Den%26rls%3Dcom.microsoft:*:IE-SearchBox%26rlz%3D1I7SKPB_en%26sa%3DN%26start%3D72%26um%3D1&ei=gSbUSfrGFZCgtgPhgb2kCg)

It doesn't take a rocket scientist to grasp what's going on here. These men were sworn to secrecy holding top secret clearance and the highest merit of honor and integrity. To jeopardize their careers by speaking the truth would have serious consequences certain to tarnish or even terminate their careers. However, as these old space cowboys near the end and their lives, their most coveted secrets are being dusted off and are coming to light. These old veterans know that the truth will set them free, which is why they are talking before death. Astronauts and pilots are some of the most credible observers and witnesses of UFOs, and are some of the most highly trained and disciplined professionals in the art of observing their surrounding airspace. What they say holds serious weight as they were not only trained by, but trusted by the U.S. government. These pilots and astronauts have no reason to fabricate lies or manufacture fictional stories, whereas the government has every reason to conceal and bury the truth. For world governments and military misinformation campaigns, it's easy for them to manipulate the truth within classified and top-secret documents because these documents are not available to the public for 25-50 years, like the JFK assassination files. Only after the holding period do the documents make their way to public view, only to have most everything with true value—the meat-n-potatoes—blackened-out, the truth murdered and becoming even harder to find. The paper trail, if any, is not going to provide any real answers to the BIG questions we all have. These skeletons in the nation's closet are labeled under the "Black Operations" tab in the government's black world accordion folder, also known to not exist publicly and never making the front page of national newspapers or headline news. We must include the government as part of the problem, not the solution, and take matters into our own hands. Otherwise, we're all just, metaphorically, singing birds that got accustomed to their cages.

This compelling chapter has hopefully assisted in opening your eyes and realizing that 1903 has lost its validity and should be amended in history books across the globe ASAP. "Since the dawn of humanity we have been in contact with extraterrestrials. Either by one on one close contact or watched from a distance by UFOs and other spacecrafts. There is a plethora of evidence of aliens being involved in our history from paintings, scrolls, sculptures, art, and stories that date back to the beginning of our earliest recordings as people on this planet. Some of the most famous works of art from the greatest artists often depict different aliens, UFOs, and other paranormal sites that can only be explained by the visiting of our alien neighbors." (http://alien-ufo-research.com/aliens_in_ancient_history/) When we finally come to a world acceptance on the UFO subject everything we've ever been taught will have to be relearned. We are only infants in the bigger picture of what's going on in the universe, and in order for us to take that next step for mankind we're going to need to be extremely open minded in revamping our beliefs and very existence. Physics, mathematical equations, religion, everything as we know it will transform and mankind will be absolutely dumbfounded. Dumbfounded and humbled by the idea that we as a human species thought we knew it all, yet we were so naively wrong.

If this chapter intrigued you then you may want to Google the "Baghdad Battery," a.k.a., the "Parthian Battery," and discover that electricity was actually invented and used 2000-years-ago in ancient light bulbs and batteries throughout Egypt and Iraq. Many believe that alien wisdom of physics, astronomy, and mathematics provided this sacred blueprint for light, most of which was guarded by high priests. "Western civilization generally credits Count Allessandro Volto with the invention of the simple battery, in 1800. However, a small jar about the size of a fist, found in the ruins of an ancient settlement near Baghdad, appears to predate Volta's battery by about 2000 years." Dozens of these "Baghdad Batteries" have been excavated and studied. (http://patentpending.blogs.com/patent_pending_blog/2004/10/the_baghdad_bat.html)

We as a society have been taught and led to believe in school that the plane was invented in 1903 and that the battery was invented in 1800. However, these claims are an illusion and are withholding the real truth. Why would we want to learn or teach incorrect facts? The truth is generally excluded from Western world ideologies, yet they need to be adopted into the creed of our schools and universities around the world. These new truths, once stomached, will instantaneously broaden our horizons and bring further respect and understanding to technology, religion, and the reality of ancient astronauts and divine intervention.

THE UFO FABRIC

Once we've accepted that UFOs are indeed the real deal and that ancient astronauts are indeed a reality, then we can start to move forward to see the feasibility of cattle mutilations, crop circles, and alien abductions. All of these compelling paranormal topics are part of the UFO fabric and deserve a chapter in my book. Even though we will just cover the tip of the iceberg on these subjects, crop circles, cattle mutilations, and alien abductions should become more transparent and aid in opening our eyes to the bigger picture.

All across North America and the world cattle mutilations and killings are taking place, and as the UFO subject heats up and slowly gains acceptance and forward momentum, more and more ranchers are coming forward to discuss the bizarre events that are taking place on their farms and ranches. Reports of UFO sightings in rancher's fields preceding the discovery of crop circles, and more importantly, the horrific findings of mutilated carcasses of cows, horses, bison, steer, and bulls have all exemplified UFO activity. Strangely enough, scavenging predators like crows, coyotes, foxes, and hyenas won't even go near the mutilated carcasses as if their sixth sense detects some anomaly that the carcass was tainted or tampered with. If you have ever watched Animal Planet, *Planet Earth*, or gone on a safari, you know that these scavengers love a free meal as they're nature's garbage disposals. These honest, hard working ranchers, with no reason to fabricate lies, who have worked on their farms for over 50 years, have been coming forward with brutal tales of their animals being mutilated in ways never seen before. Who are the perpetrators carrying out these heinous acts of malice? These ranchers are reporting that their animals are being slaughtered in a way that is much too advanced and sophisticated to be some kind of hoax or prank. They are finding their animals precision-cut (as if by laser), with no blood trails and no tire tracks or footprints coming in or out anywhere, even in the mud or snow. And, if scavenging predators were at fault then there would be blood everywhere as scavengers habitually tear and rip the flesh off the carcass. These animals have a very thick hide and through further evaluation and testing, investigators tried to mimic the precision-cut and concluded that even using a human surgical scalpel it was deemed impossible to replicate the radically advanced technology that cut the animals. Throughout testing, scientists claimed the human scalpel cutting the animals' thick hide left serrated edges as compared to the perfectly cut incisions found on the animal corpses. Investigations also proved that under a microscope the mutilated animals' hair was crispy where burnt leading investigators to further conclude that the unusual slits had to be from a high heat source like a laser. Furthermore, in the winter, the snow around the dismembered cow, steer, bison, horse, or bull is always melted away. Even worse and more telling is that ranchers and investigators have been finding their animals' mutilated carcasses with random organs and parts of the animal removed. Why are these random autopsies occurring? Witness ranchers have found missing intestines, missing lungs, hearts, tongues, and legs off their animals. Or, even more cumbersomely, incisions have been found by the dismembered animals' navels, or a left eye has been taken, or there's a missing left ear, all of which point the finger to UFO intervention. Where the ranchers' animals have been mutilated there are additional crucial clues that point to the UFO phenomenon to blame. There are so many additional clues left behind that point directly to ET subjugation, including, trees, bushes, and grasses in the surrounding adjacent areas that turn brown and lifeless. In addition, UFO footpads are commonly spotted where the craft landed near the soon-to-be dismembered carcass, a signature footprint foreign to any known conventional aircraft. Another significant clue is that the subjected animal is often found flipped over and found lying on its back with its legs kicked out in a fashion that is highly abnormal.

A recent cattle mutilation with the animal displaying the typical idiosyncrasies of dismembered body parts as well as kicked out legs from abduction and shock. Some UFOs may entail a hostile species that we would consider malicious and inhumane. Through abductions they examine and dissect our anatomy like we study lab rats.

When you add up all of these clues, the clues glue together and what's left is the reality that UFOs are the primary cause for these mutilations. Many of these ranchers claim that something toxic still resonates on the mutilation sites where no life grows or flourishes, and where the soil turns bland, unfertile, and nonviable around the site of the mutilated animal. Witnesses also claim that when in the vicinity of a mutilation site they'll often feel dizzy, light-headed, and often experience a shortness of breath.

So, what does the government think of all of this? Good question. The government has and will claim that the mutilations and dismembered carcasses, just like the crop circles, are an elaborate hoax or prank and has even claimed the culprits to be satanic cult rituals. According to John Stewart of *The Daily Show*, "We cannot ever take the governments word at face value as they're snake oil salesmen who sell snake oil as vitamin tonic." It is up to us in the civilian world to bring the truth to light as they have taken our kindness for weakness for far too long on a subject that should be shared with all.

These animal mutilations move us into position to discuss our next topic—crop circles, another eye-opening piece of the UFO fabric. Our stylish, debonair space neighbors take artistry to another realm, literally. Take a look at these crop circles pictures and the exact attention to every conceivable detail without imperfection. It doesn't take an astro-biologist or a NASA engineer to realize that there is something bigger than all of us at work here. However, and to credit the debunker community, some crop circles are synthetic and have been and can be created by man. Whether it be by a tractor or by manually stepping on the stalks of the crop, the point is that it can and has been done by humans. Yet, man-made crop circles can be readily identified with closer examination of the geometric angles and patterns exactness. Paul Dale Roberts, HPI Ghostwriter and Cerealogist says, "crop circles have been seen and documented since the 7th Century. While inside of a legitimate non-man-made crop circle, witnesses and scientists from across the globe have noticed how the grain stems from the crop are arranged in a precise concentric manner. They have also noticed that when entering a crop circle made by our space neighbors, knives and watches have been magnetized; body hairs have stood on end and people felt a titillating sensation on parts of their bodies. Also, and to further discredit the debunkers' explanation, dogs, cats, and other animals in the nearby vicinity will avoid entering a crop circle, just like with an animal mutilation site, since their built-in sixth sense warns them that something is not right. Witnesses have also heard and reported twilling sounds coming out of the crop circles." The 2002 "Alien Face" crop circle entailed an easily recognizable alien face, along with a circular grid containing some kind of binary data sequence.

The August 2002 alien face crop circle near Winchester, Hampshire UK. This creation appeared overnight and was immediately destroyed by authorities. Animals, such as dogs, would not enter the crop circle zone, an obvious sixth sense warning detection system that we humans rely on machines for.

This Alien Face formation was discovered in the middle of August in 2002 just west of Winchester (Hampshire, UK) at the Crabwood Farm. It appeared overnight and was measured to be 120 meters by 80 meters in size. You can watch the helicopter/plane flyover of the Alien Face formation, as well as the rest of the cited formations, on YouTube. The Binary Code actually works and at least three different experts with no affiliation to one another came to the same, identical conclusion. Jamie Maussan, who is one of the most respected journalists in Mexico and host of *Jamie Maussan, UFOs and Other Mysteries*, delivered their message at the 16th Annual International UFO Congress Convention and Film Festival in 2005. The deciphered code for the Alien Face crop circle reads as follows: "Beware the bearers of false presents and broken promises! Much pain but there is still time! Believe there is still good out there! We oppose deceit! The conduit is closing!" All of this powerful message is extremely humbling and we should be thankful that our space visitors are helpful enough to provide us with clues of what's to come in the future.

The August 2003 "Molecule" crop circle formation was interpreted to be an HE3 molecule. Many believe the aliens to use the HE3 Isotope in fusion reactors to produce 200 years of free energy and anti-gravity—talk about going green! This completely 3D "Molecule" formation has been analyzed as a warning of our solar system crossing into the "Galactic Plane'" in 2012 with a disastrous collision with another solar system—our binary star—found by NASA and Google Sky to be exactly where Nibiru (Planet X) and other planets revolve. If you're a hard-nosed skeptic then I implore you to log onto Google Sky or Microsoft Telescope's search function and enter the following coordinates: 5h 53m 27s, -6 10' 58. (http://www.youtube.com/watch?v=21Tzd5pp0fM) As of recently, editing has been a problem and the two companies are thought to be part of the notorious disinformation scheme, hiding vital information from the public, hiding stars around Orion.

The August 2003 molecule crop circle near Beckhampton, Wiltshire UK. Heed to the gigantism of the crop circle compared to the researchers standing within the molecule design. What if Earth's crop fields are a

blank canvass for these UFOs to leave renderings on? What if within
this otherworldly artwork there is a message trying to communicate
with us Earthlings that we are failing to receive?

The August 2003 'Molecule' crop circle...This large rendering was destroyed two days after its creation. Military officials are infamously known for demanding that farmers immediately harvest their grain, even if it's not ripe, obviously trying to delete the telling crop circle image from public view. Their efforts to cover the UFO phenomenon are commendable but in vain, as they probably didn't expect YouTube and the Internet to be such a problem for circulating the truth. The fact that these government agencies actually demand that ranchers and farmers harvest their crops in the wake of a crop circle can be used as evidentiary support for pleading the UFO case. If humans were to blame then why would the government cover up agencies waste their time in concealing and eliminating these crop circle images? The reason is that these animal mutilations and crop circles bring us closer to the truth, which is exactly what these government cover up agencies have sworn to protect.

The most intriguing and perplexing crop circle, and my personal favorite, is the "Mayan Wheel" formation found in Silbury Hill, Wiltshire UK, in August of 2004. Located in the UK, thousands of miles away from the home of the Maya and across the Atlantic Ocean, this formation is believed to depict the Mayan calendar and the end of the current cycle. In the mountains of Peru, with global warming and climate change, they have unearthed tiny green plants under the melting glacial ice that have been preserved for over five thousand years, entombed in the ice from the last great cycle. The Mayan understanding of our solar system and sun and has guided scholars to believe that our sun has cycles too, every 5,125 years. Over the course of our sun's life it has fluctuated in temperatures leading many to believe 2012 to be the commencement of the rising of our sea levels, which has happened many times in Earth's history. (http://www.youtube.com/watch?v=jBnowBwf1WI&NR=1) This prediction is more plausible than we may want to believe. Two-thirds of the Earth is currently covered by water but that ratio may go up drastically if our sun heats up and melts the trillions of gallons of water frozen in the form of glacial ice residing in our mountains as well as the North and South Pole. These crop circles are seemingly beyond human capacity with encrypted messages and "constructing of 2D patterns on the ground in order to give a 3D visualization from an aerial perspective." (http://www.cropcircleresearch.com/articles/alienface.html)

The August 2004 Mayan wheel crop circle Silbury Hill, Avebury, Wiltshire UK. One must notice the drastic size difference between the crop circle and the investigators standing in the middle of the Mayan wheel. Full disclosure of the UFO phenomenon between governments and their citizens needs to happen so that we as a collective species can move forward accelerating our involvement in deep space exploration and colonization.

Do you remember the show the *X-Files* with Fox Mulder and Dana Scully? Well, the truth is out there, and these encoded crop circle messages are providing mankind clues in order to raise consciousness. However, these messages are not going to be endorsed and sponsored by our TV news channels or newspapers. The programmed slaves in the news networks are mere foot soldiers following orders from their General (their editors). They're mere sheep following their shepherd and I would not expect a sheep that goes "baaahhhh" or a pig that goes "oink" to be on the same intellectual level as a wolf that howls. They are part of the problem, not the solution. They take orders not give them. The truth IS out there but we need to read between the lines in order to succeed.

ROSWELL

We are a tiny, fragile speck in the universe so blindly wrapped up in petty Earthly differences and bickering that we fail to look to the stars above for guidance. Plato said, "Astronomy compels the soul to look upwards and leads us from this world to another." In past generations, before the invention of TV's and computers, looking up into the night sky was normal. Now, in 2010, most have traded looking up for looking down to text message and email on their phones, and computers. If we're not looking up anymore then we're going to miss what's going on in the heavens above us. We need to acknowledge the secretive relationship between UFOs and our space exploration programs. Not since JFK have we had a decadent movement to go to the heavens and beyond and we need another serious awakening. We need a declaration, an announcement, that addresses the citizens of this great country, like the "We Choose to Go to the Moon" speech given by John F. Kennedy at Rice University in Houston, Texas on September 12, 1962.

"To be sure, all this costs us all a good deal of money. This year's space budget is three times what it was in January 1961, and it is greater than the space budget of the previous eight years combined. That budget now stands at 5 billion, 400 million dollars a year—a staggering sum, though somewhat less than we pay for cigarettes and cigars every year. Space expenditures will soon rise some more, from 40 cents per person per week to more than 50 cents a week for every man, woman and child in the United States, for we have given this program a high national priority—even though I realize that this is in some measure an act of faith and vision, for we do not now know what benefits await us. But if I were to say, my fellow citizens, that we shall send to the moon, 240 thousand miles away from the control station in Houston, a giant rocket more than 300 feet tall, the length of this football field, made of new metal alloys, some of which have not yet been invented, capable of standing heat and stresses several times more than have ever been experienced, fitted together with a precision better than the finest watch, carrying all the equipment needed for propulsion, guidance, control, communications, food and survival, on an untried mission, to an unknown celestial body, and then return it safely to earth, re-entering the atmosphere at speeds of over 25 thousand miles per hour, causing heat about half that of the temperature of the sun—almost as hot as it is here today—and do all this, and do it right, and do it first before this decade is out—then we must be bold. I'm the one who is doing all the work, so we just want you to stay cool for a minute. However, I think we're going to do it, and I think that we must pay what needs to be paid. I don't think we ought to waste any money, but I think we ought to do the job. And this will be done in the decade of the Sixties. It may be done while some of you are still here at school at this college and university. It will be done during the terms of office of some of the people who sit here on this platform. But it will be done. And it will be done before the end of this decade. And I am delighted that this university is playing a part in putting a man on the moon as part of a great national effort of the United States of America. Many years ago the great British explorer George Mallory, who was to die on Mount Everest, was asked why did he want to climb it. *He said, 'Because it is there.' Well, space is there, and we're going to climb it, and the moon and the planets are there, and new hopes for knowledge and peace are there. And, therefore, as we set sail we ask God's blessing on the most hazardous and dangerous and greatest adventure on which man has ever embarked."* (http://en.wikisource.org/wiki/We_choose_to_go_to_the_moon)

Earth, its seven continents and vast oceans, seem overwhelmingly large when you're standing at ground zero, but as you exit our atmosphere and enter into the endless abyss of space you suddenly see our planet from another perspective. One of eight planets revolving around our burning star, our sun that other civilizations see as a star in their night sky. For some alien species our star, and planets, are accessible and reachable by their advanced technology that we have yet to figure out. Their planes (i.e., interstellar vehicles, interplanetary vehicles, or UFOs) can travel to Earth from light years away as they are years ahead of us in knowledge and technology.

This view of the rising Earth greeted the Apollo 8 astronauts as they came from behind the Moon after the lunar orbit insertion burn. With this view, everything gets put into perspective...Earth, a blue sphere, full of life, seemingly floating in the black lifeless abyss of space.

There are four types of gravity in the universe that we know of: strong-force, weak-force, gravity, and electromagnetic force (http:// hyperphysics.phy-astr.gsu.edu/Hbase/forces/funfor.html#c1), with gravity being the weakest of the four and the type humans have the greatest understanding of. Our intergalactic neighbors have obviously learned how to harness the other types of gravity as a means for propulsion. UFOs are consistently spotted by witnesses around the world in areas of unusually high magnetism, also known as UFO hot spots. The UFO hot spots located across the globe—Sedona, the Bermuda Triangle, Bimini, Stonehenge, Machu Picchu, Easter Island, the ancient Egyptian pyramids, Puma Punku—are, intriguingly enough, all located on energy vortexes. This adds weight and validity to the notion that our sophisticated visitors are drawn to these areas to harness the magnetism around Earth's energy vortexes, a concept that our scientists and engineers are still trying to figure out.

Our Achilles' heel as a human race is to not think outside-the-box and unlearn what is possible. This creates an impenetrable wall, a nonviable learning platform. You and I, and our addicted-to-oil species, stop at gas stations to fill up our cars to get around and this is exactly what our intergalactic space neighbors are doing. Earth is just an exit stop to refuel off the galactic highway—a quick pit-stop to refuel and recharge. Our human cars and planes run on oil and gas while our space neighbors planes (UFOs) run on the harnessing of magnetism.

We are in the Stone Age compared to other galactic civilizations that may be 10,000 years, 1,000,000 years, or 1,000,000,000 years ahead of us on the spectrum of time. How can we be so naive as to think we're the only ones that exist in a universe of super unknowns? That way of thinking is scarily unintelligent and very unsophisticated. Some of these other alien beings have obviously learned how to harvest the power of quantum physics as UFO videos clearly point out a rubber band movement effect and an acceleration in velocity from 0-Mach 10 (ten times the speed of sound) instantaneously, hence the camera blur when a UFO is captured on camera even at 5,000 frames per second. Is it too late to learn of this radically advanced technology or have we been learning in deep parts of military intelligence circles since the Roswell UFO crash in New Mexico in 1947? Of course we've been learning about this intriguing and fascinating alien technology, but don't be looking in the newspapers anytime soon for military acknowledgements to the public that they have in fact been back/reverse engineering these craft for decades. Unfortunately, most governments think militarily and alien technology can be the difference between a country winning a war against another country, and which is why they will never go public. But, there's a very good reason behind our accelerated technological achievements in the last 100 years. The back/reverse engineering of alien technology is exactly why we've made more advances in science in the last 100 years than the last 5000 years combined.

You can see other species' advanced systems stemming into our military if you just do a little research. As of November 19, 2004, "NASA's X-43A took off from the Dryden Flight Research Center at Edwards Air Force Base, California, and created history when an unmanned experimental jet broke a world record for speed cruising over the Pacific Ocean at just under 7,000 miles per hour in a NASA test of cutting-edge scramjet engine technology. The X-43A supersonic-combustion ramjet or scramjet engine scoops up oxygen from the air rather than carrying liquid oxygen in a tank like an ordinary rocket. The design of the engine, which has no moving parts, compresses the air moving through it, so combustion can occur." These recent developments, which as of 2010 are six years old, prove our aircrafts could at least keep up with and possibly compete in the same arena as some of our visiting otherworldly alien UFOs. (www.indiadaily.com/editorial/11-19g-04.asp)

So, back to where it all began in Roswell, New Mexico, 1947. This is one of those open-your-eyes moments to search deeper and read between the lines. It is easy for the government and its staunch ties to the media to put some makeup and spin on this story, especially in a small town like Roswell, New Mexico, where they could easily dismiss the claims and fabricate a fallacy that the gullible public would buy.

The Roswell Daily Record from July 8, 1947 announcing the capture of a flying saucer. What happened in Roswell was real but relentless misinformation campaigns and cover up stories would have most of the public programmed to believe otherwise.

Was the military intelligence and top-secret community worried? You better believe it! They had to act quick to silence the truth. The last thing they wanted at this time in history, with heightened Cold War tensions, was for communist USSR to think we'd recovered an out-of-this-world extraterrestrial craft with advanced weaponry that we reverse engineer and deploy against them. So, the men in black working for clandestine government agencies took immediate control of the situation at Roswell and began their relentless disinformation campaigns. They generated a believable story about debris, not from a crashed otherworldly spacecraft, but from an experimental high-altitude surveillance balloon belonging to a classified program named "Project Mogul" or "Mogul," and thoroughly circulated their lies throughout mainstream America. The information that is pumped out into the mainstream world is carefully controlled and screened. Jeremy Ratter said, "information that we receive concerning the real world is carefully controlled," and more importantly, has been controlled since the day the printing press was invented. It's rather naive to think that our country's government and corporations would not control its media. These clandestine agencies also had to deal with and silence the witnesses from this small town, just like the eyewitnesses standing around the grassy knoll on Elm Street from the JFK assassination. If you did know or see anything you'd want to keep your mouth shut. Ask the people that were around Roswell at that time, or you could read and figure out that they all died from mysterious claims. Today there's a little more leniency and flexibility on the subject of UFOs but if you get in too deep they'll take control. They'll have you bugged and they will always be one, if not two steps ahead of you. Once you're a marked target in their cross-hairs they'll know every movement you make throughout the day, every word spoken on the phone, and every word typed on the computer. They'll know your next move before you know your next move. Once you realize that they own you is when most surrender and keep quiet in fear for the lives and well-being of themselves and their family. Most of the eyewitnesses to the crash were definitely spooked one way or another into not talking. The fact that these witnesses were being confronted by strange men claiming to work for the government is one of the biggest signs that what those witnesses saw was the real deal. Open your eyes! Why else would they use ferocious scare tactics and even kill witnesses over a downed experimental weather balloon? What they saw, they were not supposed to see. What they saw did not mesh well with certain government agencies who were trying to hide the one thing the witnesses were positive they saw.

Here's a list of Roswell residents who've been shaken down by the agencies of the government that deal with UFO cover-ups.

- Mortician Glenn Dennis said he received a death threat at the base hospital from a redheaded captain, who warned him if he talked "somebody [would] be picking [his] bones out of the sand." The following day, Sheriff Wilcox talked to his father, a personal friend, and said, "...tell your son that he doesn't know anything and hasn't seen anything at the base. They want you and your wife's name, and they want your and your children's addresses." His father told him about the conversation with the sheriff, so Dennis related the events of the previous day to him. Dennis also claimed that the nurse who confided in him about alien corpses subsequently was shipped off base and attempts to contact her by email resulted in letters returned with "deceased" marked on the envelopes.

- Frankie Rowe claims her father was a firefighter who, on a fire run outside of town encountered a wrecked craft and alien bodies. Later, after seeing a state trooper with a piece of dull, gray, metallic foil from the downed craft that "would unfold itself," she and her family were threatened into silence by military personnel who visited her house. She said they said, "They could take us out in the desert and no one would ever find us again." In her affidavit she wrote, 'I was told that if I ever talked about it, I could be taken out into the desert never to return, or that my mother and father would be taken to Orchard Park, a former POW camp." Rowe's older sister, Helen Cahill, said her parents told her a very similar story.

- Barbara Dugger, granddaughter of Sheriff George Wilcox, said her grandmother, Inez Wilcox, told her the sheriff had gone to the ranch and seen four alien bodies. Dugger said, "My grandmother said 'Don't tell anybody.' When the incident happened, the military police came to the jail house and told George and I that if we ever told anything about the incident, not only would we be killed, but our entire family would be killed."

- George 'Jud' Roberts was manager of the KGFL radio station in Roswell. He signed an affidavit where he claimed to have been threatened if he ran an interview his station had done with Brazel. "I got a call from someone in Washington, D.C. It may have been someone in the office of (New Mexico Senators) Clinton Anderson or Dennis Chavez. This person said, 'We understand that you have some information, and we want to assure you that if you release it, it's very possible that your station's license will be in jeopardy, so we suggest to you not to do it.' The person indicated that we might lose our license in as quickly as three days. I made the decision not to release the story."

- Walt Whitmore Jr., son of the KGFL station owner, also recalled how his father had hidden Brazel at their home and done a recorded interview. Whitmore Sr. was unable to get the story through on the wire and instead began broadcasting a preliminary release locally over KGFL. At this point, a long distance phone call came to the station from a man named Slowie, saying he was with the FCC in Washington. Slowie informed Whitmore that the story involved national security and that if he valued his station license he should cease transmitting it and forget about it. Immediately afterwards, another call from Washington came from Senator Dennis Chavez, who suggested he had better do what Slowie advised. (http://en.wikipedia.org/wiki/Witness_accounts_of_the_Roswell_UFO_incident).

These government men used frightening tactics to put the town of Roswell, New Mexico into a submission choke-hold. Fear ran that Do-Jo. They conjured up magic to release to the press, reinforced by scare tactics and brute force, and put a juicy worm on the end of their hook to lure the public in with a fictional, yet believable story. These government players know how to control human behavior and mindset. They know what people read in the newspaper and what they see on TV is what they'll be programmed to believe, especially if they just reiterate their lies of experimental weather balloons and military test dummies over, and over, and over again.

Major Jesse Marcel was the Roswell Intelligence Officer on duty and one of the first individuals to arrive at the crash site in 1947, a very credible firsthand eyewitness. On his deathbed he revealed everything, all of which is recorded on tape and available to the public. A portion is printed here.

"There was all kinds of stuff—small beams about three eighths or a half inch square with some sort of hieroglyphics on them that nobody could decipher. These looked something like balsa wood, and were about the same weight, except that they were not wood at all. They were very hard, although flexible, and would not burn...One thing that impressed me about the debris was the fact that a lot of it looked like parchment. It had little numbers with symbols that we had to call hieroglyphics because I could not understand them. They could not be read, they were just like symbols, something that meant something, and they were not all the same, but the same general pattern, I would say. They were pink and purple. They looked like they were painted on. These little numbers could not be broken, could not be burned. I even took my cigarette lighter and tried to burn the material we found that resembled parchment and balsa, but it would not burn—wouldn't even smoke. But something that is even more astonishing is that the pieces of metal that we brought back were so thin, just like tinfoil in a pack of cigarettes. I didn't pay too much attention to that at first, until one of the boys came to me and said, 'You know that metal that was in there? I tried to bend the stuff and it won't bend. I even tried it with a sledgehammer. You can't make a dent on it.'" (http://en.wikipedia. org/wiki/Witness_accounts_of_the_Roswell_UFO_incident)

Although far from a carbon copy of the recovered materials around Roswell, this malleable material resembles our own Earthly material known as Mylar. However, and as stated by Marsel and Marsel, Jr., this recovered material could not be burned or scratched, and more importantly, was not used in the government's alibi of high altitude spy weather balloons, also known as Project Mogul. Hopefully your eyes are starting to open a little more as we undercover yet another government lie. Major Jesse Marcel was part of the 509th Composite Group of the Roswell Army Air Field, New Mexico, which was an elite nuclear air wing bomb unit, and at the time was the only nuclear air group in the world. After the Japanese surrender ending WWII, and as of "November 1945, the 509th Composite Group relocated to Roswell, New Mexico, from the island of Tinian, which was part of the Commonwealth of the Northern Marianas Islands. This is the island perhaps best known for being the base from which the American atomic bomb attacks were launched on Japan during World War II. The 509th B-29 Superfortress bombers, the Enola Gay and Bockscar, piloted by Colonel Paul W. Tibbets and Major Charles W. Sweeney, took flight towards Hiroshima and Nagasaki, Japan carrying the first atomic bombs 'Little Boy' and 'Fat Man' deployed to be detonated over the two cities." (http://en.wikipedia.org/wiki/509th_Composite_Group) This human behavior had not been seen before, and just as human scientists study the patterns of wildlife, these otherworldly intelligent species were monitoring and studying our human nuclear behavior and were obviously observing our every move towards unleashing the world's only nuclear bombs, Fat Man and Little Boy.

However, and fortunately for us—or should I say for our military—the aliens had a malfunction and lost one or two of their aircrafts (UFOs) while on a reconnaissance mission gathering information near the Roswell Army Air Field and the world's sole nuclear air wing unit, the 509th Bomb Group. This is a crucial moment in time when our country was blessed to recover the Holy Grail of ufology—radically advanced foreign technology. This alien technology proved to be a portal to see years beyond our own earthly intellect and accomplishments, and would eventually become a platform to work off of in laboratories such as the top-secret Nevada base, Area 51, located just north of Las Vegas. From a military point of view, the key to a crashed vehicle and/or craft from another civilized part of the universe is to understand how it was created, and this is done through a process called back or reverse-engineering. This process, in a nutshell, is just about taking a finished product and figuring out how it was put together by disassembling it backwards piece by piece to understand its dynamics and origin.

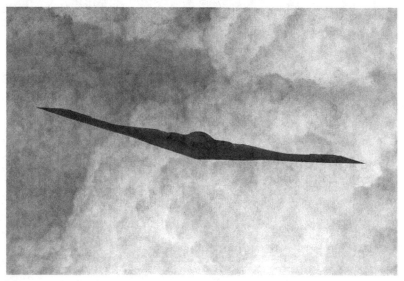

The Northrop Grumman B-2 Spirit stealth bomber (front profile).

The Northrop Grumman B-2 Spirit stealth bomber (side profile).

Take a look at this picture of a B-2 stealth. Looks alien, huh? Well, it's close but it's manmade from reverse engineering and is not quite as sophisticated as actual UFO crafts; however, the blueprint for this B-2 stealth craft is alien and otherworldly in origin. For those fortunate enough to be selected to back-engineer a UFO, this up-close-and-personal encounter, which would be completely mind blowing to the average John Q. Citizen, would be psychologically altering. Once you've seen some of the biggest secrets that our military has kept from the public, I doubt a regular 9 to 5 job would ever suffice. "The work conducted on recovered space vehicles has broadened and stemmed into our everyday lives. Technology originally earmarked for the military winds up as the most basic and everyday consumer products. From a military viewpoint, night-vision, microchips, Kevlar, bulletproof vests and armor, semi-conductors, fiber optics, lasers, stealth (i.e., B-2 Stealth Bomber, F-117 Stealth Fighter, F-22 Raptor, F-35 Joint Strike Fighter, Project Aurora), and many other metal alloys can all be attributed to the alien technological savvy. Through the reverse-engineering of their UFOs and technology, their blueprints were ascertained." (1997 New York Times Best Seller *The Day After Roswell* by Colonel Philip Corso and co-author Bill Birnes of the History Channel's *UFO Hunters*).

In the astounding book *The Day After Roswell*, Colonel Corso and Birnes, both trailblazers for breaking open the UFO subject, advocate that NASA and the American military have been designing and tinkering with alien technology—designing plasma beam weaponry—from shot down and recovered UFOs. Furthermore, in 1961 Colonel Corso was posted to the Pentagon to the Office of Foreign Technology where he was ordered by his superiors to share alien secrets with military contractors, thus leading to an incredible array of inventions from the reverse-engineering. Phillip Corso called it "applied engineering." What he meant was to give this radically advanced technology to industries that want it and encourage them to take credit for the discoveries and for the patents. Corso also advocates that this alien technology that was to be stemmed into certain companies, especially defense contracting companies, would not under any circumstances be traceable back to the alien technology. They were to be purposely misled to believe the inventions were conceived by human minds. (www.bibliotecapleyades.net/sociopolitica/dayafterroswell/dayafter17. htm)

AREA 51

Area 51 was deemed non-existent by our own government for years and was only recently admitted to exist, most likely because civilian owned satellites proving that something does indeed exist out in the Nevada desert just north of Las Vegas—with the second longest runway in the world at 23,000 feet long, I may add. (http:// wiki.answers.com/Q/What_is_the_world's_longest_runway) The operations and experiments being conducted there are extremely classified and never make the headline news. Satellite imagery from civilian funded organizations clearly see a base, which is mostly submerged as an underground facility in the Nevada desert. The government is doing classified work within the labyrinth of Area 51, but recent covert and top secret black operations are underway in new, underground bunker complexes near the Bradshaw Ranch just west of Sedona or underneath Dulce, New Mexico. When I say "underground bunker complex," think "Vietnam rat tunnels" to get a picture in your head. Now take that image and enhance it to see an underground lair, fully equipped with sustainable living quarters and state-of-the-art technologically advanced systems. Looking around, you'd never even know you were underground. The work force for Area 51 flies out of the Las Vegas McCarran International Airport to the heavily guarded impregnable fortress of Area 51. Try to walk within the Area 51 perimeter past the "Use of Deadly Force Authorized" signs and you'll be intercepted by security forces, detained, fined, possibly imprisoned. We don't need to look to Area 51 to know UFOs exist. The most promising, plausible evidence has been passed along from earlier civilizations.

The infamous Area 51 'Use of Deadly Force Authorized' sign. This is a multi-level, state-of-the-art research facility, most of which is concealed within an underground labyrinth, and has some of the most genius and brilliant minds employed doing top-secret, classified projects.

DULCE

If extraterrestrials were indeed observing human behavioral patterns, then they would quickly realize that we are very predictable. For example, humans sleep to recharge every night and at that time our guard is pretty much down. We're vulnerable when we're not observing our surroundings and extraterrestrials know this typical human behavior. They would see that we tend to reside and populate on the surface of the planet. They would also observe that we dominate Earth's airspace operating airplanes that litter the skies from New York to Hong Kong. They know our ways and our behaviors, so why would they set up shop where humans congregate? Extraterrestrials would also quickly discover that Earth's oceans are unoccupied and relatively vacant from mass human activity. We also do not tend to live underground, which is why Dulce, New Mexico is the next piece to unraveling the enigma. Considered a more secretive Area 51 and known by insiders as "Section D," Dulce is a seven-level underground research facility deemed nonexistent by our own government. A base so secret that they will kill you on site, without hesitation mind you, for attempting to infringe upon their business. If you thought the surveillance that encompasses Area 51 was impregnable, Dulce, New Mexico is the zenith and epitome of top-secret and classified. This is the location where the things that "don't exist but do exist" take place.

Open your eyes to a subterranean world of intricate tunnels and sub-cities created by huge, steel-encased worms called boring machines. These nuclear powered boring machines burrow through deep underground rock, heating the rock to a molten state, which quickly cools after the machine moves on. These machines bore the holes, remove the earth, and pave the inside of the tunnel with precast concrete segments. Living quarters, spacious parks, lakes, and wooded areas have already been constructed underground, and an ex-security officer, who worked underground in the Area 51/Groom Lake area, claimed to have seen a baseball diamond and an Olympic-sized swimming pool in one of the caverns a mile below the Nevada desert.

A U.S. Air Force Tunnel Boring Machine (TBM). It is tangible proof that the U.S. military has used TBMs for secret military tunnel systems. This photo was taken December 14, 1982, some 28 years ago. The TBMs of 2010 are much larger and much more technologically advanced compared to the earlier predecessor. TBMs working for clandestine black agencies have casted a network of sophisticated underground "Doomsday" tunnel systems that span from LA to NYC. If the surface of the planet becomes inhospitable, our species will be forced to dwell within mountains and within the Earth's crust. We will learn to live underground like ants. We must adapt to survive.

Dulce, New Mexico, is the perfect cover town to conceal black operation exercises underground. A small community of only 900, most people have never even heard of this remote town. Yet, there's a dark underbelly of the small town. Dulce is located at 7,000 feet in elevation beneath the Archuleta Mesa and concealed within the Jicarilla Apache Indian Reservation. The black world knows this Jicarilla Apache Indian Reservation, which is located on top of the Continental Divide and engulfed by national forests and river systems, will misdirect the public's eye in order to preserve the enigma found underneath Dulce's candy-coated layer. This small isolated town in northern New Mexico has one hotel and few stores, but beneath its artificial surface there lies a deep and dark secret. That secret is said to involve a joint government-alien biogenetic laboratory constructed to carry out bizarre experiments on humans and animals. Other similar bases exist in Colorado, Nevada, and Arizona. New Mexico State Police Officer Gabe Valdez can vouch for the area being host to a multitude of mysterious cattle mutilations, and furthermore, investigators claim the area to be a hotspot for UFO activity.

Ex-security officers and informants who have worked in the Dulce facility have claimed this to be an underground mecca for over 18,000 "greys," a reptilian-humanoid-alien-entity capable of being devious and not adhering to agreements. A portion of their description follows.

> The underground compound is designed to have increased security as one descends to the lower levels and there are over 3,000 real time video cameras deployed throughout the complex. Levels 5, 6, and 7 are the levels where the aliens are housed and it has been said by numerous ex-employees of the base that most signs on the doors and hallways are in the alien language, yet a universal symbol system is used and understood by both species, human and alien. After the second level, everyone is weighed in the nude, then given a uniform. Visitors are clearly marked and given an off-white jump suit with a zipper. The weight of the individual is put on an I.D. Card each day and harshly scrutinized. The individual's weight is monitored and any change is noted, and if the individual is three pounds over the initial recorded weight a physical exam and X-ray is mandatory. In addition, scales are located in front of all sensitive areas and are built into the floor near doorways and door control panels. The individual places their ID card into the slot, and then proceeds to enter a numerical code into the keyboard. The person's weight and code must be synchronized to the ID card or the door will not open. Any glitch or discrepancy will summon

security immediately. No one is allowed to carry anything into sensitive areas and all supplies are put on a conveyor belt and thoroughly X-rayed and investigated. The same process exists visa versa when exiting the facility. Furthermore, all of Dulce's elevators are created without cables and are magnetically controlled. The magnetic housing system is fabricated within the walls of the elevator shaft, and there are no normal electrical controls. Since the radically advanced technology was not understood by the humans, the aliens assisted in the design and construction. The humans involved in the construction process watched in awe as the assisting alien project engineers pieced together and assembled structures that baffled them, yet functioned to a T when put together. Everything is controlled by advanced magnetics, including the lighting for the underground labyrinth. There are no regular light bulbs and the tunnel systems are illuminated by phosphorus units with broad structureless emission bands. Some of the deeper tunnels use a phosphorus pentoxide to temporarily illuminate areas, and for reasons unknown the alien entities will not go near these areas.

The ex-security officers and informants go on to state, "Level 1 contains the garage for street maintenance, level 2 contains the garage for trains, shuttles, tunnel-boring machines and disc maintenance. Level 4 entails studies on human-aura research, including all aspects of telepathy, hypnosis, and dreams. They have the capability to separate the bioplasmic body from the physical body to place an 'alien entity' life-force-matrix within a human body after removing the 'soul' life-force-matrix of the human being. Furthermore, they can introduce data and programmed reactions into your mind, or if you prefer the Dulce Base lingo, information impregnation or 'Dream Library.'" (www.abovetopsecret.com/forum/thread61316/pg1)

Level 6 is privately called "Nightmare Hall" in the Dulce Base loop. This level holds the genetic labs, where experiments are executed on fish, seals, birds, and mice that are vastly altered from their original form. There are multi-armed and multi-legged humans and several cages of humanoid bat-like creatures as tall as seven feet. The aliens have taught the humans an extraordinary amount about genetics, both helpful and dangerous. People truly have witnessed monsters that have been genetically engineered in "Nightmare Halls" across our country and the world. In addition, the ex-security officers and informants claim, "The grey and reptoid species are highly analytical and technologically oriented and are intensely involved with computing and bio-engineering sciences. They conduct what we humans would consider to be extremely inhumane, unethical experiments without regard towards other living creatures." These insiders who worked for the Dulce Base left with great haste after working in the horrific and haunting underground environments, thus starting the "Dulce Wars." Unfortunately, many of these insiders who formed a secret resistance group knew too much and had to be eliminated by the rogue black elements sworn to keep the base a secret at all costs. "Over time they were assassinated or died under mysterious circumstances." (www. abovetopsecret.com/forum/thread61316/pg1) These insiders who had been traumatized during their years of work at Dulce had this place dialed, even knowing its affiliates within our principal government organizations. These insiders stated that the Dulce Underground Labs are run by the Department of Energy and that the chief of the genetic experiments for Dulce and Los Alamos is Larry Deaven. These ex-security guards and informants who saw this mind altering world go on to say that many UFO abductees have been used in genetic experiments where often the humans are kept in cages on Level 7. Row after row of thousands of humans, human-mixture remains, and embryos of humanoids are kept in cold storage. One of the sources claims, "I frequently encountered humans in cages, usually dazed or drugged, but sometimes they cried and begged for help. We were told they were helplessly insane, and involved in high-risk drug tests to cure insanity. We were told to never speak to them at all. At the beginning we believed that story. Finally, in 1978, a small group of workers discovered the truth and that began the 'Dulce Wars.' Intriguingly enough, the sources also went on to declare that the aliens don't want Earth's land, the gold, the minerals, or the water that we possess, nor the human and animal life. However, what they DO want is the raw magnetic power that surges on and through the Earth. The aliens harvest this magical power in a way unknown to us, and most importantly, the aliens recognize this magnetic power as more valuable than any other commodity on our globe." (www.subversiveelement.com/Dulce.html)

Now, put the pieces together and open your eyes to see the direct correlation between UFOs, abductions, animal mutilations, and Earth's many energy vortexes that are a beacon for extremely high levels of magnetism. These energy vortexes are obviously some sort of gas station for these alien beings and their planes or UFOs, which harvest and harness magnetism. The technologies that are feasible and viable to these alien entities are still relatively unknown and undiscovered to our primitive human species. This is where we all must open our eyes to see this world, not of science-fiction, but of science-fact. This is reality and it's happening here on Earth right under our noses. Recently, research teams have gone up to the Dulce vicinity and the Archuleta Mesa to conduct sounding tests to penetrate underground, and eerily enough, preliminary and tentative computer analysis on the underbelly of Dulce indicates deep cavities and catacombs under the mesa, thus confirming what we've known for far too long—a strange world exists beneath our feet. Whether or not you want to open your eyes and see this living nightmare is your choice. If you're looking for truth and want to ask our government for an answer then you've already become prey for their disinformation campaigns. They'll eat you and your questions up for breakfast and smell your stench of weakness a mile away.

WASHINGTON D.C. UFOS

Throughout this chapter I will reveal some declassified tangible evidence and proof regarding a cluster of UFOs over Washington D.C. in 1952. This is an extremely captivating and compelling chapter based around the true events that occurred in 1952, five years after the Roswell, New Mexico UFO frenzy occurred. We must remember that at this point in time, America and the world were just seven years out of WWII and had no stealth aircraft besides the U-2 spy plane that could've been mistaken for UFOs.

The statement that UFOs normally only appear in desolate areas is definitely not plausible, especially when considering the 1952 buzzing of the White House, Capitol building, and the Pentagon which you can watch on YouTube. http://www.youtube.com/watch?v=sTZ7O9cfpPQ. The first incident occurred on July 19 and 20, with the second mass-sighting occurring shortly after on July 26 and 27, both of which made front-page headlines in newspapers across the nation and around the world. The sightings were confirmed by ground and airplane radar as well as by visual reports from pilots that were sent in to validate the objects. Edward Nugent, an air-traffic controller at Washington National Airport, and his superior, Harry Barnes, a senior air-traffic controller, spotted seven objects on their radar the night of July 19. Air-traffic controller Nugent officially stated, "We knew immediately that a very strange situation existed...their movements were completely radical compared to those of ordinary aircraft."

An array of photographs were taken from all over Washington D.C., clearly proving the anomalies to be authentic and genuine. (Reference picture on back cover.) Furthermore, third party verifications proved that the pictures were not counterfeit or fraudulent. It's imperative to know that at this time in our country's history, our government had acknowledged through official reports that they believed the UFO sightings studied since 1948 showed that the unknown flying objects were interplanetary devices. Seemingly defying the very clandestine governmental agencies that were so intent on keeping UFO existence a secret, the UFOs over Washington D.C. proved to be one of the most revealing events and cases in UFO history. The irrefutable radar returns were seen and verified at both the Washington National Airport as well as at Andrews Air Force Base. The monotonous routine of doing things just became surreal. Witnessing government officials were at a loss for words to account for what was happening over their own highly sanitized and regulated air space, as this event seemed to defy all logic. The blips on their radar screens usually traveled around 100 miles per hour. The witnessing radar operators and government officials were left dumbfounded when the UFOs displayed the ability to reach the astonishing speed of 7,200 miles per hour when accelerating. They quickly realized that the capabilities of the UFOs were far beyond our military's technological proficiency at the time. Then, just when the bizarre couldn't get any more bizarre, it did. The interstellar vehicles buzzing the White House, Pentagon, and Capitol Building vanished from eye sight and disappeared off the radar screens over one of the most highly fortified airspaces in the world. These alien airplanes, or UFOs, had what we are currently trying to reverse engineer and model our fleet after in 2010, a chameleon-like cloaking mechanism as well as the unfathomable ability to become invisible to the eye and to radar. Now, our military in 2010 has stealth that evades enemy radar but this form of stealth more than fifty years ago, was unheard of.

Invisibility is not taken lightly, especially within the military-industrial complex and national security arenas. The "imminent threat to national security flags" go up immediately when an unidentified flying object is able to evade and penetrate the world's most advanced military and radar systems. The UFOs' ability to show technological dominance and air superiority directly over our country's capital, Washington D.C., makes us wonder if these otherworldly beings were showing off. Were these UFOs blatantly showing off our vulnerabilities and weaknesses by showcasing their absolute supremacy over our nation's capital? If not, then why didn't these UFOs display hostility and attack us and our primitive defenses? For these otherworldly beings to showcase their UFOs' mind-boggling ability to become invisible, directly over our capital suggests they were bragging. To "flex their muscle" over the most sensitive and patrolled airspace in the world immediately dispelled any notion that we (the USA) were the world's greatest superpower. Invisibility was often thought to be impossible, a science fiction concept thought to only occur in comic books and movies, but today we know that to be a fallacy. It can be accomplished, and in 2010 scientists and engineers are close to unlocking the secrets of invisibility—the ultimate stealth. If you've ever seen the movie *Signs* with Mel Gibson and Joaquin Phoenix then you'll probably know what I'm talking about. Do you remember the scene where the bird unknowingly hits an invisible UFO and falls dead to the Earth from the invisible craft hovering above Mexico City? Well, this is the same type of setting that occurred in Washington D.C. in 1952 with UFO crafts becoming invisible and hovering directly over our most prized and coveted city. Now, our black world scientists and engineers working in quarantined, classified environments like Area 51 and Dulce have been busy bees, diligently working to harness this technology and channel it into our own military. This radically advanced alien technology from 1952 was and has been ascertained through reverse-engineering and is something that we've incorporated into our military as the stealth that we currently use today to escape enemy radar detection.

The US Air Force Air Defense Command was first notified of what was occurring in 1952 by Andrews Air Force Base and immediately summoned several F-94 night fliers which were ordered to hunt down and verify the subject of the radar sightings. However, repairs being done on a runway delayed their response to intercepting the unknown bogeys. By the time our first fighter jets were off the ground the UFOs were nowhere to be seen. When our interceptor planes ran low on fuel and returned to their airbase, the UFOs returned, as if taunting our antiquated defenses. Senior air-traffic controller Harry Barnes believed "the UFOs were monitoring radio traffic and behaving accordingly." This doesn't suggest that these alien UFOs were intelligent, it's implicit. For hours, our US planes chased the illusive targets, yet without success. According to official reports, our pilots could actually see the perplexing objects, but as they approached, the lights of the UFOs vanished.

The Cedar Rapids Gazette *from July 29, 1952 speaks volumes. More so, and even more telling than the* Cedar Rapids Gazette, *was* The Washington Post *front page from Monday, July 28, 1952 which read* "'Saucer' Outran Jet, Pilot Reveals." *People need to open their eyes to see that this squadron of UFOs were able to penetrate restricted airspace over Washington D.C., and made themselves known to the world's superpower with flybys over America's capital.*

There are pilot accounts of actual dogfights between our US planes and the UFOs, with our planes being ridiculously out-maneuvered. After the first wave of UFOs there was a quiet week, but the feeling of disbelief resonated strongly with the military and aviation circles. Then, and to prove it wasn't just a fluke, on July 26, 1952, they came back again. And, just like the first occurrence there were multiple radar confirmations of the unidentified objects, and once again F-94s were dispatched to confront the invading UFOs. The outcome was the same as the first encounter with our pilots feeling the same vexing feeling as the week before. As soon as the intercepting F-94 pilots approached the UFOs, the lights of the pursued UFOs blackened out. To add to the frustration of our pilots, some of the UFO pilots were very audacious and brazen, suggested in an air to ground radio transmission: "They've surrounded my plane, what should I do?" The UFOs were seemingly just toying with our pilots and planes and I tend to wonder if any of the aliens were laughing aloud inside their UFOs at the primitive humans trying to catch them.

The importance and significance of the events over Washington D.C. in 1952 produced an Air Force press conference on July 29, and just like the hokey press conference held after the Phoenix Lights in 1997, the ridicule card was played to trump the paranormal event. Due to the mass sightings throughout the entire Washington D.C. vicinity, the public believed they had every right to expect an answer to why our Air Force was unable to prevail over the unknown objects so easily seen speeding throughout our skies. Major John A. Samford was in charge of the conference and he provided an answer to the paranormal event that was less than adequate from the public's viewpoint. Yet, we are well aware today of the government's jaded protocol, nefarious non-disclosure routines, and especially their notorious misinformation campaigns. It's the same song and dance today as in 1952 and is exactly why *Open Your Eyes: To 2012 and Beyond* was crafted to fuse the correlating relationship between 2012, UFOs, and religion. We know the government wants prudence and the people want candor on the subject of UFOs. We know now that they'll never reveal the truth because no one would ever trust the government again for keeping a secret of that magnitude hidden from them for all those years. Remember that the government lied to us before, denying the existence of the top-secret base, Area 51, up until 1995, according to the Travel Channel.

The status quo of denial, ridicule, and misinformation on the UFO topic will remain the government etiquette until the day the aliens make themselves known to the mainstream world. This is what we all want but it most likely will not happen because of a clandestine governmental force that regulates alien interaction with humans. The Air Force's explanation for the mass sightings of 1952 was a "temperature inversion." They claimed that this weather phenomena could be illustrated by ground lights once they reached the clouds giving the illusion of lighted craft flying in the sky. If this bogus misdirecting explanation is to be accepted, we would have had our scrambled F-94 jets flying at mirages in the sky. The eager, naive, and gullible public, that trusted the government, accepted this explanation and shelved the alternative that we were being invaded by otherworldly beings. Naturally, those who favored the UFO explanation laughed and didn't subscribe to the Air Force's bunk explanation. How do claims of seeing a "red-cigar shaped object" or a "huge fiery-orange sphere" or "a light that was changing from red to orange to green to red again" possibly be a "temperature inversion?" When we apply our common sense and logic, everything screams out "cover up!" Even Project Blue Book, a UFO study committee, joined in later saying that the "temperature inversion" explanation was completely bogus and that the Washington D.C. sightings were labeled "unexplained." (http://en.wikipedia.org/wiki/1952_Washington_D.C._UFO_incident)

The mass UFO waves over Washington D.C. were some of the largest sightings of all time, and were observed and photographed by many credible witnesses, both civilian and military. The witnesses were of "high" caliber, including, Air Force and other military personnel trained in the art of thorough observation and identification, thus making the D.C. sightings one of the strongest and most legitimate cases for the world of ufology. We've come to the point where the typical "temperature inversion and mirage" explanations are an insult to our intelligence. They might as well spit in our faces. These government agencies want to act as the controlling wolf and they want us to be the manipulated, cowardly sheep, but those days are over. Their failure to include "we the people" in these awesome revelations has once again woken up "the sleeping giant.'" The battle to disclose the correlating relationship between 2012, UFOs, and religion rages on. They have summoned an army of darkness to hide the truth and now it's up to us to raise our own flag and to summon our own army of crusaders to reveal the truth. (http://ufos.about.com/od/visualproofphotosvideo/p/washingtondc.htm) There's a war going on outside between Heaven and Hell. Which side do you choose?

PILOTS AND ASTRONAUTS AND UFOS

Let's talk for a moment on this next heated topic, which is an extremely valuable piece to the UFO puzzle. The riveting relationship between UFOs, astronauts, and pilots is a formidable adversary to any UFO critic or debunker community. The plethora of eyewitness accounts and high-caliber credibility of methodically trained pilots and astronauts, most trained and trusted by our government, are second to none. If you're wondering why we don't hear or read more about this in the news, I'll tell you. Due to the high level security environments that these professional individuals work in, taking orders based on rank is protocol and orders are followed based on a chain of command, period. You salute brass above your rank on the hierarchy and you are only allowed into restricted areas based on your specific level of security clearance. Everything, and I mean everything, is cleansed, rinsed, and sanitized before it ever reaches the media, especially about UFOs. The agencies that these astronauts and pilots work for are extremely crafty about how they conduct themselves in front of the media and public. Lying and embellishment of the truth is a monotonous circus routine for them at this point, since they've been doing it for so long. Directed by the government's ruthless misinformation and cover-up campaigns, and to misdirect the public's eye, they act as sculptors that sculpt believable stories for the awaiting press and news conferences. The messenger who delivers the fictitious story to the awaiting media forums is just that, a messenger—a delivery boy. All this puppet has to do is deliver a message and then sit back and field a few questions with extremely vague answers. If it were Major League Baseball this messenger would be a Gold Glove Award fielder. The real government players who are directing the show, and who are in charge of the messenger, are behind the scenes, behind the curtain. Systematic non-disclosure regulation so that no prized information ever leaks to media sources.

Regardless, what these pilots and astronauts have seen should be celebrated by all. Furthermore, the inquiring public deserves to know more about this subject and the intimate relationship between UFOs, astronauts, and pilots. If a ranking officer orders a subordinate not to talk about UFOs and be silent about their encounter, they listen. That's what these government agencies bank on—silence. However, they weren't banking on many of these retired veterans, nearing the end of their lives, and providing the public with top-secret UFO information they've been harboring inside their brains' vaults for too long. Can you imagine holding the greatest secret of all time inside your brain but you can't tell a soul, not even your direct family members? For many people in this world, the inability to divulge a secret of that magnitude would eat them alive and they wouldn't be able to sleep at night. Most of these individuals would not qualify for any kind of top-secret, high-level security clearance, either. Gossip cannot exist in the black operations world. Many current astronauts and pilots keep silent not only because of direct orders and fear of a court martial, but also out of respect for their superiors, as well as to not tarnish their reputations or branch of military service. Now, astronauts and some pilots, both civilian and military, have been cleared with some of the highest level security clearance based on their credentials. Much of what they've seen is classified and top-secret.

People, we need to get into our brains and erase what the government has told us. Why must we delete parts of what the government has told us? Well, that's an outstanding question. Certain areas of our own government excel in controlling, regulating, and manipulating the public through the bias and spin of TV, media, newspapers, and radio. The major players of our government who regulate and control these forums know that the majority of people are going to believe what they see on TV, what they read in newspapers or magazines, or what they hear on the radio. These are the major platforms from which they launch their propaganda and poisonous rhetoric. Nonetheless, are we going to believe what the government tells us after all we've been through and all the lies they've fed to us? We must learn from past mistakes in order to open our eyes. Metaphorically speaking, the point of *Open Your Eyes* is to bring the facts and the truth to the table so that we can see what we're eating, in this case, what the astronauts and pilots have been eating. For far too long we've been eating what the government has been feeding us, and believe me, they haven't included a ingredient list on what they've been serving us. When they've altered our way of thinking to believe what they want us to believe, they've won and are victorious.

I don't know about you, but I'm a spirited competitor and hate losing and strive diligently to come out on top a winner, no matter how tough the battle may be. We can't be called out on strikes and must go down swinging, and as Malcolm Muggeridge said, "never forget that only dead fish swim with the stream." The world would have its eyes opened to an entirely new realm of possibilities if our government, like other world governments, would reveal the truth about UFO encounters. Unfortunately, all these dark riders and henchmen employed under the dark side of the force of our government have committed perjury to the American public, but since they have the authoritative power and control the top-secret and classified paper trail it's damn near impossible to summon these players to court without tangible, plausible evidence. They rule with an iron fist and we need more than just accusations to stand a chance in court against a ruthless and tyrannical military industrial complex. To extract information through the legal system and through the court system would not bear any fruit, and all your efforts would die in vain.

IF we want real answers we must bypass the traditional method of asking for information and go directly to the source, the retired astronauts and pilots. Active duty astronauts and pilots are still sworn to secrecy and follow strict non-disclosure protocol, so asking them about UFO activity is pointless and would be a joke. However, the retired astronauts and pilots are the valuable first hand witnesses, the gatekeepers to the multitude of UFO encounters that occur to this day in the skies above us and in space. They hold the keys and combination to unlocking the secrets of the UFO enigma. Once that vault door is opened and the truth is revealed it will precipitate upon the world's people and way of thinking. Therefore, I implore everyone to think more clearly, free from our habitual and complacent mentalities. We must take a stand to reclaim the ability to set the truth free without being chastised for it. If a rumor is going around and being spread about someone or something and it sticks for years, chances are it's sincere and real and not just gossip. That's what we have with UFOs and their encounters with pilots and astronauts. There is definitely more than meets the eye.

The UFO rumor and myth has been around since the beginning of time, long before we took flight with the conventional aircraft, so chances are there's a genuine reason for why the rumor hasn't been dispelled. Another rumor that didn't wither away and die was the the Roswell UFO crash of 1947 that many believe to be authentic. Since 99.9 percent of us aren't in the intelligence community, it's up to us to bring this compelling relationship between UFOs, ex-astronauts, and ex-pilots into the limelight. I don't know about you, but I've seen our human planes AND I've seen their alien planes (UFOs) and all I'm advocating is that if we just open up the UFO subject to a broader audience, maybe we can learn from our aeronautically inclined space neighbors. We need to revitalize and revamp how we fly through our atmosphere as well as space. Our current look and way of flying is ridiculously outdated and in serious need of a face lift. Since the Wright Brothers' invention of the plane in 1903, airplanes have pretty much had the same look, especially our space shuttles. Our classic, outdated space shuttle is the equivalent to still driving around in a Ford Model T relic. Meanwhile, our alien astronaut space neighbors are cruising through the universe in their interstellar Mercedes-like UFOs or their interplanetary Bentleys, tricked out with all the high-end luxury options.

The outdated space shuttle design is in desperate need of a facelift and overhaul in order to propel our species into the heavens in order to join other interstellar communities of the universe. Other species looking at our space shuttle see this means of transportation as primitive and defunct. From their perspective and from behind their eyes, it's like we're still getting around using the Ford Model T car.

When we do finally open this ufology subject up to the public, millions of jobs will be created to further advance and expedite the human race into space and beyond. Lucky for us, many countries have started unveiling the black curtain and have begun releasing documents pertaining to UFOs in order to discuss the phenomenon more publicly. Some of these specific countries to finally disclose their UFO files to the public and media include: Belgium, France, Brazil, Mexico, and most recently, the British. Many of these released files are direct accounts from astronauts and pilots, and these accounts are the encounters that we need to broadcast more openly throughout the media forums.

The Internet has also been a huge asset in circulating truth and for opening people's eyes to the UFO phenomenon. Public interest and understanding of UFOs is without a doubt increasing, especially with the testimonies of extremely credible eyewitness pilots and astronauts.

To solve this puzzle, credible witnesses come first and foremost, and they are the astronauts. There have been many astronauts to enter the heavens above our atmosphere, but only an elite dozen have ever walked on the moon. Or did they? Let's take a look at the tip of the iceberg on the moon landing subject. We know there was a motive to create a counterfeit and intricately staged moon landing with the heated USSR vs. USA Space Race during the beginning of the Cold War. The USSR vs. USA rivalry was a neck and neck, ruthless race to pioneer the new frontier of space, and each side would do anything to trump the other side—hence the nuclear arms buildup created for one purpose—an Armageddon-like showdown. The Soviets reached the space benchmark first and successfully put the first satellite into orbit with Sputnik. In turn, it was up to the USA to trump the Soviet's latest achievement. The question is this, could, at a time when the majority of US citizens trusted the government, the moon landing have been filmed in a covert Hollywood-like studio with a Steven-Spielberg-like, gifted director to have the psychological advantage over the USSR? After all, the USA was engaged in a serious psychological warfare chess game with the Soviets during the Cold War. Just KNOW that the moon landing, authentic or fabricated, is a hot topic. So, raise questions and stir the shit storm in order to shake the coconut out of the tree. The problem is that most don't shake the tree hard enough to get any results. BUT, if we shake the tree with some ferocity, determination, and persistence, we may get some answers that fall from the pillars of the government. We must raise enough awareness to create a conquering movement, a relentless quest for the raw, pristine truth. But we must know that when we bark up that tree, we must bark loud and hard, knowing that the government is trying to murder the truth that we seek. Justice and truth don't come automatically, and the truth often poses a threat to power.

So, and with the moon landing conspiracy aside, let's get back to the linking relationship between astronauts and UFOs. One of these space pioneers was Dr. Edgar Mitchell, Ph.D, a distinguished American and former Apollo 14 astronaut and the sixth man to walk on the moon. Dr. Mitchell has openly confirmed the existence of other species in our universe and has stated that our government has kept us in the dark for over six decades. Now an old man rejoicing in the end of his days, Dr. Mitchell's not too worried about his personal safety anymore as he doesn't believe the government is eliminating people like in the past. He states that the other known species are not hostile and that if they were combative we wouldn't have the technology to defend ourselves. You can listen to Dr. Ed Mitchell's statement via the Internet. (http://www.youtube.com/watch?v=Q2uL9QqBl6g&feature=related) You can also listen to Apollo 11 astronaut Buzz Aldrin, famously acclaimed for being the second man to walk on the moon. (http://www.youtube.com/watch?v=XlkV1ybBnHI&feature=related & http://www.youtube.com/watch?v=Np45b2Xt-Ww&feature=related)

Buzz Aldrin jokingly states that there was no way they could just call down to Houston and say over the radio "We've got a light, a UFO, following us around up here" as it would've been complete pandemonium back on Earth and could have endangered the moon mission. Aldrin said that standard NASA protocol for the astronauts was to keep silent on the radio waves that could be subjected to public interception and eavesdropping. Their orders were to wait until they were back behind closed doors for the UFO debriefing. Take note that at this point in time, even with Vietnam, King, Kennedy, and Kent State, most people still trusted the US government and wouldn't doubt Big Brother's judgment. With that said, many of the elite government agencies wielded too much power and their nefarious schemes flew under the public's radar, unnoticed.

Just like today, complete secrecy and loyal oath are the norm for intelligence and black operation officials. These agencies keep their employees on a tight leash. If a trusted individual opened his mouth to rat and snitch out top-secret and classified UFO information, then he'd be toiling with demonic forces. That would certainly lead to the use of no-mercy, nightmare scare tactics on the individual and his family. Even worse, and if that individual knew too much, he'd get clipped and be six feet under with a fabricated, fictional death disguised as a heart attack, suicide, drug overdose, car crash, cancer, food poisoning, or whatever. The black operations world has a plethora of untraceable ways to orchestrate the extermination of an individual, and that substance wouldn't be detectable in an autopsy. So, when the people read the newspaper and see that some person died from a heart attack, that's most likely where their thinking process ends. But, I urge us all to dive in deeper to unveil the truths behind these disguised murders. These malevolent scare tactics are the reason why active duty personnel astronauts and pilots aren't talking, and is exactly why retired astronauts and pilots who are close to the end of their lives are finally talking. With death from old age so close, there aren't that many reasons anymore for these retired astronauts and pilots to still be afraid of opening their UFO vaults for the world. What astronauts and pilots say counts, and counts big.

The Phoenix Lights

The Phoenix Lights event forever changed the lives of thousands of Phoenix, Arizona residents, and is yet another invaluable satellite orbiting around the UFO phenomenon. In March of 1997, daily monotonous routine was interrupted when a massive V-shaped object was videotaped and photographed across the Phoenix area. Phoenix witnesses to the unknown craft described it as a giant, yet silent flying V-shaped mothership bigger than our largest aircraft carriers at sea. Some witnesses even described the unknown monstrosity as so big that a squadron of our B-52 long range bombers could fit on one of the wings of the massive V-shaped UFO. To add credibility to the Phoenix Lights subject, I cite the most credible, notable witness of the thousands of Phoenix witnesses, former Arizona Governor and Air Force veteran pilot Fife Symington. Fife Symington, the Arizona Governor at the time of the Phoenix Lights in 1997, witnessed firsthand the sightings that perplexed him along with thousands of other Phoenix residents to this day. We need to understand the professional stature of a governor and what it means to come out and openly announce a UFO encounter to the public and the media. This is not the typical non-disclosure etiquette and is a testament to the validity of the high-profile case, that there was something tangible that occurred and triggered Fife Symington to break protocol. You can watch former Arizona Governor Fife Symington discuss the Phoenix Lights on YouTube. (http://www.youtube.com/watch?v=W3zotvpZLnY&NR=1)

A rendering of the 1997 Phoenix Lights spectacle that appeared in USA Today. The former Arizona Governor Fife Symington confirmed that he too saw this object and stated to CNN "In 1997, during my second term as governor of Arizona, I saw something that defied logic and challenged my reality. I witnessed a massive delta-shaped, craft silently navigate over Squaw Peak, a mountain range in Phoenix, Arizona. It was truly breathtaking. I was absolutely stunned because I was turning to the west looking for the distant Phoenix Lights. To my astonishment this apparition appeared; this dramatically large, very distinctive leading edge with some enormous lights was traveling through the

*Arizona sky" (http://www.cnn.com/2007/TECH/science/11/09/
simington.ufocommentary/index.html)*

*We must encourage and commend more high ranking officials, such
as former Arizona Governor Symington, for challenging the pillars of
power to bring about truth on a subject owned, guarded, and horded
by the black world and all its affiliates that are privy to classified and
top secret programs.*

We must realize that when you're a governor and decide to go public
with a touchy, ridiculed subject, like UFOs, you're opening yourself
up to a world of harsh scrutiny from all angles by the public media.
Fortunately for us in this case, with crusaders like Fife Symington, as
well as many other truth-seeking officials coming forth as of recent
times, ascertaining the truth was much more important than being
ridiculed as a "wacko" and tarnished by the media. However, ex-
Governor Symington knew he wasn't the lone witness to the Phoenix
Lights of 1997, and because of that it made it easier for him to come out
and discuss the UFO. There were thousands of other Phoenix residents
lucky enough to witness the Phoenix Lights. You see, as a witness to a
life-altering paranormal event, it's always easier to come forward when
there are other witnesses who saw exactly what you saw. In turn, more
witnesses add more credibility and also means that listening individuals
will most likely respect and take your word at face value. This would
be much harder to accomplish if there was only one witness, as it's
always more difficult to accept one person's witnessing testimony at
face value. Even with an impeccable record, especially when dealing
with the "things that don't exist but do," one witness will not suffice
and can easily be discredited. That's why the Phoenix Lights of 1997 is
such a celebrated and highly unusual case. The Phoenix Lights case not
only involves a mass UFO sighting over the heavily populated city of
Phoenix, Arizona, but it also involves many credible witnesses that work
a host of honest jobs, including, military personnel and police officers.
Discrediting such a plethora of credible eyewitnesses would be a tough
task for any critic or debunker community.

However, the government denounced the sightings, former Governor Symington's claims, along with thousands of others, as flares dropped from a plane during a military training exercise. It comes as no surprise that further investigations proved the flare allegations to be erroneous. There were NO military training exercises being conducted anywhere in or around the nearby vicinities of the UFO sightings. The government even provided a dog and pony show at the June 19, 1997 press conference that turned into a media circus when they brought out a human dressed up in an alien costume, ridiculing and mocking the widely seen event. This is where, in my opinion, the people were deceived and misguided. The government misdirected our eyes elsewhere and we "dropped the ball" when we should have stood up to the system in numbers with some serious conviction. Whatever was seen by the Arizona Governor and thousands of other Phoenix witnesses struck a nerve with certain elements of our government and was quickly silenced. We surrendered too easily when we had a golden opportunity to strike while the iron was hot. Government cover-up protocol to neutralize the excitement and to keep the Phoenix Lights silent epitomized the UFO status quo. This has happened time and time again where the truth gets murdered right under our noses. We've seen it before in the past and we need to become more aware and keener of these government cover-up idiosyncrasies. Aren't we tired yet of being told what to see, what to hear, and what to think? Isn't it about time "we the people" stood up for the truth? As Ella Wheeler Wilcox said, "To sin by silence when we should protest makes cowards out of men."

The thousands of credible Phoenix residents that witnessed the massive, hard-to-miss craft that blocked and unblocked the stars as it flew over the Phoenix Valley in 1997 will never forget what they saw and will never stop believing, no matter how much the government's misinformation juggernaut tries to brainwash them and control their thinking through media spin and propaganda. The fraternity of credible and high caliber witnesses know what they saw, and what they saw were not aircraft flares from military training exercises.

However, there is one man-made, still-classified "black" craft that could have fit the bill for what was seen, and although the sizes don't accurately match up, it's the only HUMAN craft in our arsenal that comes close to describing what was seen over Phoenix—the TR-3B Astra.

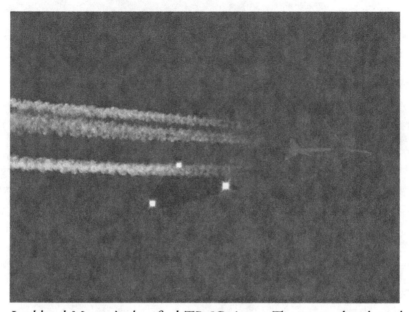

Lockheed Martin's classified TR-3B Astra. The triangular shaped nuclear powered aerospace platform was developed under the top secret Aurora Program. This still classified program is revolutionizing the way we travel. This top secret craft is 50 years ahead of its time and is a direct result of reverse engineering otherworldly propulsion systems. Make no mistake, this black world aircraft is the epitome of the things that don't exist publicly but do exist behind closed doors. This is the realm of the black world.

This "best of the best," cutting-edge craft is a direct result of the reverse-engineering of alien ingenuity and will most likely not be seen showcased at public air shows for another 50 years. The TR-3B Astra is still top-secret and highly classified, falling into the black world's realm of "things that don't exist but do." Built in the early '90s, this innovative stealth craft is right out of a science-fiction story. There have been three known 600 foot operational models built for the TR-3B Astra. This cunning craft can hover indefinitely, change its size at will, and has visual stealth giving it the unique cloaking ability to show itself, hide itself, and even make itself look like another object or aircraft. Most importantly, the TR-3B Astra has a Magnetic Field Disrupter, which disrupts or neutralizes the effects of gravity on itself, lowering its weight by 89 percent. The Astra is used for high-altitude reconnaissance at around 120,000 feet and reportedly flies comfortably at speeds of Mach 9. It is capable of achieving these radical speeds by traversing through less atmosphere at higher elevations. It can do this because it does not have the typical air inlets that we currently see on conventional aircrafts. The Astra has three multi-mode rocket engines mounted under each corner of the craft that use either hydrogen, methane, or oxygen as the propellant. (www.abovetopsecret.com/forum/thread164110/pg1) We don't have an exact blueprint outlining the unique dynamics of this cutting-edge craft, but we have enough information to paint a solid picture of what's going on in the black world behind closed doors in research facilities. What Phoenix residents saw, including the former governor, WAS an unparalleled and unprecedented craft. The only real question left that needs answering is whether the massive triangle craft seen over the Valley of the Sun in 1997 was the human knock-off prototype or the extraterrestrial, alien version?

This chapter has only provided the icing on the cake for the bizarre Phoenix Lights mass sighting of 1997, and is yet another riveting piece of the puzzle regarding the giant elephant in the room. The sobering reality of UFO truth will certainly bring transparency to the government's cover-up charade and collapse the house of cards built on lies. We continue to climb and march uphill through the flak in a quest for answers and truths.

KECKSBURG "PENNSYLVANIA'S ROSWELL"

This next chapter takes a look at "Pennsylvania's Roswell." Kecksburg, Pennsylvania, is a small rural town like Roswell, New

Mexico, that was changed forever when an unidentified flying object crashed in the town's woods on December 9, 1969. For better or worse, the attention garnished by the 1969 UFO event put the small town on the map, but its people were never the same.

Before the crash and before the UFO entered the Kecksburg airspace, local authorities confirmed on tape that reports had come in from thousands of witnesses in the surrounding areas of Detroit and upper Michigan, northern Ohio, and Windsor and Ontario, Canada. Intriguingly, all of these areas are nearby the abundant fresh water supply of the Great Lakes, which many ufologists believe to be attractive to UFOs. Many ufologists believe that water is an important ingredient needed for the UFOs' advanced propulsion systems. The FAA (Federal Aviation Administration) also confirmed that 23 reports from aircraft pilots, first starting at 4:44 PM, had seen the unknown bogey in the sky. In addition, the nearby town of Greensburg, just north of Kecksburg, received an onslaught of calls regarding a UFO sighting. This very bright light that started over Lake Erie was described by dozens of eyewitnesses as a "fireball or a star on fire" that eventually smashed into the wooded area of the small town. Kecksburg local eyewitnesses rushed to scene of the accident where the "long streak of orange light" ended, with most thinking that a plane crash landed in the woods of their quiet town. At this point, the Kecksburg witnesses had no idea that what had fallen from the sky was actually a UFO—not a downed aircraft.

With the possibility of a downed aircraft, the residents of Kecksburg geared up for survival mode to try and save any surviving passengers from the wreckage. Reports from local witnesses state that the UFO was indeed a physical object making controlled S-turns and appeared to be moving around the skies strategically as if to land. Furthermore, where the downed UFO had descended in the Kecksburg woods, the trees and tree limbs were snapped and broken in the exact angle that witnesses had described in their testimonies. Many of the towns witnesses, like Bill Weaver, recall a heavy and immediate manifestation of military personnel, some military branches being readily identified while others were unknown. Some saw the Army's trademark star symbol on jeeps and trucks, as well as state police, and other unknown, yet presumably military vehicles thought to be from the Air Force and NASA. In addition, if there was a downed aircraft in the Kecksburg woods then where was the NTSB (National Transportation Safety Board)?

Many witnesses wondered how the military personnel had gotten there so punctually to take control of the situation of the supposed downed aircraft. A plethora of credible witnesses "including fire fighters, newspaper reporters, and a news director at radio station WHJB, who was on the scene taping interviews, described the heavy military presence at the crash site, the cordoning off of the area, and the retrieval of an object transported by an Army flatbed truck. Many witnesses have been brave enough to come forward and provide signed affidavits for Kecksburg investigator Stan Gordon, who has been working on the case for over three decades." (www. ufoevidence.org/topics/Kecksburg.htm) Local news director and reporter John Murphy, of the radio station WHJB, was promptly on the scene collecting live interviews on tape, as well as taking pictures of the crashed object. Murphy may have been in too deep because not only were his evidentiary pictures confiscated, but immediately after the incident the situation escalated when two unidentified men in black paid him a visit at his radio station. When an individual, like Murphy, knows too much about the "things that don't exist but do," the dark riders come for you. Why would our government's clandestine agencies summon their lawless henchmen to pay a visit Murphy if it was just a plane that had crashed into the Kecksburg woods in 1969? They wouldn't. Why would they send out their dark riders to confiscate his photographs? Obviously, to conceal and hide the truth.

Murphy's closest friends say they don't know what was said to him, because what was said to Murphy was behind closed doors, but they noticed an immediate difference in his behavior after he had been approached. In addition to knowing too much sacred information, and with the possible threat of launching his eyewitness testimony to the world through his WHJB radio station platform, news director and reporter John Murphy was killed while crossing a highway in California. John Murphy's death reeks of a cover up. It's vile, putrid, and stinks like a bog. The nature and cause of John Murphy's death is shadowed with ambiguity. He was eliminated because in the eyes of the dark riders summoned from the black world of our government, Murphy was a threat to national security. John Murphy's ex-wife had said that John had extremely revealing pictures detailing the crashed UFO, which apparently was too much for the government's cover-up agencies to handle.

Many of the Kecksburg witnesses were pressured NOT to talk about the incident, and many didn't want to attract public attention or gain notoriety regarding what they had seen. However, before the military convoy and other local officials had arrived at the UFO crash site, the locals were the first on the scene. Witnesses Bill Bulebush, Bob Gaty, Robert Blystone and dozens of the town's citizens heard hissing sounds as they saw the bright, flaming fireball streak overhead their small town. Witness Robert Blystone claims to have seen smoke and dust pluming out of the Kecksburg woods, a common claim among the town's witnesses. Many also claimed that what they saw was a blue smoke similar to that of a welders light changing in hues from bright to dull, as well as the smell of sulfur permeating throughout the air. The key Kecksburg witnesses of December 9, 1969, who were all independently interviewed, reported the same story—seeing a windowless, bronze-gold colored acorn, a bell-shaped object with no seams, rivets, bolts, or nuts and a ring around the object entailing hieroglyphic symbols and inscriptions, similar to ancient Egyptian hieroglyphics. As the December night went on, more and more of the witnesses started to know that something of great importance to the military, possibly not conceived from this Earth, had crashed into their woods. The military, seemingly directed by unidentified officials, took immediate control of the situation. Dozens of the town's citizens were soon removed from the crash zone and ordered to stay behind the yellow tape. A perimeter was immediately set up by military officials and other authorities, not allowing any reporters or civilian witnesses to observe the site. What was so important to the military in the Kecksburg woods that was going to great lengths to conceal?

The official explanation that was aired on the news and ran in the newspapers was that a meteor had crashed into the Kecksburg woods on that winter night in December 1969. Government misinformation campaigns and cover-up agencies have been trained and know how to program a human mind. This conduct and behavior is more than expected from the government cover-up agencies always trying to downplay the seriousness of what was seen. It's all lies and an insult to our intelligence. Any logical, rational, common-sense-thinking human being knows that meteors don't intelligently fly around the entire Great Lakes area, as seen by thousands of witnesses. Why would a meteor be transported by a military convoy on a flatbed truck? Why would armed soldiers respond to a meteorite crash? How would a meteor have any of the true, tell-tale UFO insignias that were described by dozens of eyewitnesses? Why were witnesses threatened not to talk? Why would local news director and reporter John Murphy be murdered? Why would the local newspaper change its story, like with Roswell, New Mexico, to claim that nothing fell from the sky and that nothing was found? The Greensburg Tribune-Review newspaper from the following day of December 10, 1965, stated "Unidentified Flying Object Falls Near Kecksburg—Army Ropes Off Area."

If a meteor traveling at thousands of miles per hour from outer space did crash into the Kecksburg woods on that night of December 9, 1969, it would've smashed deep into the Earth's crust, splintering into a zillion microscopic pieces. Eyewitnesses described a bell or acorn-shaped object transported away by an Army flatbed truck, which would've been much too large to be a meteor. In addition, if the meteor theory were true then there'd be disintegrated meteor debris and particles left as evidence to be found and studied, and there would've also been individuals in protective biological hazard suits to protect themselves from any foreign, harmful entities derived from space.

In addition to the meteor alibi, stubborn, shortsighted debunker communities and cover-up affiliates will advocate that what crashed in the Kecksburg woods was a Soviet Venus probe called Cosmos 96 that re-entered Earth's airspace over Canada and eventually crashed into the Kecksburg woods. This theory was proved NOT to be consistent and accurate with the Kecksburg UFO case and has been verified to be a fallacy. The more excuses and lies they manufacture to feed to the public only destroys the rapport between our government and its people. The Soviet Venus probe Cosmos 96 reentered over Canada on the same date but at around 3:18 AM, while the sightings and crash at Kecksburg occurred half a day later at around 4:47 PM (www.ufoevidence.org/documents/doc1300. htm and www.theblackvault.com/wiki/index.php/Kecksburg,_ Pennsylvania_(12-09-1965) & History Channel). The research clearly proves, without a doubt, that the hours didn't match, nor were the flight path coordinates synchronized. Furthermore, the Russians have even verified that Cosmos 96 was not the source of what fell that day. Sorry debunkers, I know you may not want to hear it, but you need to open your eyes to what you don't want to see or believe. Do the research and follow the trail like a bloodhound. Get away from and avoid the speculation, the hearsay, the embellishments and fabrications, and once you've steered clear of these roadblocks you will come to the sobering realization that the facts don't lie. Remember, the key Kecksburg witnesses of December 9, 1969, who were all independently interviewed, reported the same story. These small town folks had no reason to lie. "Pennsylvania's Roswell" was not a meteor and it wasn't the Soviet Venus probe Cosmos 96. It was exactly what the key Kecksburg eyewitnesses described—a bell-like, acorn-shaped UFO.

In order to open our eyes to what really happened in Kecksburg, Pennsylvania, we need to jump into our time machine and travel back to Nazi Germany during WWII. Why? Because the Nazis were already reverse-engineering the exact bell-like, acorn-shaped object that key witnesses described seeing in the Kecksburg woods in 1969. The Nazis called it the "Die Glocke" and Adolf Hitler had his Nazi scientists working around the clock trying to back/reverse engineer the "Die Glocke" UFO. The Nazi scientists were tinkering with a new propulsion system and beginning to understand the dynamics of what they were dealing with. Fortunately for the Allies, and for the world, WWII ended and Adolf Hitler committed suicide before the Nazis were able to fully harness the radically advanced alien technology. With such a progressive project in the works, one could easily speculate that the Nazi air force, the Luftwaffe, would've reigned supreme with complete air domination. Air superiority dictates much in wars, and the Nazi swastika may have still been a common sight in 2010.

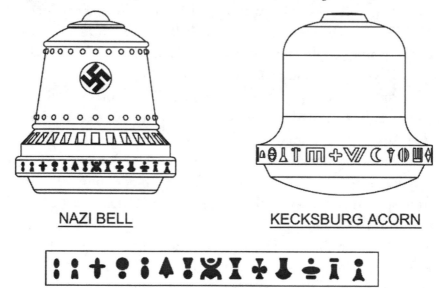

NAZI BELL   **KECKSBURG ACORN**

NOTE: STRANGE INSCRIPTIONS WERE FOUND ON BOTH THE NAZI BELL AND KECKSBURG ACORN

The Nazi 'Die Glocke' aka 'The Bell' shows a striking resemblance to the Kecksburg, PA acorn UFO.

With the seize and capture of Germany at the end of WWII, Nazi Germany's renowned scientists became a celebrated prize to obtain. The race was on between the Americans and the Soviets to capture as many Nazi scientists as possible so that we too could begin to understand the alien technology that they were tinkering with. What eventually grew from these Nazi blueprints was the Space Race and eventually, the Cold War. In America, these knowledgeable, former-Nazi scientists became employed for defense contracting companies like NASA, Boeing, Bell, Lockheed Martin, etc., developing new systems that completely revolutionized space technology. Many of these former Nazi scientists were also put in charge of classified developments at top-secret facilities within Area 51 and Dulce, New Mexico, among others. So, it's not a question of whether it was a Soviet probe or a meteor that crashed that December night in Kecksburg, PA 1969. The bigger question is: was it an alien ship or was it a man-made version of the "Die Glocke?" And if it was a man-made prototype of the bell-like, acorn-shaped "Die Glocke," then why were there hieroglyphic inscriptions?

Whether the Kecksburg UFO was terrestrial or extraterrestrial— who knows without seeing the bodies—but the origin of the "Die Glocke" that Nazi scientists were diligently working on in WWII was absolutely otherworldly and alien in origin. Our technology is where it is today thanks to our alien neighbors, but we could be so much further ahead, to the stars and beyond, if civilians could be introduced to the "things that don't exist but do" world. Have the government's best scientists take civilian protégées under their wing for the collective world effort to exponentially advance our space exploration programs. If the government and the civilian worlds work together harmoniously and integrate ideas, trust me, the discovered wonders and achievements will appear as if they're right out of a science-fiction book. We could have a Team Planet Earth vs. Team Planet "X" on ESPN's Intergalactic SportsCenter in no time at all. We all just need to open our eyes to the bigger picture, in the government and in the civilian world, so that we can get in the cosmic game and stop sitting on the sidelines.

CHICAGO O'HARE INTERNATIONAL AIRPORT AND TINLEY PARK, ILLINOIS

The next spoke on the *Open Your Eyes* wheel brings us to Chicago. These next two compelling pieces of the puzzle are key sightings from the Chicago area, both of which garnered national media attention. On Tuesday November 7, 2006, a UFO was spotted by several pilots, supervisors, baggage handlers, mechanics, flight attendants, and additional airport workers over the United Airlines Terminal. The UFO was spotted hovering silently for over two minutes 700 feet, over the C concourse, Gate C-17 around 4:30 PM, while it was still light outside.

The Chicago O'Hare Airport UFO was seen by a multitude of credible witnesses, including pilots and military personnel. According to the agencies that have sworn at all cost to keep the ufology subject a secret, what was seen was not supposed to be seen by the public. Every time a mass sighting occurs the black world sends out its henchmen with their toolboxes to rinse, cleanse, and sanitize the situation so that what you read in the papers and what you hear on TV is a fabrication of the truth. Swamp gas, temperature inversions, weather phenomenon, have all been past alibis. They are Sith Lord tacticians of psychological warfare including the use of misdirection, cover ups, and the programming of human minds. They have much more than just a hammer in their black operative's toolbox.

The dark gray cylindrical disc was reportedly seen lingering around the low-lying clouds, blending into the 1600-foot, overcast cloud ceiling. The witnesses claimed that the flying saucer that had penetrated restricted airspace over one of the world's busiest airports suddenly jetted off vertically, without noise, and punched an "eerie" open hole through the low-lying overcast clouds. The gaping hole created by the exuberant amount of force created by the propulsion system from the UFO eventually disappeared as the wind meshed and blended the clouds back together. One could easily see why our selfish military agencies don't want to share this knowledge with the civilian world; these crafts are the epitome of stealth. They want to hoard the UFO technology and eventually use it against our enemies. These UFOs are silent, they're elusive, they don't appear on radar, and they supersede all our conventional and military aircraft. After the November 7, 2006 sighting, United Airlines and the FAA both denied that they had any information on the O'Hare Airport UFO sighting. However, after the Chicago Tribune filed a Freedom of Information Act (FOIA) the FAA flip-flopped and manufactured an alibi to blanket the truth to silence all the hype and excitement. The FAA claimed and concluded that the metallic saucer was the result of a "weather phenomenon," the typical excuse used to sidestep the colossal truth.

In addition to their fraudulence, the FAA stated that the agency would not be further investigating the sighting, a direct contradiction to their protocol to investigate all airspace security breaches. Their suspicious actions to downplay the sighting as a weather phenomenon, and more importantly, to not take the United Airlines employees' testimonies seriously infuriated many, and I don't blame them. The FAA, like NASA, is the pinnacle of airspace secrecy and will continue to look down upon the mass population and feed us feeble excuses for what witnesses claimed to have seen. Their brazen demeanor and patronizing attitude is why we must learn to open our eyes and not seek answers from agencies who conceal the truth. Mind control is a powerful tool that they constantly deploy against the people. They depend on us to be manipulated and taken advantage of. They condemn and discredit us for witnessing the impossible and habitually stonewall our inquisitions to ascertain what was seen. These cover-up agencies obviously see UFO activity as greatly important to their agenda, which is why they'll never stop mandating the cover up. Further investigations should have been conducted.

Any security breach over restricted and controlled airspace warrants a thorough investigation. So, why did the FAA disregard protocol on Tuesday November 7, 2006 when a UFO made itself visible while it was still light out? If 'we the people' rise up in the millions, we can make a stand and pry open the UFO subject to the civilian world. But, our strength has to be power in numbers as we march to open the perilous vaulted black world door. What happens when we rise up in the millions and march on Area 51? What happens when we are no longer intimidated by the "Use of Deadly Force Authorized" signs? There will be stiff resistance as we summon an army of crusaders to battle an army of darkness, and it's absolutely paramount that our crusade does not fail. For too long we have played their game, choked on their rhetoric, and have been victims of their hypocrisy. When we go to war for our cause, surrendering is not an option because what lies behind that vaulted door will change everything about how we live, how we think, and most importantly, how we see ourselves playing a role in the vast spectrum of the universe. If we don't fight we'll never know the truth, and the truth is always worth fighting for, even if it means that some people will perish. That's the sacrifice the crusading army will have to accept, but as long as the truth is eventually unveiled the deaths will not have been in vain.

These UFOs and extraterrestrials have been visiting our planet since the beginning of time, long before the birth of Christ. There's a vital message that the black world is withholding from the people that affects every living creature. What's entailed in that crucial message revolves around December 21, 2012. Mother Earth may be in trouble, her well-being in jeopardy, and we must know the message to survive.

In order to decipher what's in that eye-opening message, we must clash with the black world to get access before it's too late.

The 2004 Tinley Park, Illinois UFO sightings are very significant. Just like the Chicago O'Hare UFO sighting of 2006, the sightings were seen by thousands of people, not just one or two witnesses that could easily be discredited. The 2004 Tinley Park UFO sightings were well documented and reported about in the *Chicago Sun Times*, *Chicago Magazine*, and appeared on several news channels throughout the Chicago area. On August 21, 2004, Tinley Park, Illinois became yet another town thrown into the UFO limelight. The mass sighting is now known as the "Tinley Park Lights" and occurred in and around the surrounding areas of Tinley and Oak Parks, about 30 minutes south of Chicago. The first of many sightings occurred on August 21, 2004, but additional sightings of the identical object were seen two months later on October 31, 2004, about a year later on October 1, 2005, and then again on October 31, 2006. Four sightings within two years has deemed Tinley Park a hotspot for paranormal activity. The UFO that was seen by thousands of witnesses and on four different occasions defied the FAA standards for signature navigation lights required for conventional aircraft. Throughout the sightings in the same geographic area, the collective verdict from witnesses was that a giant triangle was seen navigating with three, silent, self-luminescent red and red-orange lights at a low to intermediate altitude for about an hour. The massive isosceles triangle with unconventional flight characteristics was later calculated from the pictures and videos to be approximately 1,500 feet in diameter. During each of the sightings the behemoth craft was stealthy enough to elude radars, as well as evade the carefully controlled Class Bravo airspace at both Midway and Chicago O'Hare International Airports. Strangely enough, the same triangle UFO was seen earlier in British Columbia, Canada and Houston, Texas, as well as several days later in Australia. Why were these destinations chosen by the triangle UFO? What does the UFOs pattern reveal? Regardless of the pattern, the worldwide-witnessed event demonstrates the speeds at which these crafts are able to travel, almost as if Earth is a zoo and they're just jumping from one attraction to the next.

The sighting that really put Tinley Park on the UFO hotspot map was the mass sighting of Saturday August 21, 2004, when the massive triangle appeared over the populated 28,000-seat First Midwest Bank Amphitheater, or Tweeter Center, where an Ozzy Ozbourne concert had just ended. People of all professions captured multiple angled pictures and videos of the anomaly. The plethora of striking evidence from all angles closed the door for illumination flares, the typical excuse used to cover up UFO reports. Furthermore, "video and witness accounts do not seem to present a slow, windborne descent normally associated with illumination flares, and video and photographs do not seem to suggest persistent relative order between the objects over the course of the event, moving about in a way inconsistent with gravity-bound objects retarded by parachutes." (http://en.wikipedia.org/wiki/Tinley_Park_Lights) When I was serving in the US Marine Corps Infantry we used plenty of illumination flares, and let me tell you firsthand, illumination flares are NOT going to be deployed by our military over such a populous, metropolitan area, or in an area with an abundance of air traffic like Chicago's O'Hare International Airport, one of the busiest airports in the world. In addition, the weather phenomenon excuse could not be counted on by the cover-up agencies as the weather was perfectly clear that autumn day of August 21, 2004. As a Chicago native, I realize it's a rare day when it's absolutely beautiful outside, but we got lucky. If the weather had not cooperated on that August day, the truth would've most likely been buried under the "weather phenomenon" excuse.

Since the mass Tinley Park sighting of August 21, 2004, civilian world scientists and researchers, not subjected to non-disclosure military protocol, have done their homework. Scientific researchers, who've applied state-of-the-art technological methods in conducting their research, have ruled out weather balloons, they've ruled out flares, they've ruled out weather phenomenon, they've ruled out celestial bodies, they've ruled out mass hallucinations, they've ruled out computer-generated fakes, and they've ruled out the possibility that the Tinley Park Lights could be a hoax. Let's come out and just openly say it—it's a UFO. Those who've traditionally learned from the orthodox books in schools and universities have been taught to believe in certain scientific parameters with limitations to what is possible. Well, the time has come to unlearn what we've learned. We need to take another look at the facts at hand and adopt an entirely new creed of what is actually possible. Mass sightings, although rare, are extremely treasured in the ufology community because more people of higher merit and credibility will come forward in the community if they know that they will not be ridiculed. It's always easier for an individual to come forward when they're not alone in witnessing a UFO. A cross demographic of doctors, lawyers, nurses, aviation personnel, and military personnel who witnessed the baffling Tinley Park Lights bring these sightings into the realm of being genuine, a truth that's hard for stubborn skeptics to stomach. I wasn't able to recover a single picture off the Internet for this 'Tinley Park Lights' chapter to depict what was seen on any of those occurrences, NOT ONE PICTURE despite the thousands of pictures that were taken from the thousands of witnesses. If nothing is going on as the black world and it's government affiliates would have us believe then why would the black world pirates hijack and cleanse all the evidence from the Internet? We MUST have the courage to follow our own path, otherwise we're just pawns floating along on a conveyor belt of conformity.

CHAPTER 4: THE BIGGEST CATCH IN THE SEA

USOs (Unidentified Submerged Objects) in the Earth's Oceans

Most of this next chapter is without a doubt one of the biggest pieces to the *Open Your Eyes: To 2012 and Beyond* puzzle. What is learned in this chapter should leave an indelible mark and open your eyes to an untamed underwater world we have yet to conquer.

"Earth is supposedly 4.5 billion years old, has a surface area of almost 197,000,000 square miles and over two-thirds of it is covered by water. The deep sea floor alone covers about 60 percent of the Earth's surface and about 116,000,000 square miles, making it one of the most extensive ecosystems in the world. Its sheer size and inaccessibility also make it one of the least-known ecosystems. The deep sea is one case where out of sight should not mean out of mind." (http://nationalzoo.si.edu/Publications/ZooGoer/2005/2/whaleworms.cfm) As of 2010 a vast majority of Earth's seas remain an unexplored mystery, especially the deep sea trenches, less than one percent of which has been explored. "We know more about the secrets and enigmas of the moon's lunar surface then we do about the Earth's waters." In order to open our eyes to the magnitude of this USO (Unidentified Submerged Object) chapter, and really make it sing, let's step back for a moment. We must use the Three Rs, Reiteration, Repetition, and Redundancy, to reprogram our minds, unlearn what we've learned, and have the truth resonate.

We must cement the date 1903 in our brains for two reasons: first reason because it was the year the Wright Brothers invented the first airplane. The second being the "fact" that prior to the invention of the conventional airplane in 1903, nothing flew. This "first in flight" ideology is a fallacy that's being taught as a reality in schools and universities around the world. Yet, for as long as history goes back, there have been eyewitness reports of UFOs in the skies centuries before humans took flight, and as long as there have been UFO reports there have been similar reports of USOs in Earth's oceans and seas. UFOs are synonymous with USOs and as Bill Birnes, publisher of *UFO Magazine* and co-author of *The Day After Roswell*, advocates "UFOs and USOs are probably the same things. A UFO becomes a USO when it is no longer flying and submerges." Each and every country that has a Navy is VERY intrigued by this subject. As nuclear physicist and UFO researcher Stanton Friedman puts it, "It would be nice if the Navy would tell us about all their observations of such crafts. We have reports of USOs going into and out of the water, but we don't have any of the technical data. Flying saucers that are above the ground, people see them, but what's underwater, the Navy sees them, and the Navy isn't talking about what its finding." A USO is basically a submarine, airplane, and space shuttle all-rolled-in-to-one and is able to transfer from one medium to another. From a human world viewpoint, these USOs are equivalent to nothing in our military arsenal. Our submarines would have to be impervious to the ocean's pressure, without a "collapse depth" or "crush depth," and have the ability to breach the water's surface and fly around the atmosphere and space.

If you're curious as to how deep our current submarines can dive you will not be impressed. Even the strongest American modern nuclear submarines (of the Seawolf Class) have a crush depth of 730 meters (2,400 feet), and in 2010 the 7,000 foot depth is considered to be the absolute crush depth for even the best submarines. This 7,000 foot depth equates to not even a mile and a half. With the deepest part of the ocean at 35,813 feet, and an American submarine Seawolf Class crush depth of 2,400 feet, I think it's fair to say we need to open our eyes to the feasibility of USOs hiding out in the depths of the oceans. However, a small submarine funded by the US Navy, the Trieste, carrying two passengers, Jacques Piccard and Lt. Don Walsh, made it to the deepest point in the ocean, the Challenger Deep in the Marianas Trench, a few hundred miles east of the Philippines, 10,916 meters (35,813 feet) below sea level. Not only did the Trieste reach the impossible depths of the Marianas Trench but the sub also revealed that life does exist in the deepest, darkest trenches of the world's oceans. So, clearly a submarine can be engineered to make it as deep as it's theoretically possible to go, as well as discover a viable platform for flourishing deep sea marine life. The problem is that this occurred about a half century ago and since the Trieste retirement in 1966, the few deep-sea submersibles that are out there have been robotic and mostly unmanned. (www.wisegeek.com/what-is-the-deepest-depth-a-submarine-can-go.htm)

"There's a very good reason for a whole society of creatures, advanced creatures, living under the water because they can, because nobody goes there," claims Bill Birnes of *UFO Hunters*. Furthermore, underwater USOs have been tracked on sonar moving at supersonic speeds at incredible depths, which human scientists say is possible and technologically feasible. There have also been reports that the Lost City of Atlantis is a secret USO base and that the legend of Atlantis is based on knowledge that such a USO hub exists today.

The Santa Catalina Channel, home to the Redondo Trench, extends 26 miles in the Pacific Ocean separating Catalina Island from Los Angeles. Scientists, scholars, and experts believe that these non-translucent waters to be as deep as Mount Everest is high (29,035 feet) and may conceal some of the world's most intriguing mysteries.

Locals to the area claim the area to be a hotbed for USOs entering and exiting the channel. Witnesses have reported seeing USOs stealthily exiting the water before blasting off silently into space. On June 14th, 1992 at 10:24pm over Santa Monica Bay, multiple witnesses reported to police departments as far away as Malibu of seeing over 200 bright, disk shaped objects exiting the water without noise. These crafts, according to eyewitnesses, levitated silently over the water before jetting off into the upper atmosphere and out of sight. Around the Santa Catalina Channel there have also been eyewitness reports of enormous USO motherships coming to the ocean's surface and having dozens of smaller crafts depart from the mothership. It's highly likely that within the unknown, unexplored depths of the oceans, USOs are residing. Studies prove that the incredible depths of the Redondo Trench, as well as the murky, dark waters, to be ideal hiding places for anyone or anything that wanted to stay hidden away out of sight. Most standard sonar devices equipped on ships and submarines are only capable of tracking down to a mile in depth, so anything below that is beyond our reach. If we're going to find USOs in the depths of our oceans then we have to start looking harder. We need to start a massive search with numerous battalions of deep sea, unmanned submersible drones armed with cameras and the latest technological breakthroughs. These cameras need to also provide us—the public, not the government—with a live, unedited feed from what the submarines are seeing in the ocean's depths. We've got to go fishing for these USOs and we're most likely going to need a lure or some type of bait. If USOs and UFOs are indeed attracted to nuclear material then we should use nuclear matter that is safe and contained to lure these ocean dwellers to our camera. A courteous and cordial message to these USOs also couldn't hurt upon first contact just so they know we're not trying to harm them and only mean to communicate peacefully.

Firsthand witnesses in a 1960 Argentinian Naval incident claimed to have seen USOs multiply and break apart from one main mothership, only to vanish over the Golfo Nuevo, 650 miles south of Buenos Aires.

This event garnered the attention of the Soviet leader at the time, Nikita Khrushchev, who immediately sent his aides to get information on what had occurred in Argentina. The manifestations of these smaller crafts from a USO mothership resembles our aircraft carriers where one giant vessel harbors a plethora of other smaller crafts. "The aircraft carrier USS Ronald Regan can house a complement of 5,500 sailors and over 90 planes and helicopters from one Nimitz Class aircraft carrier." (http://wiki.answers.com/Q/How_many_troops_ can_the_AIRCRAFT_CARRIER_USS_ronald_reagan_hold) The day is soon approaching when our aircraft carriers will display the same astonishing technological savvy that these USO motherships display.

"It's fascinating to think of the underwater UFOs because they know a lot about this planet that you and I don't know," advocates retired nuclear physicist and UFO researcher Stanton Friedman, who is one of the most renowned names in the ufology community. Another renowned individual in the USO community was Ivan T. Sanderson, author of the 1970 book *Invisible Residents*. Sanderson's book was the first to analyze the reports and behavior of USOs. His research brought the subject from ridicule to reality, especially with the documentation of credible, firsthand witness testimonies. These witnesses weren't degenerate drug addicts, they were military professionals trained in identifying and observing their surrounding targets. Sanderson's book pioneered the research of USOs using two primary theories. The first theory being that there are USOs here on Earth that have either evolved along with the planet or came from space and made their home in Earth's oceans long ago. His research addressed the reality that 50 percent of UFOs were actually USOs seen over bodies of water. Sanderson's second principle theory was, and still is, the most compelling. Ivan T. Sanderson claimed there was evidence showing that several crucial points around the globe, when taken together, formed an unseen invisible map of triangles that he identified as "vile vortices." By locating areas where ships and planes had disappeared, Sanderson was able to conclude that USO sightings were linked to the triangular vile vortices where strange magnetic anomalies occurred. It turned out that Sanderson was dead on. In 2010, we know these irregular areas to be called "energy vortexes." Many of these peculiar vile vortices contain some of the most treacherous and turbulent seas on the face of the Earth, and after 12 years of research, Sanderson concluded that there was a clear correlation between the unusually high number of USO reports and areas of high gravitational or vortic pull on the Earth. Some of the vile vortices, located in the most inhospitable seas on Earth were claimed to be theoretical USO bases.

The naturally hostile seas act as a mask, concealing the silent, unspoken beauty that lies beneath the chaos. And, according to author Steven Greer, they're "very deep and undetectable where they've been observing what we're doing." Sanderson researched the link he firmly believed to be no coincidence until his questionable death of brain cancer in 1973. Why was his death questionable, you ask? As we've all opened our eyes to by know, the black world delegates will not hesitate to reach into their toolbox to eliminate, sanitize, and silence these types of high profile situations.

Interestingly enough, during WWII, Ivan Sanderson was a commander of the British Naval Intelligence Service and was also a part of the British Security Coordination. (www.absoluteastronomy. com/topics/Ivan_T._Sanderson) The British Naval Intelligence Service is the United Kingdom's sister agency to the USA's Office of Naval Intelligence, or ONI. Sanderson had a bunch of ties, friends and foes, in the Office of Strategic Services (OSS), which was the forerunner of the Central Intelligence Agency (CIA). (www. cryptomundo.com/cryptozoo-news/james-bond-cz/) As a renowned cryptozoologist, he was in direct communications with these intelligence communities and was getting information from them, as well as feeding intelligence information back to them. Speculation has continued today as to whether secret government operatives rigged his death in order to remove his files, thus destroying the best collection of deep sea USO evidence ever compiled. Nonetheless, we carry the flag for Ivan T. Anderson as his diligent research resuscitated the UFO and USO topics to bring them back into the limelight. Ivan T. Sanderson was a crusader for truth and was murdered for getting too close to the USO subject. In my opinion, Sanderson deserves the Medal of Honor for his fearless sacrifice of attempting to go against the grain and bring the truth into the public spotlight. Sanderson's death was not in vain as he has passed the USO torch to all of us to continue the uphill battle against the black world's wretched army of darkness. What's most important about Ivan T. Sanderson is the footprint and legacy that he left behind on the breakthrough subject of USOs. Ivan T. Sanderson, you will not be forgotten.

In March of 1963, a United States Navy submarine exercise was taking place 100 miles off of Puerto Rico when suddenly one of the submarines from the naval fleet broke from its route in order to track an object on sonar traveling at speeds of 150 knots. But it wasn't the speed that truly amazed and perplexed the sailors aboard the pursuing US sub. It was the incredible depth at which it was traveling—20,000 feet—well beyond the pursuing US submarine's crush depth. Bruce Maccabee was an optical physicist with the US Navy and recalls, "It gave the acoustic signature of a single propeller type of motion through the water and it was tracked to depths down to 20,000 feet, whereas a typical crush depth for a submarine is 7,000 feet. Whatever it was, it was exceeding the technical capabilities of submarines at the time and even today." The USO was shadowed and tracked for four days by the entire carrier group, but after midnight on the fourth day's pursuit the USO disappeared never to appear on radar again.

On November 11, 1972, a fast moving sub-like object was detected on sonar in the Sonya Fjord off the west coast of Norway. It was tracked by the Norwegian Navy for two weeks. During that two week period, a fleet of Norwegian surface ships and specially equipped submarines and helicopters were summoned to hunt the USO. On November 20, 1972, the heart rates of the sailors jumped through the roof when the USO was seen visually for the first time. The encounter utterly shocked witnesses aboard the naval vessels who reported seeing a massive, silent cigar shaped object. Remember this is 1972, an era without the Internet, without computers, without cell phones, and without wireless technology. Once the eye opening visual had been confirmed, the Norwegian Navy's armada immediately fired torpedoes and guns at the unknown bogey, and once the USO submerged beneath the surface they started deploying depth charges. The Norwegian Navy then attempted to block and seal off the fjord and trap the USO but to no avail. After the 14th day of the pursuit the USO vanished and escaped the Norwegian Navy's airtight net.

Why are we, the humans, trying to be so hostile and destructive towards these USOs? Why did a ship from the Norwegian Navy act as the aggressor and fire upon the USO? What happened to the rules of engagement and not firing upon an object until fired on? What happened to protocol?

Christopher Columbus is a name most people associate with a holiday and an extra day off of work. However, what most don't know is that Christopher Columbus' voyage is synonymous with USO activity. Christopher Columbus, his royal steward Pero Gutierrez, and the rest of his crew were all witnesses to the USO activity that shadowed their galleon. Fortunately for those of us trying to shed light on the USO subject, Christopher Columbus recorded much of his eyewitness reports in his personal journal. Remember that this was the year 1492, 411 years before 1903 and the Wright Brother's invention of the plane. On October 11, 1492, at around 10:00 PM, Christopher Columbus and his crew of three ships were traversing across one of the deepest trenches in the Atlantic Ocean. The three-ship envoy was led by Columbus and his flagship, the Santa Maria, which was sailing directly above a four-mile-deep ravine. This mysterious and perilous area would later be known as the Bermuda Triangle.

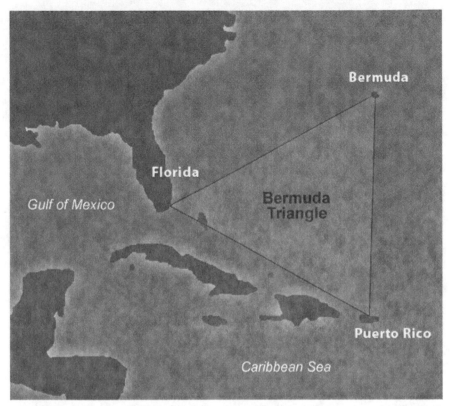

The Bermuda Triangle embodies paranormal activity and is also located on top of an energy vortex, also known as a vile vortices, where mysterious disappearances have plagued ships, planes, etc. Many believe that these turbulent waters act as a shield and deterrent to a greater force at work below the ocean's surface. Many researchers adamantly believe that a USO hub exists under the treacherous waters of the Bermuda Triangle. Christopher Columbus was just one witness of many to witness USO and UFO activity on their 1492 journey to the New World.

This puzzling and infamously hazardous area is associated with extreme danger. Captains of planes and ships make it a point to steer their planes and vessels clear of this area that is synonymous with ambiguity and paranormal activity. The Triangle is now known as a graveyard which has entombed dozens of planes and ships at the bottom of its murky abyss. But Columbus was not aware of this. Neither he nor his crew had any idea that this area was located on top of an energy vortex and was a magnet for UFO and USO activity. Yet, Columbus details how "unearthly lights" were seen by himself as well as witnesses aboard the Santa Maria, all of which startled the crew of 120 aboard the three Spanish ships. They witnessed a "disc-shaped object" exiting the ocean, transitioning to the sky with a great flash and level of brilliance unlike anything known at the time. What did Columbus and his crew encounter while crossing the Bermuda Triangle? If you're pondering the notion of an otherworldly craft, then you're exactly right. And to clarify, otherworldly visitors does mean "aliens" but does not necessarily refer to the stereotypical "little green men."

Within five hours after the USO encounter, and while crossing the treacherous Bermuda Triangle, Christopher Columbus had discovered the New World. To our good fortune, Christopher Columbus kept a log of several USO incidents throughout his voyage, all of which can be found with archivists at Fordham University. His journey took over two months and the October 11 sighting was far from the only one. On September 10, 1492, which was the halfway point of the journey, another sighting was logged by Columbus, as well as on September 11, 17, and 20. Why was the most fabled nautical voyage plagued by such strange events? Were the otherworldly vessels tracking and observing Columbus' three-ship fleet? Why wasn't this revelatory information shared with the mass public? Remember that in 1492 the laws were much different than today's. An era of regal kings, ruthless conquerors, and iron-fisted rulers, not presidents and democracies. If we lived in 1492, our American freedom of speech rights would get you imprisoned, or killed, and if it were the latter of the two options you'd be executed by being burned at the stake or sent to the gallows to be hung. Stanton Friedman adds, "If Christopher Columbus saw a strange thing come out of the water fly around his ship and then take off, would he have told anybody about it? They would have locked him up in the brig instantly. The guy's crazy, cause things can't do that." Lucky for us in America 2010, freedom of speech and the ability to question authority DOES exist.

One of the earliest USO reports is known to be from 329 BC, long before the birth of Jesus Christ and obviously long before submarines and airplanes were invented. In 329 BC Alexander the Great had an indelible mark left on his life when he witnessed "shining shield-like objects flying into and out of the Jaxartes River in India." In 329 BC!!! Alexander the Great spent the last six years of his life scouring for evidence to the mysterious event he witnessed. Most UFO witnesses today can relate to Alexander the Great's feeling of not getting closure to an event that changed their lives forever. Many researchers conclude, however, that Alexander the Great had another goal with his underwater expeditions—to find and conquer the one kingdom that eluded him, the Lost City of Atlantis. What Alexander the Great probably didn't realize was the link between USOs and the Lost City of Atlantis. If he had found Atlantis, he would've found USO activity.

To this day, researchers and those spearheading the USO investigations continue to speculate that Atlantis is a major hub for USO activity. Remember that even our best American submarines in 2010 have a crush depth of 7,000 feet, whereas the deepest ocean trench in the world is 35,813 feet below sea level. Try and fathom this astonishing depth. The Marianas Trench is deeper below sea level than the height of Mount Everest above sea level. We don't know as much about our oceans as we may think we do. Less than one percent of Earth's deep sea trenches have been explored. But what may seem impossible to the average John Q. Citizen may actually be very possible, especially with the tightly sealed mouths of the naval intelligence communities throughout the world. USOs are part of the naval intelligence communities just as UFOs are part of the air force intelligence communities, all of which fall into the black operations world of "things that don't exist but do."

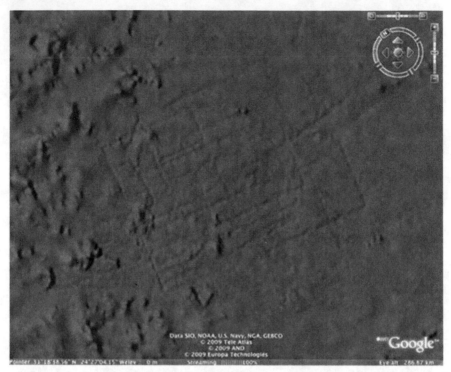

A deep sea floor bed scan reveals the real possibility that the Lost City of Atlantis has been discovered 600 miles west of Morocco. We must strike while the iron's hot. This is the time to mobilize a civilian owned and operated fleet of unmanned deep sea submersible drones to plunge to the depths of the oceans to find out once and for all if these UFOs and USOs have been living under our noses in our oceans for thousands of years. With less than 1 percent of the deep sea floor explored, I'd say there's a lot of room for new discoveries.

The Lost City of Atlantis' supposed location near the Mediterranean Sea would've provided a conducive position to observe early human civilizations and shipping routes. "The Mediterranean was the cradle of ancient civilizations. The Phoenician traders traveled back and forth between the Middle East and Greece across the Mediterranean. If there were a culture of either aliens or original inhabitants of planet Earth who wanted to seed the planet, to seed humanity with myth, the Mediterranean is a natural base for them to set up an underwater facility," advocates Bill Birnes of *UFO*

Hunters, one of the most respected and renown names in the game. The Mediterranean Sea and its surrounding area are shrouded in USO mystery. The ancient Athenians were not the first to record USOs in the oceans. "Researchers and experts believe recorded sightings are documented in hieroglyphics and drawing inscriptions in the 2,000-year-old Temple of Osiris at Abydos in Giza. According to UFO researchers and Atlantis proponents, the inscriptions and hieroglyphic illustrations discovered depict highly developed crafts, specifically a helicopter, a submarine, some form of flying saucer, and a jet plane." (http://www.catchpenny.org/abydos.html)

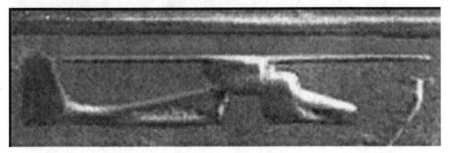

The ancient hieroglyphic illustration of a helicopter found in the 2,000-year-old Temple of Osiris at Abydos in Giza. Helicopters were not supposed to exist at this period in time. (Reference picture on page 43.)

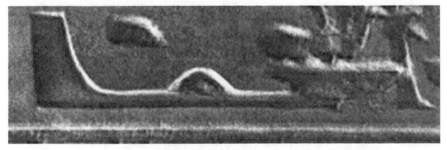

The archaic hieroglyphic rendering of an advanced flying vehicle found in the 2,000-year-old Temple of Osiris at Abydos in Giza. Our adopted Western beliefs are full of taught fallacies that many shortsighted individuals consider to be the infallible truth. (Reference picture on page 43.)

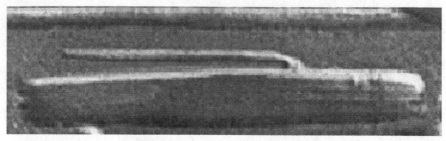

An ancient hieroglyph of a submarine, tank, or UFO found in the 2,000-year-old Temple of Osiris at Abydos in Giza. (Reference picture on page 43.)

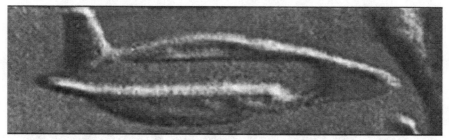

An ancient hieroglyphic inscription of an advanced flying machine found in the 2,000-year-old Temple of Osiris at Abydos in Giza. (Reference picture on page 43.)

Remember, since there weren't any cameras, video cameras, or phones at this time, these archaic renderings were the ancient civilizations' way of recording and documenting what they saw. Don't be deceived by what the manipulative government cover-up agencies claim them to be. If the cliché "a picture speaks a thousand words" is true, then these eye opening and extremely revealing pictures of highly developed crafts found encrypted in the 2,000-year-old Temple of Osiris at Abydos in Giza prove the ancient astronaut theory and past visitations to be a reality. Why else would these hieroglyphic renderings and detailed inscriptions be etched into the Temple of Osiris' walls? How could anyone at this period in time have any clue or idea as to what a helicopter, a submarine, a flying saucer, AND a jet plane would look like? How could anyone detail all four images when none had even been conceived or invented yet? The pictures are spot on in description, need no deciphering, and are a testament to what these ancient civilizations saw. What they saw they recorded, and what they recorded will change everything.

Search your heart and gut feelings to find the pristine, uncorrupted truth within, free from contaminated propaganda and media spin. As Bob Marley said, we must "emancipate ourselves from mental slavery. None but ourselves can free our minds." We're reaching a crucial point of critical mass on the UFO and USO subjects as the copious amount of compiled evidence is becoming impossible to refute and dismiss. What baffled and mystified Christopher Columbus in 1492 and Alexander the Great in 329 BC still captivates and enthralls individuals in 2010.

The list of USO sightings from Ivan T. Sanderson's groundbreaking book *Invisible Residents*, as well as the breakthrough research provided through the History Channel's *UFO Hunters*, goes on to include one of the earliest European USO cases from a series of English sightings in the 11th Century. In 1067 AD Englishmen out in the countryside reported seeing a "flaming object in the sky that blanketed the countryside with a brilliant light." Standing there in awe, the witnesses claimed to observe the object moving up and down in the sky before disappearing into the sea. This encounter is a small piece to the UFO and USO puzzle, but a piece nonetheless, needed to cement the fact that objects were flying around in the skies and moving around in the oceans long before the inventions of the plane and submarine.

In the 20th Century, the first reported USO encounter appeared well documented in the *Philadelphia Inquirer* with headlines of the paper reading "Electric Cloud Enveloped Ship." On August 1st, 1904, a British cargo ship, the Mohican, was en route to Philadelphia when the ship encountered a strange object. According to the *Philadelphia Inquirer* and eyewitness testimonies, the ship was "enshrouded in a strange metallic vapor which glowed like phosphorous." Testimonies state that as the USO neared the ship the crew was paralyzed and couldn't move while the cloud was around the ship. The *Philadelphia Inquirer* also printed that the ships' "compass revolved with the speed of an electric motor and the sailors were unable to raise pieces of steel from the magnetized decks." The USO was seen by every man aboard the Mohican and the ship's captain, Captain Urcubart, confirmed that the report was "vouched for by every man of the crew." Mechanical failure is now known to be a common occurrence within energy vortexes and UFO/USO encounters. Unfortunately, we do not have the technology available to the public and the civilian world to measure and detect energy vortexes. We only know that energy vortexes ARE energy vortexes from the strange events that occur while in the presence of such highly magnetized and abnormal areas. On October 30, 1906, shortly after the Mohican's bizarre USO encounter, the SS St. Andrew and her entire crew witnessed a USO off Nova Scotia, Canada and was captured within the pages of the New York *Times*.

The 1906 SS St. Andrew case moves us into position to discuss the next event, an event that has been deemed and celebrated as the most important USO sighting by numerous renown cryptozoologists and ufologists alike—the October 4, 1967, Shag Harbor Incident in Nova Scotia, Canada. Known to be the "Roswell of USOs," Shag Harbor is a small fishing village in Nova Scotia on the east coast of Canada and was put on the map by one of the most extraordinary USO cases in history. The events that took place around Nova Scotia, specifically Shag Harbor, took place throughout October 4 and the following weeks. According to the History Channel's interview with Chris Styles, UFO researcher and co-author of *Dark Object,* "the reason that the Shag Harbor incident came to the forefront and kind of eclipsed the importance of the other sightings from the night of the UFOs is simply the fact that it's the one case where something came down over the sky and crashed into the water. You know...it made a noise, it made a flash. It's also unique in the sense that nobody reported a UFO. Several calls came in very quickly to the nearby Royal Canadian Mounted Police Detachment and those reports said simply that people had seen lights or perhaps an aircraft had crashed into the water. The interest and concern was totally for the possibility of survivors.

Nobody reported a UFO." The Royal Canadian Mounted Police officers who witnessed the perceived plane crash from the shoreline immediately went into "rescue mode" and quickly headed out in boats with the help from local fisherman, like Norm Smith. "They searched for more than an hour until the Coast Guard Cutter 101 from Clark's Harbor on Cape Sable Island arrived on the scene about an hour into the search. They had a report from the RCC, or Rescue Coordination Center in Halifax, the capital city of Nova Scotia, for RCMP Constable Ron O'Brian who was on patrol at the time. The RCC report stated, 'No aircraft, private, commercial or military had been reported missing anywhere along the eastern seaboard of Canada or the northern United States.'" (www.theufochronicles.com/2008/06/shag-harbour-from-obscurity-to.html) The RCC report was directed towards the six fishing boats scouring Shag Harbor for survivors, and when the news spread to the men on the fishing boats, a puzzled feeling engulfed them. Without a downed aircraft, what were they looking for? If they weren't orchestrating a rescue operation then, what did witnesses see crash and submerge into the harbor?

During the night of October 4, 1967, reports of UFOs were called in and reported all across Nova Scotia from various folks in the surrounding vicinities, not just Shag Harbor. Of the many key witnesses from October 4, 1967 there are less than a handful of surviving, civilian, firsthand witnesses today: Chris Styles, Norm Smith, Dave Kendrick, and Laurie Wickens. Norm Smith and Dave Kendrick witnessed firsthand an "unusual object hanging at a 45 degree angle, pointing down towards Shag Harbour. They noted four to five amber or orange colored lights flashing sequentially and what, for a moment, Norm thought might be the windows of an airliner." (http://leapingrealeyes.blogspot.com/2006/03/ufo-crash-at-shag-harbour.html) However, on Friday, October 6, with the arrival of seven Canadian divers dispatched from Halifax, and with the RCC report two days prior of no reported downed aircraft, it was becoming clear to the eyewitnesses that they were no longer searching for a crashed airplane but a downed UFO.

The unknown will always excite and stimulate the imagination. If there was no plane crash, why would divers from Halifax be brought in? The news of a downed UFO in Shag Harbor spread like wildfire throughout the world and brought with it a Roswell, New Mexico-like media circus. The government reports for the USO incident claim that the anomaly traversed from the south to the north along the Nova Scotia shoreline, and at one point the object stopped and hovered. Then, at around 11:20 PM, the USO entered the water at a 45 degree angle, 300 yards off shore. "The object, according to Chris Styles and numerous other witnesses, also appeared to be leaving a trail of dense yellow foam" similar to the thickness of human shaving cream. The government reports go on to state that the USO stayed in the Shag Harbor for a weeks' time, resting on the floor of the sea. The report claims that a second craft entered the water to rendezvous with the other USO for possible repairs. The two crafts then broke the surface of the water and flew away over the Gulf of Maine. The government's primary documents for the Shag Harbor investigation stated that the object discovered was not a result of flares, floats, downed aircraft, or any known object.

Another hotspot for more recent USO activity is Puerto Rico, which has become a mecca for USO manifestations. Puerto Rico has been a magnet for attracting an abundant amount of USO activity, which, in turn, has placed the island at the center of the USO debate. Remember, Puerto Rico is located on the southern most point of the Bermuda Triangle, a known energy vortex with a long legacy of USO activity. This activity includes hundreds of cases of USOs entering and exiting the surrounding Puerto Rican waters. Many ufologists claim that the deep, unexplored waters of the southern Bermuda Triangle link not only past disappearances of planes and ships that went missing, but conceal and house a major USO hub beneath the treacherous waters. The hundreds of credible witnesses and testimonies have brought Puerto Rico into the limelight and raised the flag of awareness for USO activity across the globe.

Another astounding USO case occurred in late 1969 during the United States' ice-breaking training exercise, "Operation Deep Freeze" near Antarctica. US Navy sailors aboard the USS Calaterra witnessed a massive USO, at least 100 feet long, break through three yards of solid Antarctic ice. The highly trained and credible sailors say it punched through the seemingly impenetrable ice with such haste that it'd be impossible to duplicate with human technology. Similar cases have been reported by navies around the world. Since many of these cases involve a UFO hovering near or around small and large bodies of water, experts agree that USOs must need water as a fuel source. The unparalleled dynamics of these sophisticated crafts in Earth's oceans seem to defy all principles of modern physics. Experts and witnesses alike are mesmerized by the abilities of these radically advanced vessels and how they're able to travel at supersonic velocities at extreme depths, as well as the ability to pass through ice blocks with impunity. According to UFO guru Bill Birnes, "These kind of crafts, extensively, can travel underneath the water because they are impervious to water, just like they're impervious to gamma rays, cosmic rays, and impervious to anything that gets in the way of their traveling in space. So, the engines wouldn't be engines as you and I imagine engines. They would be generators generating a magnetic force creating a magnetic envelope around the craft that repels the Earth's natural magnetism, hence, allowing them to accelerate, decelerate, climb, fall, and navigate through the water." Nuclear physicist Stanton Friedman concurs with Birnes' advocation, adding, "by exerting forces of the surrounding fluid, sea water, nice, electrically conducting fluid, you control the drag, you control the flow, the speed, the lift. You can get around all the problems of high-speed motion under the water. A magneto-aerodynamic system would work similar to the electromagnetic submarine that was successfully tested." This hypothetical statement was proven to be true and the achievement was well documented in a TIME magazine article titled "Run Silent, Run Electromagnetic." The article goes on to state, "like a well trained-dolphin, the miniature experimental submarine maneuvered docilely around the waters of California's Santa Barbara water basin. No propellers, no jets were visible along its sleek, 10-foot-long haul, yet the sub was obviously moving under its own power, gliding silently at about two miles per hour, three feet under the surface. There was not a motor on board, but the odd little boat was being propelled by the same electrical phenomenon that causes rotors in electric motors to turn: electromagnetic force." (www.time.com/time/magazine/article/0,9171,842848,00.html)

So, obviously mankind is paying attention and learning from our alien neighbors who don't subscribe to the "addicted to oil" ideology. We have apparently made some progress in harnessing electromagnetic force. Through the building and testing of the first electromagnetic sub in 1966—with no moving parts—we have taken a giant leap forward in our underwater travels. We've learned from our savvy alien neighbors that we need to take advantage of harvesting the ocean's salt water and its natural ability to conduct electricity. As Stanton Friedman confirms, "the principle here is that salt water is electrically conducting fluid. You push against the sea water by Newton's Laws... it pushes back and off you go." "Water is a great magnetic conduit. In fact, if they were traveling using a process called 'diamagnetism,' which is a weak repelling force, then water would enhance that force and could explain why these crafts can navigate these waters so well," claims ufology maverick Bill Birnes. In order to fathom this technology and fully grasp the concept of diamagnetism, I strenuously implore you to watch the video demonstration online. (http://video.google.com/videoplay?docid=-4131097019486262141) I guarantee that after watching this video, the breakthrough subject will become much more transparent. The laws of Earthly physics change drastically when submerged underwater. For example, for an object five feet in diameter to travel at the speed of sound—which equates to 768 miles per hour or about one mile in five seconds—an engine must produce 15,000 horsepower in the air. However, it would take 1,000,000 horsepower to move the same object to the speed of sound underwater. Marko Princevac, who is a professor of mechanical engineering at the University of California, Riverside, has done numerous studies on the ideal shape to streamline underwater travel. He concluded throughout extensive research that the best shape proved to be that similar to NASA's return capsules from the lunar modules, a big cone or acorn shape. What was the shape of the object eyewitnesses saw firsthand being taken away on the back of a flatbed truck escorted by a convoy of military jeeps in Kecksburg, Pennsylvania? That's right, it was an acorn and cone shaped object tattooed in hieroglyphic inscription, which was destined to be headed for a laboratory for reverse-engineering.

Our knowledge of the raw power of this subject is minuscule compared to the vast understanding that the extraterrestrials have achieved with their UFO and USOs. Our terrestrial, indigenous neighbors, or extraterrestrial visitors, can obviously travel from one medium to another without barriers or limitations, with advanced technology that we humans are desperately in need of. There may come a point in time around December 21, 2012, when we will need to have that type of technology to save our species. We are certainly going to need THEIR help. We need to have an End of Days accord with them. If we cannot save ourselves we are going to need to call upon our sophisticated neighbors to be a major part of our contingency plan. If we both inhabit Earth, then both species share a responsibility to befriend one another, fraternize, and become teammates in order to get a survival game plan ready. Apparently, our human agenda is not their agenda and they mean us no harm. Through the extraterrestrials' eyes, the human race is still classified as a neutral or mild threat to their species, which is why they seek refuge in our oceans. As author and researcher Bill Birnes puts it, "USO sightings continue all around the world to this day. They continue to come out of the water and they continue to be seen by witnesses around the world. If they're hostile and have come here to conquer Earth they would've done it a million years ago. We might be their creations for all we know...The Earth is conquered, we work for them, they live here, this is their planet." Are these terrestrial or extraterrestrial creatures the real landlords of Earth and we're just tenants?

Some of the most important USO encounters were the sightings that our naval servicemen witnessed aboard one of the world's first ships in the naval fleet to have nuclear weapons as a part of their armament. The USS Franklin D. Roosevelt was a Midway Class Aircraft Carrier armed with some of the most advanced technology of its time. Commissioned after WWII in October of 1945, the 1000-foot-long, 64,000-ton behemoth was constructed in the New York naval shipyards. The former radar operator of the F.D.R, Harry Jordan, states, "The FDR was a very capable ship in every stretch of imagination. She was an experimental floating active laboratory for the entire navy department." Jordan was one of the many USO witnesses aboard the nuclear-armed USS FDR. "I have no doubt about the existence of UFOs and their interaction with the FDR, and there have been many other sailors who've had the same experiences I have had." Another witness to the inexplicable paranormal activity aboard the nuclear aircraft carrier was Chet Grusinski. "There's probably a good connection with the USS FDR and the nuclear weapons and the UFO sightings. It was a magnet for UFOs," claims Grusinski, who served aboard the Midway Class Carrier from July 1958-December 1960 as a fireman and metal-works engineer. Grusinski, along with a cluster of other naval personnel aboard the carrier, witnessed a massive USO craft in September of 1958 by Guantanamo Bay, Cuba.

This eye-opening incident has plagued him ever since and, thanks to the History Channel, Chet Grusinski gave his first camera interview revealing what occurred during the September 1958 encounter. Remember that these naval witnesses are extremely credible witnesses. They know what enemy vessels and aircraft look like and have been tested and evaluated in their specific field of expertise. The chosen individuals aboard one of the world's first nuclear aircraft carriers would not have been aboard if they did not hold the highest credentials of merit and honor. Fireman Grusinski recalls the USO encounter, "We were down below decks that evening between 8:00

and 9:00 PM…It was dark outside….a bunch of men come running up the ladder from the engine room, and my buddy then said, "Hey Red, why don't you go up there and see what's going on?' So, I followed those men all the way up the ladder, up to the hangar deck, all the way up to the flight deck." The witnessing sailors stared directly at the UFO, mesmerized by a cigar-shaped UFO traversing silently towards them, maneuvering at speeds not derived from any man made aircraft. Keep in mind that the FDR crew was elaborately trained in the art of identifying their surrounding targets. Grusinski goes on, "We had no air operation going on on the flight deck so it was quiet up there, and this thing just came right at us and I could see what the light was when it came at our ship. It was a row of windows with figures inside, and they got close enough I could feel the heat on my face…and those figures looking at us through those windows. And the impression that I got was that those figures looking at us were not human beings. And then this thing turned a bright red, orange color and I could see the shape of it. It was a cigar shape when it turned colors and then it just took off like that."

The reports from the sailors that night also claim that the object rose from the ocean without volume and remained silent throughout the 45-second encounter. In 1958, this type of stealth technology had not yet been discovered and explored by our military. Of the more than 25 witnesses most were quickly transferred off the FDR, and in retrospect we know why the witnesses were split up and relocated elsewhere. What seemed inconspicuous then is very conspicuous now and seen as a black world power play.

Jordan states that within hours of the extraordinary USO sighting the ships' logbook had been altered. As a former US Marine, let me tell you this is a tell-tale sign of a cover up. Jordan goes on to tell the History Channel, "When I got the deck log a lot of things were blackened out on the log books…there was nothing there. And the witnesses were transferred off ship, and they probably, I imagine they had to sign some papers to say something about it, but I never had to sign anything like that. Maybe because I didn't say that much about it." The same situation occurred with Grusinski, "I'm still trying to find these men on the flight deck. I didn't have to sign any papers...I wasn't transferred off the ship. I've got a lot of 'Whys? What Happened? Why?' That's what it is...That's why I've been spending all these years doing research on her." Fifty years later, and still without closure, his search for answers continues along with the rest of the crew that witnessed the unidentified object.

Included within the FDR's menu of onboard advancement options Seaman First Class Jordan stated to the History Channel, "she also had the capability of jamming rockets, intercontinental ballistic missiles (ICBMs), and even the capability to break though counter measures being put upon us by Soviet block countries. The Roosevelt definitely attracted UFOs because of all the technical equipment and all of the armaments that she had, and also nuclear weapons." In his first camera interview, with the History Channel, since his 1963 USO episode, Jordan went on record revealing what happened that strange day. "I do remember the incident and the details of it because it just stays with you when you've gone through this." Anyone, like myself, who's ever lost a family member or friend in an unexpected and sudden death knows that unforgettable feeling and the psychological trauma that forever resonates. It's traumatically sealed within the brain's vault. Just like with 9/11, moments like that are frozen in your mind and are preserved forever and are very hard to forget. On October 2, 1963, at 2:00 AM, off the coast of Sardinia, Harry Jordan stood guard methodically watching over his radar equipment. "Everything was normal and routine until an unidentified object suddenly appeared on his radar monitor." The unknown airborne bogey was 600 miles down range traveling at an altitude of 80,000 feet, an unreachable ceiling for conventional aircraft in the '60s. "The first blip came on about 2 and a half hours into the watch. It was 600 miles from the ship at 80,000 feet, then it can into 300 miles at about 35,000 feet, and it came into about 10 miles at 10,000-15,000 feet from the ship off our port side. I reported it to the watch commander at the time and he came over and went through the same process and confirmed it and reported it to the Officer of the Deck on the Bridge. Then the Officer of the Deck on the Bridge woke up the Captain after the contact started to move. This thing was covering 10 miles in just a few seconds and it was traveling about 4,000 miles per hour. It was making right-angled turns and it was almost like a Z-Pattern...if you took about four Zs and lined them across your scope. So, I could tell she was going pretty fast, and then so when she stops they didn't have any heat signature. OK? This was highly unusual." Immediately after Jordan's report was confirmed by the Officer of the Deck on the Bridge, Jordan claims that the Captain ordered the launch of a pair of Phantom 2 jets to analyze and intercept the unidentified bogeys. "They went to afterburners and then launched one right after the other. They left the Rosie and headed up on a course of about 0-1-2, so then I thought immediately that there might be something new going on here because that wasn't following protocol as far as normal ship operations that I was used to." The blip on his screen then literally disappeared in a flash once the Phantom 2 interceptor jets got closer to the UFO's location. Jordan says, "It was being recorded on the view board up on the right hand side in CIC, and then the contact winked out about twenty, thirty seconds after and I could hear one of the pilots say, 'What the....' and that's all I heard."

Strangely enough, when approached, these crafts exemplified a type of ultimate stealth and a chameleon-cloaking mechanism, giving them the ability to disappear completely off the FDR's radar grid, also appearing invisible to the human eye. "The Phantom 2s landed and then it winked on again off the port side of the ship, and someone yelled out in CIC, you know, 'What the hell is that!' And I bet you had 15 people out there with binoculars, looking." Then at 2:32 AM, and within full view of the crew, the UFO reportedly levitated for a moment, several hundred feet from the ship, before vanishing again. Jordan says he "saw the Z-Pattern and it stop...it winked out and then it was gone. I know what the fingerprints are of the electronics on the Soviet aircraft, Korean aircraft, Chinese

MIGs, you name it. If it'd been a meteor it would've burned up in the atmosphere and I have seen meteors streak across the scope, but it only happens in about 2-3 seconds...I mean it's gone." The stunning enigmatic encounter quickly became an X-file as Jordan recorded the episode into his logbook at 2:36 AM as a "UFO Incident." Seconds after recording the information into his logbook, Jordan's commanding officer burst in through the door and stated, according to Jordan, "'Jordan, what did you put in your log?' And I had 'UFO' in there and I had the contact number of the time. I held it out in front of the commander and he says, 'You can take that out.' My commander acknowledged to me, in not so many terms, that 'Yeah Jordan, that's what it was. But NO Jordan, nobody else is to know... period.' I had too much respect for him and the Navy to say anything about it for over 20 years. This is an historical moment for the US Navy and it was just left out of the logs." The fact that Jordan's commanding officer condoned the doctoring of the logbooks is apparent that the Navy has been sanitizing these USO encounters for longer than we think. Steven M. Greer, author of the book *Disclosure* states, "I've interviewed three people separately who have been on the FDR where large UFOs have been seen over the ship, observing it, making its presence known, and at times interfering with what appears to be some of the electronics on the ship." According to USO researcher Carl Feindt "the FDR was the first aircraft carrier to carry nuclear weapons and UFOs seem to be drawn to anything that's nuclear related." With so many reports claiming that UFOs and USOs are attracted to nuclear material, it looks like we've found our bait for when we go fishing for our advanced alien neighbors who reside in Earth's oceans. Of course when we do go fishing at USO hotspots like Puerto Rico, we're going to go fishing with battalions of civilian-owned and operated, unmanned drones and ROVs (Remotely Operated Vehicles). In addition, are intentions cannot be destructive or malicious towards the USO species. Our civilian-world agenda CANNOT be to detonate nuclear weapons aimed at the USOs, but rather to use the nuclear material to lure them to our fishing line with our proposed message…a harmless bait and switch tactic. It is absolutely paramount for our species' survival to find out what these USOs know about the once-every-25,800-year great galactic alignment set to commence on December 21, 2012.

The first instance of the USOs' apparent nuclear attraction occurred during NATO operations in the North Sea near Denmark. In case you're unfamiliar with NATO, the North Atlantic Treaty Organization is a military alliance of democratic states in Europe and North America. During September of 1952 NATO initiated "Operation Mainbrace," the first cooperative multilateral maneuver since WWII. Operation Mainbrace involved an armada of over 200 ships, 1000 planes, and over 80,000 men from NATO member nations. Throughout the joint training exercises the technologically advanced USS FDR paved the way for the armada of combined forces. Renowned ufologist Bill Birnes tells, "The FDR was part of a NATO exercise off Denmark called Operation Mainbrace. The FDR and the RAF and British aircraft carriers were witnesses to one of the most incredible multiple USO sightings in history. The Ministry of Defense in the UK actually wrote it up as a USO sighting. She was part of a task force sealing off the Russian submarine access through the North Sea into the Atlantic. It's extremely important because what if there had been a USO base underneath the North Sea in that area north of Europe. We were surveilling them…they were surveilling us."

The list of USO encounters goes on with the USS FDR, which throughout her commission was a beacon for UFO and USO attraction. On September 13, 1952, the Danish Destroyer, Villamose, was navigating waters in the Baltic Sea north of Bornham Island. The commander and crew members swore to have seen a luminous triangular craft traveling at unfathomable speeds above the water in close proximity to the main fleet. The reported bluish object traveled westward and then suddenly shifted southeast coming directly towards the FDR. Over the next week, the conglomerate fleet, spearheaded by the nuclear-armed FDR, witnessed several more sightings ranging from Denmark to the air operations command bases in Scotland. On September 20, 1952, at 7:30 PM, three Danish officers witnessed a shiny disc-shaped object, unlike anything in their convention arsenal, rise from the sea and pass over them headed in the direction of the NATO fleet and the FDR. The rapidly moving metallic UFO headed east until it disappeared into the cloud layer. The next day, September 21, six British pilots flying over the North Sea spotted a shiny, spherical object rise from the water to court the FDR again. Once this craft approached the fleet's location, and the FDR, the six British pilots followed protocol and gave chase, protecting the airspace around their naval assets cruising the sea below, but to no avail. USS FDR veteran Harry Jordan spoke to a witness over 40 years ago and recalls the surreal occurrence. "They had a sonar contact from three or four destroyers and they couldn't figure what the hell it was because it was moving with them and the damn thing was like a quarter-mile wide. A quarter-mile wide and it came up out of the water and flew up!" Renown UFO researcher Bill Birnes also adds, "after Operation Mainbrace, there were so many sailors who saw the objects and airmen from the RAF who saw the objects. This wasn't just one or two people. These were crew members on the USS FDR, so this is one of those very famous multiple sightings where everybody saw these objects."

Attached to the FDR to document the operation was journalist Wallace Litwin. Litwin was also a key eyewitness to the paranormal activity. As a journalist, Wallace Litwin's weapons of choice were a camera, pen, and paper. Litwin wasted no time at all springing into action, and when the anomaly appeared at 11:00 AM on September 20, 1952, he pointed his 35mm Canon camera at the horizon. He captured two images of the disc seemingly defying all rules of gravity. However, no official report was ever filed, so as to not leave any paper trail. Fireman Chet Grusinski recalls when journalist Litwin captured the apparition, "Wallace Litwin took photos of the flying disc over the USS FDR in Operation Mainbrace and I've got copies of his photographs here. It shows the object going over the ship and you see the ship's super structure and part of a wing of an airplane. Just like a bright light going over the ship with a forward control but disc-shaped." What was this estranged romance with the USS FDR and these USOs? Was the attraction that brought these crafts to the FDR simply nuclear?

A majority of the military witnesses uniformly concur that the USOs were observing their naval exercises at close range. Reports reveal that even Supreme Allied Commander General Dwight D. Eisenhower, before his presidency and while touring aboard the USS FDR, witnessed the surreal attraction between the nuclear aircraft carrier and the USOs. Now, if you're a general or just an average Joe sailing with the world's most powerful Navy, the US Navy, it must be a humbling feeling when one finds out that there is a stronger presence out there. The USS FDR was the best of the best, but finding out that, even with all of her state-of-the-art amenities and technological wonders, she couldn't even get in the ring to compete with the USO must have been appalling. Why? Because the FDR lost the title belt and was no longer the top dog. The witnessing sailors must have realized how vulnerable and completely defenseless they were, subjected to the will of the superior USO race.

However, from all these situations and encounters we've learned that the bulk of these visitors are not hostile. Our human race would have no choice but to surrender and be enslaved if this was the USO species' agenda, which apparently it is not. Obviously, our sea inhabitants and space neighbors are superior to us in the technological department, which is why our jaws always drop to the floor when we try to comprehend their elegant, ballerina-like spectacles above and below the water's surface. What they have our military wants. The black world is literally obsessed with getting their hands on the USO technology so they can reverse-engineer it and leverage it, militarily, against their adversaries. According to Bill Birnes, "the military, in fact, the militaries of all First World nations treat these things as threats. They can penetrate airspace, go into highly secure areas, out-fly our fastest jets. Does that mean they're hostile?"

It's really sad and pathetic that the black world hides this topic from the civilian world. What's even worse is that these clandestine agencies are the chosen ambassadors that speak for the human race and hold our very existence in the palm of their hands. The black world believes this subject to be their exclusive right, their prerogative. Operation Mainbrace's files and documents are mostly still classified. They obviously don't believe the civilian world should be "in the loop" or involved in researching the ufology subject. They want the general public to keep out of THEIR business. What I'm advocating is that this subject is not solely THEIR business but a phenomenon entitled to all inhabitants of Earth to share equally. Yet, when dealing with UFOs and USOs we've ventured on into the black world's territory, into the lion's den, where standard protocol does not exist. The strong proclivity to disregard standard protocol is indicative that UFOs and USOs are THE MOST IMPORTANT item on the black world's agenda. And, if UFOs and USOs are the most important item on the black world's agenda then it should be a serious priority and major area of research within the civilian world's agenda as well. But these untamed and ferocious lions don't want to share the fresh meat of this ufology subject, and they don't care that we're hungry because in a land of predators the lion never fears the jackal. According to author Steven Greer, "the people who are the serious witnesses to operations and events have been afraid to come forward, both because they've been threatened, and they're also afraid of being ridiculed."

The status quo denial of black world government agencies is UNACCEPTABLE. The condescending approach they use in dealing with UFOs, USOs, and December 21, 2012, could be the downfall of our species, and is UNACCEPTABLE. Something calamitous and of catastrophic proportions, foreseen by many prophets proclaiming dire predictions, is about to happen to Mother Earth—and these USOs are evidently aware of it. And, if the Earth is in trouble, we need to ascertain what's going on by whatever means necessary. Hopefully, these ocean dwelling USOs act benevolently towards us and our need for their help in deciphering the December 21, 2012, doomsday event. According to Bill Birnes, "does it mean that somehow there's an event coming on planet Earth, a cataclysmic end of time, and somehow the USOs are coming out of the Earth because the Earth itself is in trouble? Maybe we're nearing the End of Days." How long have these advanced creatures been here? Most importantly, how can we contact them without government interference before the End of Days?

Author and UFO/USO researcher Preston Dennett advocates that "some believe it's easier for us to land a man on the moon or to create a moon base than to land a man on the bottom of the ocean." Lauren Coleman, friend of Ivan T. Sanderson and author of *Mysterious America* says, "USOs have been in history for a long, long time and as associate and friend of mine, Ivan T. Sanderson, did a study of them long ago. They are there all the time. They're in the data. They're a part of the phenomena." And to further back up Sanderson and Coleman's claims, Bill Birnes gives additional insight on the situation by stating, "Even more frightening than extraterrestrials is what Ivan T. Sanderson said when he wrote the book *Invisible Residents.* They're not extraterrestrial...they're already here. Do USOs mean that living underneath the surface of planet Earth is a whole civilization of creatures, entities, and aliens for whom Earth is home, just as it's home for us on the surface? USOs might be indigenous to planet Earth. They were here before we were, and these are residents who've been here for millions of years, probably before life evolved on the surface of the planet." A foreseen, predicted event of apocalyptic proportions is about to happen to Mother Earth and these USOs are apparently aware of it. If the Earth is in trouble then we need to fraternize with this alien species by whatever means necessary in order to get a lucid explanation of what we're dealing with. If they've been here since the beginning, then they've seen this before. If we learn from them, we survive, but if we try and freelance our survival and "wing it" we will become shadows and dust quicker than we all may want to believe.

December 21, 2012, is right around the corner. The sand in our hourglass of existence is quickly diminishing.

The hour is upon us to make a decision, even without permission. We must not wait for the emotionally colorblind black world to help us. They're already plotting their survival contingency plan without our consent. In their survival game plan, only the perennial all-star types in the civilian world will merit an invitation and be granted access to their underground life-sustaining complexes, while everyone else gets the short end of the stick and must fend for themselves like animals. The fact that these underground life-sustaining bunker complexes have been built should open our eyes to the seriousness of what's about to occur, and apparently what the black world has known all along. The black world has been preparing for the end by building these life-sustaining underground complexes for quite some time. What has the civilian world done to prepare? When the surreal becomes real and the end collapses itself upon our way of life it will be too late for a viable plan. Time is not on our side at this point. It's time to go fishing for USOs and for answers. I'd be willing to bet my life that we find more than we ever thought to be possible. If we're wrong, we're wrong and I'll be the first to admit it, BUT if we're right then our way of life just might be saved and preserved to shine another day. If we spent one tenth of the time fishing for aliens as the paparazzi does chasing celebrities, we'd have some real answers. However, the black world knows and exploits our weaknesses. They know all too well that small, shortsighted minds talk about people and are engrossed in gossip and vanity, and are easy targets for mind subjugation. We must not be deceived again, and we must OPEN OUR EYES before our history IS history. (History Channel)

CHAPTER 5: OUR UNTAMED GALACTIC BACKYARD

BLACK HOLES

With a once-every-25,800-year celestial alignment happening on the winter solstice of 2012, what lives in the heavens is cause for great concern. Even more intriguing is that only in the last decade have western astronomers discovered a massive black hole in the center of our milky way. In the year 2000, conclusive evidence proved that there are rogue, renegade black holes right in our own cosmic backyard. Remember, light that travels at 186,000 miles per second cannot escape a black hole's wrath. So to have a black hole roaming in such close proximity to our own solar system and Earth is bound to raise some eyebrows. "Black holes, which are invisible, are the cosmos' greatest threat. When gravity wins and collapses a star, a black hole forms and its gravitational grip pulls everything inside." This is like a predator coming into our campsite to feast on us without us being able to defend ourselves. There is no defense from a black hole. If it came down to it, the Earth would lose against a black hole... period. A black hole's power is unmerciful and would suck the Earth's shield, our atmosphere, right off and then continue to dissolve human beings and all life forms by molecular disintegration. In his book, *The*

Day After Roswell, Phillip Corso notes that, "black holes, the ultra dense remains of stars that have collapsed upon themselves, swallow up light and gravity and, compress them like a galactic compactor into something that only subatomic particle physicists can describe and that can't actually be 'seen.' Only their effects can be determined from the way light and gravity seem to behave around them. So, you guess that a black hole might be present in a specific region of space when light and gravity around it bend almost like the way water circulates around the drain at the bottom of your sink."

What we don't know can destroy us and our most formidable enemies in our cosmic backyard are roaming black holes. The fact that we know so little about the dynamics of a black hole, especially in our own galaxy, is what makes them such an unknown variable. And, with such an unknown, unpredictable variable it's almost impossible to predict the outcome. They are unknown, devastatingly dangerous forces of the universe completely unmerciful to any object that crosses their path.

GAMMA-RAY BURSTS (GRBs)

What we don't know can kill us. The heavens above are shrouded in astonishing mystery with new clues to the universe's puzzle being discovered daily. Astronomers and scientists in the astrophysicist community are realizing just how fragile we are. In the great scale of the universe there are so many formidable adversaries to our Earth and way of life. Scientists acknowledge that the phenomenal powers of the universe greatly overwhelm the powers that human beings wield.

Known in the astrophysicist community as GRBs, gamma-ray bursts are a complex, intriguing mystery and only in the past few years have scientists begun to understand their power and magnitude. A gamma-ray burst is a radioactive light, brighter than a trillion suns, traveling at the speed of light, 186,000 miles per second. This light, occurring from an extinguished star, cuts through and traumatizes galactic space, and takes only a few milliseconds to occur. In the final collapse of a star, thus leading to its death, it releases an energy output so great that it poses a serious threat to our Earth as a global, killing nemesis. The sun is the engine of life. Scientists estimate there are 100 billion stars in our galaxy. Furthermore, there are 100 billion galaxies in our ever-expanding universe. So, 100 billion stars in our galaxy multiplied by 100 billion galaxies equals the realistic possibility of Earth having to sustain a GRB. With such an inconceivable number of stars in the universe GRBs are bound to happen—they're inevitable. However, with Earth's 4.5-billion-year history, historians claim that we haven't had a direct hit from a GRB and that the chances of being struck in the near future are very slim. However, it may not be a GRB from a collapsing star that we have to worry about; we may accidently inflict a GRB upon the Earth in the nuclear holocaust many predict to occur in WWIII. Humans have seen this man-made horror before, and sadly, we probably won't learn from it until it's too late.

The major GRBs the Earth and its inhabitants have endured have been from the two atom bombs dropped over Japan to end WWII in August of 1945. With the atom bomb dropped on Hiroshima 66,000 people died instantly but the death tolls eventually surpassed 200,000 from close contact with the atom bomb's gamma radiation.

We know the closest star system to Earth is Alpha Centauri, located about 4.37 light years away. Alpha Centauri A and B are 4.37 light years away, while the system's third, much dimmer star, the red dwarf Proxima Centauri is located a mere 4.22 light years away (FYI, a light year is roughly 6 trillion miles or nearly 10 trillion kilometers). If it hypothetically collapsed creating a GRB, the gamma radiation would singe our ozone layer and render us defenseless against severe gamma radiation (unless you have SPF 1,000,000,000). If you looked at the potency of gamma radiation on a chart or scale it would be located at the very top, with x-rays, microwaves, and radio/wireless signals all falling below gamma. Our ozone layer, which is so undervalued and taken for granted, currently deflects an array of harmful elements from space aimed at Earth. Without our protective shield, our way of life would quickly collapse. Hazardously decrepit radioactive conditions from the

GRB fallout would deem plant life on land unsustainable for years, thus leading to the collapse of our livestock. Without the livestock the human race would eventually topple over. The end result would most likely be a World War over food with famine running rampant. Banks and the value of a dollar would be worthless—all value would be in food and the Earth would only be able to sustain five to ten percent of the current world population. In 2010, the global population is around 6.7 billion (http://en.wikipedia.org/wiki/World_population) which would mean that of 6.7 billion only 335-670 million people would survive, if they were lucky. The same would occur, without the monetary issue, within our oceans, starting with the GRBs killing off phytoplankton residing at the ocean's surface where the sunlight is most abundant for the photosynthetic process to occur. Phytoplankton are a crucial ingredient for the survival of the oceanic food chain and ecosystem. These tiny, "microscopic plants grow abundantly in oceans around the world and are the foundation of the marine food chain. Small fish, and some species of whale, depend on the phytoplankton as food. The ocean's larger fish eat the smaller fish and the humans catch and eat many of the larger fish. Since phytoplankton depend on certain conditions for growth, they are a good indicator of change in their environment. For these reasons, and because they exert a global-scale influence on climate, phytoplankton are of primary interest to oceanographers and Earth scientists around the world." (http://earthobservatory.nasa.gov/Features/Phytoplankton/) A majority of the oxygen that we depend on to survive is produced from phytoplankton which converts the global warming gas carbon dioxide into oxygen. Across the map it would be an unfathomable deterioration of the food chain with famine affecting all biological forms of life on Earth. As phytoplankton die, in turn so do the fish and mammals that depend on them for food and oxygen.

With new, radically advanced state-of-the-art satellite tracking in 2010, astronomers and likeminded individuals have tracked and located a constant barrage of GRBs throughout the universe. Recently, as of September 2008, a huge gamma-ray blast—equivalent to 9,000 dying suns— was spotted 12.2 billion light years from Earth. This deep space, gigantic explosion was detected by the NASA's Fermi telescope, and scientists are claiming it to be the biggest gamma-ray burst ever detected. Astrophysicists are claiming that the spectacular blast that occurred in September 2008 in the Carina constellation, produced energies ranging from 3,000 to more than five billion times that of visible light. NASA astrophysicist Frank Reddy says, "visible light has an energy range of between two and three electron volts and these were in the millions and billions of electron volts. If you think about it in terms of energy, x-rays are more energetic because they penetrate matter. These things don't stop for anything—they just bore through and that's why we can see them from enormous distances." (http://news.yahoo.com/s/afp/20090219/sc_afp/sciencespaceastronomy)

With many more GRBs being found than scientists ever anticipated, some have theorized that many of these GRBs may not only be collapsing stars but may also be alien warfare deep in space. It could be possible for another species from another distant galaxy to be a million years ahead of us technologically. So, for their species to harness the raw power of gamma-rays could be plausible, which, of course, human scientists are just discovering the magnitude of. Between natural and manmade gamma ray bursts both from collapsing stars all over the universe as well as in our nuclear bombs, there's plenty of reason for Earth's habitants to be alarmed.

NASA AND NIBIRU A.K.A PLANET X

NASA, the prestigious government agency, is the zenith of space exploration and secrecy. They only leak a sliver of what they've seen in space to the public. NASA has actually known since 1983 of the December 21, 2012, lurking date and in 1983 they launched the IRAS (Infrared Astronomical Satellite) which located a very large object the size of Jupiter nearby. This object was named Planet X, otherwise known as Nibiru, derived from a binary failed star orbiting our Sun at a great distance. This binary object is a sub-brown dwarf, a.k.a., the Dark Star, and it is the cause of many effects on our solar system. You should familiarize yourself with Nibiru as NASA has kept us in the dark for over 25 years. Silence and non-disclosure is standard protocol for the elite government agency.

Since its discovery in 1983, Nibiru has been tracked in infrared observatories lurking around the Kuiper Belt and is now speeding right towards us set to enter our inner solar system in 2012. The inner solar system includes the terrestrial planets of Mercury, Venus, Earth, Mars, and the asteroid belt. With Nibiru's convergence into our backyard, NASA is predicting a sharp increase in the number of sunspots and killer solar flares, releasing proton storms. These "extreme solar eruptions entailing killer solar flares that unleash proton storms are bound to cause electrical and power grid failures as well as knock out communications with satellite disruptions," pretty much shorting-out all the digital and wireless toys that we all take for granted. (http://www.nasa.gov/home/hqnews/2009/jan/HQ_09-001_Severe_Space_Weather_prt.htm)

Nibiru a.k.a. Planet X's projected trajectory is forecasted to converge on Earth during the winter solstice starting December 21, 2012 with its

*gravitational pull on the Earth reaching critical mass in 2013. Think
about this, if the moon's gravitational pull on the Earth can create
the ocean tides then try and fathom the disruption caused by a giant
planet cutting through our solar system during a once every 25,800 year
galactic alignment? Coincidence or fate that we're about to reap?*

Others foresee that once Planet Nibiru cuts through our inner
solar system in 2012 and passes between the Sun and our Earth,
which is to occur during a once every 25,800 year great galactic
alignment, an event of Biblical proportions will unfold. Millions, or
even billions, could die. "Earthquakes, drought, famine, wars, social
collapse, even killer solar flares will be caused by Planet X blasting
through the core of our solar system." (http://www.universetoday.
com/2008/05/25/2012-no-planet-x/) Furthermore, Nibiru was able to
be seen by the naked eye around May 15, 2009, as a reddish object.
However, it will be shielded from most and only be visible from the
very remote southern location of Earth. By May of 2011 Nibiru will
be seen by all of Earth's peoples. Impossible you say? Understand that
it's easy to manipulate a population's perception that's never been to
space and beyond. There's only a small fraction of our population, a
sliver far less than 1 percent, that's been privileged as astronauts and
cosmonauts to blast off into the endlessness of space. So, what do we
really know? We only know what NASA has told us and what we've
read or heard about, and believe me, we didn't get the full story about
what's going on up there. It has been rumored that the space agency
predicts that two-thirds of the world population will be lost with
the upcoming events of 2012. We must get ready for what the Jews
call the "End of Days" and what the Christians call "Armageddon"
(http://www.youtube.com/watch?v=d3bv_YbVQPI&feature=related).
All indicators, signs, and arrows direct us to 2012...Tick, tock, tick,
tock, tick, tock...The sand in our hourglass of time is quickly running
out. We all must open our eyes and wake up!

CHAPTER 6: THE WORLD AS WE DON'T SEE IT

EARTH IS A GAS STATION FOR UFOs

What is the main attraction that lures UFOs to Earth? Why are UFOs often seen near large bodies of water, both fresh and salt? Why are UFOs also commonly seen near or around energy vortexes? Are these interstellar visitors harvesting an unseen energy or type of gravity that's needed to propel their UFO vehicles? Could this mysterious energy—that we know so little about—be the equivalent to the gasoline needed for humans to propel cars? Could it be that Earth is a gas station and an exit off the intergalactic highway for these UFOs? Is it just that simple? Think about it.

What's impossible to us may be very possible to them. What's obtainable to them may be out of reach to us. What they consider to be no big deal, we may consider to be a huge deal. What they take for granted as reality, we humans still see as science fiction. What's normal to them may be abnormal to us. We must remember that not too long ago what humans thought to be impossible is now very possible, and now taken for granted as normal. What am I referring to? I'm referring to our wireless technology where an invisible beam and signal provides the user with a plethora of information that allows the users to interconnect and interface on a global scale, a technological wonder that we basically take for granted and consider normal in today's day of 2010. This was not always so, just ask your grandparents. Many elders see this technology as unfathomable and it's easy to see why. In the last 100 years, our species has made more advances than in the last 5,000 years combined. Why is this? Let me assure everyone that our species had more than a little help from our interstellar neighbors who've left an indelible mark on our way of life. Throughout the reverse engineering processes that the black world has been conducting in secrecy for over half a century, this alien technology has precipitated into our military as well as into the consumer world. Yet, there is so much more to learn and so much more to gain from our intergalactic neighbors. Their interest in our planet is still an enigma full of ambiguity and raises so many questions. The forces of power that we have yet to wield stir the imagination of what is possible, and could eventually transform our way of life to where we see traveling to Jupiter and its 63 moons, or Saturn and its 61 moons, or another galaxy as no big deal and normal. You might have a business trip on one of Jupiter's moons, or you and your family are taking a trip to see Saturn's rings, or you and your friends are planning on taking a vacation to another galaxy. This is an exciting time to be alive. Our human species is about to reach the stars and beyond and finally become a part of the interstellar community.

Many of these UFOs have been seen clearly manifesting and maneuvering around thunderstorms packed with lightning and electricity in the air. These UFOs have been seen from satellites, the International Space Station, and from the space shuttle high-resolution cameras swarming to electrically charged storms in order to harvest electromagnetic energy, a form of gravity that produces an electrically charged magnetic field. These crafts have been captured from our cameras and satellites in space, docking and stalling-out on the storms, in order to extract energy out of the electrical storms on Earth. It's a sight to see and truly opens the eyes to what is possible. What appears to just be a storm to you and me may actually be a gas station for these otherworldly vehicles. With UFOs flocking to these raw energy fields, almost as if they're pirates hijacking the electromagnetic force of the storm, it makes our addicted-to-oil species seem like a Stone Age civilization. What if these otherworldly visitors see us the way we see the primitive Stone Age caveman? Remember, there are four types of gravity in the universe (gravity, strong forces, weak forces, and electromagnetic force) and we only know a small portion about them. Nonetheless, as soon as we understand the dynamics of all types of gravity and learn how to harness its raw power, like our sophisticated intergalactic neighbors, it will certainly lead our species to the frontier of space and beyond.

A Sixth Sense

Some of the most powerful forces in the universe are invisible to the naked eye, and just because you can't see or detect something doesn't mean it doesn't exist. We cannot see God in the physical form, nor can we see the forces of gravity that surround us. We cannot see our wireless Internet signals, but we consider them to be real without being able to touch or see them. That said, UFOs are tangible and actually capable of being seen and touched, yet move much too fast for our eyes to detect. These elusive crafts are just one spoke on the enormous panorama-of-life wheel that is veiled from normal human eyesight. You need an apparatus, like a microscope or a high-resolution camera, to see a different domain that the human eye is not capable of detecting. The human body is an incredible creation but we we're only so blessed. For example, a dog's nose is four times keener than our nose with 250 million smell receptors while our human nose only has 60 million. Why is it that animals, fish, mammals, and reptiles have a built in sixth sense and know hours before a storm, earthquake, or a hurricane strikes? Russian scientist Vladimir Vernadsky claimed in the middle of the past century that man's impact on the natural world had taken the scale of a geological disaster. A recent series of underwater earthquakes and the mammoth tsunami in December 2004, showed human beings their place. The king of the world turned out to be helpless and defenseless against nature. Furthermore, people were unable to predict it, at least several hours in advance. Scientists noticed, though, that the tsunami disaster of 2004 killed very few animals, whereas the number of human victims was immense, over 300,000 people.

There are a lot of hypotheses to explain such a mysterious phenomenon. People have long paid attention to animals' ability to react to imminent natural dangers. The first incident was documented in the year 2000 B.C. The ancient manuscript says that people noticed weasels suddenly disappeared from their usual habitats in Crete shortly before a very powerful earthquake rocked the island. Snakes suddenly appeared on the surface of the ground in the winter of 1975 in China. Snakes are cold-blooded animals; they hide in shelters and become dormant for winter periods. Local authorities treated such a violation of biological norms seriously and evacuated residents. As it turned out later, the snakes forecast a mammoth earthquake, which measured 7.3 on the Richter scale. History proves that animals possess a remarkable ability to foresee not only earthquakes, but tsunamis as well. There were incidents when animals abandoned valleys prior to avalanching. London residents paid attention to cats and dogs' behavior before air raids during the WWII years. A beacon worker in South India said in December 2004 that he had seen a large flock of antelopes fleeing the coastal area towards the nearest hills just several hours before the tsunami disaster. Eyewitnesses say that elephants were trumpeting, breaking chains and escaping inland in Thailand. Having a presentiment of a forthcoming natural disaster, flamingos left their lowlands and flew in the direction of mountainous areas as well. Employees of the Malaysian zoo noticed that all the animals were behaving strangely, hiding in their shelters and refusing to go out. The tsunami disaster killed over 30,000 people in Sri Lanka. However, almost all local elephants, deer and other wild animals survived the monstrous attack of tidal waves. It is worth mentioning that only one wild boar of 2,000 animals of an Indian reserve was killed in the 2004 tsunami disaster. According to US biologists, 14 sharks that were kept under regular observation for several years left their usual places of living 12 hours before Hurricane Charlie hit Florida. The sharks disappeared in deep waters of the ocean and returned two weeks later even though they had never left their natural habitat before.

Animals obviously have a natural sixth sense and can detect looming danger better than humans and all of our technology. The tsunami disaster of December 26, 2004, made scientists look deeper into the mystery. Researchers have already proved that different animal species living all over the world possess the surprising ability to envisage natural catastrophes.

Unlike humans, wild animals can perceive a lot more information about the world around them. Their senses are a lot better, they can sense vibrations at huge distances; even a slight change in the atmospheric pressure will not remain unnoticed for animals. They have a built in warning system, barometer, and advanced set of sensory equipment that they're born with. Their major advantage is an ability to read atmospheric conditions and see natural warnings, which helps them avoid the storm of nature. Biologists believe that it is impossible to obtain such a capability, although the knowledge of animal instincts could bring good to people. Scientists also noticed that wild animals have a much better reaction to imminent dangers in comparison with domestic animals. Domestic animals live under the strong influence of human culture. It is not ruled out that a human being used to be as sensitive to natural changes as wild animals are now. Ancient people probably had this animal instinct as well. Perhaps they knew where to run and hide in order to save themselves from earthquakes and volcano eruptions. Some people suffer from terrible pain in the joints before powerful landslides, for example. Others suffer from internal hemorrhage or high temperature before a natural disaster. Children and extrasensory individuals are the most "talented tellers" of forthcoming natural disasters in this respect. (http://english.pravda. ru/science/19/94/377/15403_tsunami.html)

These animals and extraordinary individuals with an extrasensory gift obviously have the ability to see and sense something that most humans cannot. They trust their built-in internal senses whereas we trust the Weather Channel and NOAA (National Oceanic and Atmospheric Administration) to guide and steer us away from disastrous storms. But, just because our human eyes can't see an object like a UFO or our bodies don't detect something doesn't mean that it isn't there. We're a blessed species but our human senses only go so far.

NOTHING IS IMPOSSIBLE IN A UNIVERSE OF UNKNOWNS

Human behavioral patterns are so predictable. Most people are seriously dependent on electronics for their day to day lives. Whether in front of their TVs, sitting in front of their computers, playing video games, talking on the phone or text messaging, it has become a dependency that most of us take for granted. However, if we were being observed and monitored from another species then our habitual way of life would be easy to predict and foresee, making their attack all the easier. An EMP, or electromagnetic pulse, which cripples electrical circuitry, would easily cripple our love for our digital and wireless toys. Furthermore, our way of communicating would be thrown back to the handwritten-letter era, delivered by horseback. Everything electronic would no longer work. Satellite, cell phone, TV, and wireless Internet signals gone. A great depiction of the havoc and chaos an EMP is capable of creating is captured within Steven Spielberg's movie *War of the Worlds*. Any true enemy of ours would study our affairs and quickly realize that our true weakness is electronics. Many people in America live, breath, and sleep electronics. That's why we should familiarize ourselves with the seriousness behind the word EMP, or electromagnetic pulse, and the fallout from losing all electronics. What we don't know can kill us, especially if another species has the ability to wield powers that we have not yet harnessed and only begun to understand. They may not breathe oxygen or drink water, which are essential building blocks for life with our human species. If you're more of a visual learner and relate better by watching a movie, then watch the science-fiction blockbuster thriller *Alien* movies starring Sigourney Weaver. These movies may seem fictional to many at the moment, but these movies show that aliens are an entity entirely opposite to the human creation. In these *Alien* movies the aliens' anatomy has some sort of extremely vile and toxic acid for blood that erodes steel. Their way of breeding is even more appalling, and I am speculating here, but I believe most humans would consider their alien way of procreating as sadistically animated. Humans know that our blood is red, full of hemoglobin, pumped by our heart and circulated throughout our arteries and veins. Our systematic way of breeding is normal to us but an alien species may consider it impossible.

What we're going to realize when we open our eyes to space travel is that humans are just one creation of many residing within the universe. Our human anatomy contains a unique blucprint and is most likely completely different from our alien neighbors. It is often wiser to unlearn than to learn. We have been programmed through school to have certain psychological limitations of the possibilities, which in turn dictate human life and our way of thinking. Humans weren't supposed to jump out of airplanes until we made the impossible possible, and humans weren't supposed to swim with sharks outside of a cage until we made the impossible possible, all of which were limitations tattooed on our brains. Don't let these limitations of our human race govern the limitations of an unknown alien race. Remember that our current standard periodic table of the elements contains 117 elements (http://en.wikipedia.org/wiki/Periodic_table), so think outside the box and try to fathom the concept of another species or civilization having 300 elements, or 1,000 elements, or only five elements completely foreign to Earth's elements. The greatest discovery one can make is that nothing is impossible. We must all open our eyes and think outside the box to discover that anything is possible in a universe of unknowns.

CHAPTER 7: WHAT WE DO IN LIFE ECHOES IN ETERNITY

EARTH IS A BATTLEFIELD

How strong is your devotion to God? Are you engaged in a close relationship with God or are you walking distant from the divine? The reason I ask is because we all must open our eyes to see the ongoing war of good vs. evil that can be seen everywhere today. Earth has become a recruiting depot for the final battle of Armageddon, and it's time to take a side. Recruiters for both sides are everywhere, advocating one side over the other. God's Angels are in full recruit mode as are Satan's wretched henchmen. Both sides have deployed their top delegates to win over the souls of men. The stage has been set for the grand finale. With that said, when the battlefield is presented to us what side will you be standing on? Do you choose the light or the darkness? I ask because in the upcoming End of Days that declaration will become the fate of your soul. For many, including myself, God has been the coach for this life and has been the source of raw inspiration and motivation. Many times He has carried us throughout the darkest times of our lives, and He has given us hope for redemption when the pain body of darkness and defeat had invaded and tried to conquer our minds. Too many times God and His Angels have carried us, at the lowest and weakest points of our lives along His white sandy beaches with only their footprints in the sand. And I'm a 6'6"-210-pound, giant human being so I'm not all that light to carry, Angel or not. For many of us mortals, whenever we've asked for His higher power and guidance He has always heeded our alarming call, even when we have turned our backs on Him in our unseasoned and foolish stages of dealing with temptation and debauchery brought on by the Devil's lure. Furthermore, the fact that God has never turned his back on us, and has always been there for us unconditionally, has won over our souls through his unparalleled loyalty. He has coached us to not let the Devil's temptation blind us and infiltrate our lives, and throughout our experiences we have learned to become attentive listeners with God. He has taught us that one can actually say a lot by saying very little. If and when we speak, we ask God questions and then we sit back and take notes from the heavenly Father. A lot of notes, indeed. Who better to learn and be mentored from? Many of us were once lost, and psychologically devoured by the dark side. Nonetheless, we were given a second chance. Now many of us are back in the game and spiritually enlightened with the power of God and His Angels walking beside us. This "once we were lost and now we are found" feeling has resuscitated our fidelity in our relationship with the divine and, in turn, has shown us our paths, our destinies. I can vouch that He is the director and wielder of my pen as His message to our world flows through me in the words you currently read. With age, I've learned to listen more and talk less, and through this process have started to hear His message more and more. Why do we usually ask God for some material thing or for some form of personal help instead of asking the bigger question, "What can we do for you, God?" What can we do to help cross off some of the items on your never-ending to-do list? We need to ask this rarely asked question more often to Him because we should all be eternally grateful for all the times He has saved us when we've asked him to, and more importantly, for the life He has given us on Earth. If an individual hates God, or has alienated Him out of their lives, then they may need to open their eyes to see that the Devil is smiling at his working ploy. The Devil is a master tactician in deceiving the human mind by attacking individual weaknesses and exploiting that vulnerability. Lucifer will try any method to win over man's soul in order to build an army of darkness. His venomous will is carried out by his wretched emissaries that have been sent to our world to recruit human soldiers. God has proved to believers like myself, time and time again, that everything about the spiritual world is more real than this world. It only takes once, but once you get a glimpse and open your eyes to the spiritual side of life everything, is more authentic, more beautiful, and much more lucid. Colors are much more vivid, edges are sharper, and emotions are enhanced to crystal clear. As John Fogerty once said, "You can ponder perpetual motion, fix your mind on a crystal day." Church, to many, may be a moot point, or seen as a money-making business by some, but church is besides the point. God is not just found in the church as his presence and aura can be seen and felt all around us. The church itself is just a holistic symbol. However, if you can't find God's presence outside of church then you can always rely on finding God within His temple of worship found within a church. To channel God outside of the church you just have to keep your eyes and ears open to get a good gage on the unspoken beauty where He resides. The natural therapeutic unspoken beauty in this world of wonders is a good starting point to start finding God, especially if you're not a fan of church. God is the most beautiful decorator I have ever known. Too many fail to see the quality of architectural genius provided to them through God's flawless vision and creation of this Earth. I'm talking about the raw beauty of this world, the true art from God's hand. Michelangelo, Vincent Van Gogh, Salvador Dali, and Leonardo DaVinci are all top-shelf, original artists but God's majestic beauty is unparalleled and cannot be trumped. Ansel Adams has an exquisite eye for capturing God's pristine beauty in his black and white photos. Nonetheless, God has proven to be the highest-caliber landscape architect with work both magnificent and world-renowned. Time and time again I have asked God what I can do for Him (since he has given me so much already) and in return He has repeatedly beckoned His call to me. I've listened for a response to my prayers and am guided in God's direction. His purpose for me is to write and educate people to open their eyes through the use of my pen. I am to use my pen as a vehicle to raise awareness and create change, especially to an event in time that could change our very existence. I previously aspired to get involved in politics out of the US Marine Corps to create real change, but I eventually realized that most politicians are as crooked as a question mark and usually don't keep their word to their constituents. As Michael Carleone in *The Godfather* said, "Politics and crime—they're the same thing." In addition, and according to talk show host turned political speaker Jerry Springer, "As soon as politics becomes your career you become intellectually dishonest." I have acted on His call to use my writing as a platform to launch an awakening. After all, God is my couth master and I am His mortal puppet and tool to be used as He pleases to better mankind. Hopefully, when all is said and done and my life's torch has burned dim, I will have left this world in better condition than I found it in. Maybe then God will smile and applaud from above, and if I'm lucky, maybe I'll earn a VIP seat in Heaven. So, and with God's blessing on my pen, fasten your seat belts because something that hasn't happened in 25,800 years is about to happen. There's still time to mend your relationship with God before Armageddon is upon us. Search your soul and make an honest declaration to yourself. Once you've chosen your side, say it with conviction. Pledge your unconditional allegiance and don't become a victim of your own hypocrisy. War is upon us.

THE DEVIL WALKS AMONG US

We are not what was intended. God has his hands on the strings but somewhere along the line the Devil manifested and manipulated our lives. The world we know is a battlefield, an ongoing war of good vs. evil where us humans are constantly torn between the two sides in a grueling test of faith. Many of us are walking contradictions caught in the middle of God's light and Satan's darkness. We can see examples all around us and know why Eve couldn't resist tasting the apple that the Devil lured and tempted her with. We should not denounce God when torment precipitates upon our lives. Many of us are victims of our own hypocrisy, claiming to be one way and then behind closed doors professing an entirely different creed and belief. Know that you only are what you are when no one is looking. We must be steadfast in our beliefs, crystalline and pure, and not be sidetracked by the strong, intoxicating aroma that the Devil has conjured and mastered. We must be able to survive Satan's temptations at the height of his powers, and many believe the signs point to a growing evil that has become more prevalent in recent years. Found within the Bible's New Testament is the Book of Revelations. These Biblical Revelations foretell of an End of Days showdown between good and evil. Many believe the revelatory omens seen today to be a sign that the end is near. The stage is currently in the process of being set for an ultimate clash, possibly stemming from the natural disaster fallout from December 21, 2012. The fallout from the great cosmic alignment of 2012 and polar shift will lead the world into WWIII, and during this point we will all be vulnerable prey to the Anti-Christ. Satan, according to the Bible, is the greatest deceiver and liar the world has ever known and will prey on man. However, according to ancient texts from the Jews, Christians, and Muslims, the scriptures emphatically speak of a divine emissary that will be sent to combat the evil and army of darkness. Many believe the long awaited messiah to be Jesus, the savior of Nazareth, who will lead the battle of Armageddon against Satan's top lieutenant, the Anti-Christ. The time frame for this grand finale is likely to occur within our lifetimes and the sand in our hourglass of time is quickly running out. We all need to open our eyes to unite for a cause greater than ourselves. Why is the saying "religion dividing instead of uniting" so true in our 2010 world? We need to flip that saying around before we enter into this major transitional period of uncertainty where the Devil walks among us.

DON'T JUDGE A BOOK BY ITS COVER

In America now, we are judged and scrutinized according to our material wealth and assets. We are all born into this world as naked human beings at birth yet we transform into designer and name-brand everything. Why has our culture become obsessed with this vain narcissistic lifestyle that only praises sin? When did we sell our souls to the Devil for material wealth? At what point in time did the Devil get his hands on the strings? In with the new, out with the old, a never-ending cycle of impulse buys. The programmed chip inside the brain has unlimited needs and wants for materialistic possessions and is constantly reloaded with the new needs and wants seen on TV and from our culture's relentless and poisonous advertising campaigns. Why has our culture created this vanity juggernaut that exhibits malevolence over benevolence? Who was the architect behind this? The once-naked human that was seen by all the other naked humans as equal has started to differentiate itself from the pack. The individual is no longer naked, now wearing an expensive tailored suit or designer dress, sporting a top-shelf watch or a high-end necklace, and driving an expensive car. However, his once-naked counterpart is now wearing clothes from Wal-Mart and driving around in a car that is a 15-year-old rust bucket. Prejudging begins to commence as the once naked individuals take material shape and form, creating their so-called identities. In today's America, judging a book by its cover has become commonplace as the substance (pages) inside of the book (person) are never opened and read, yet genius could be inside if one were to venture in. For example, if an individual has awful acne, or their teeth aren't perfectly straight and aligned, or a woman isn't wearing UGG boots, then they might be judged as a lesser person for it, which is actually sickening to believe but easy to see with our country's superficial, shallow culture. This infectious culture has created a world where imperfections aren't allowed to exist. However, imperfections are what make the humans so beautiful. In my home town of Silverthorne, Colorado, which is in Summit County by the

Breckenridge and Keystone Ski Resorts, there is a 56-year-old street evangelist named Milton Kapner (a.k.a. Brother Nathaniel) who wears white gloves, a black robe, and can be seen dancing on the streets waving his crucifix and American flag in jubilee.

Street evangelist Brother Nathanael a.k.a. Milton Kapner. Too many individuals in America 2010 habitually judge a book by its cover. "Do not judge, or you too will be judged. For in the same way you judge others, you will be judged, and with the measure you use, it will be measured to you." (Matthew 7:1) Let God, the celestial prosecutor, judge the souls of mortals.

This unique, heralded priest braves the harsh mountainous elements throughout the year, through thick and thin, to strongly praise God, Jesus Christ, and America. Now, when I was in the Marine Corps Infantry, God and Country were advocated on a daily basis and were the backbone and foundation of our beliefs. Every time I drive by this holy advocate I wave to him and make the sign of the cross to show my respect not only to him but to God and to our country. However, Brother Nathaniel has been a victim of unadulterated hate. He has been harassed and called crazy, has had his life threatened, and was even shot in the face in January of 2007, yet he's still out there stronger than ever delivering his passionate message every morning or evening. What if Brother Nathaniel is one of God's emissaries or Angels sent to view and analyze our world? However, too many of these "haters" are the epitome of what I'm getting at. They're judging a book by its cover without understanding the pages within. This, unfortunately, is the case in the world we live in. Where we live and how we live is dictated by one's looks, material wealth and assets.

THE DEVIL LIVES IN AMERICA

The brutal honesty is that Satan Calls America "Home Sweet Home." The deadly sins that claim the souls of mortals are committed so cavalierly in America without even thinking twice about the ramifications of our actions and the repercussions against our souls. We need to open our eyes to see the sinful turmoil that has engulfed many of us. Many of us are not alone, however, as greed began early with Judas selling Jesus out to the Roman centurions and high priests for 30 pieces of silver, a bribe which he later returned after he realized what he had done to Jesus (http://bible.cc/matthew/27-3. htm). The beautiful thing about life is that God allows u-turns, it's never too late to rediscover yourself or this world. It's easy to forget what the most important thing in life is, which is life itself and to leave this world in a better place than we found it in. However, our country today has an out-of-control capitalistic mindset where we are breeding and infusing the population, especially the youth, with a poisonous ideology. Some believe that Adam Smith, Scottish economist and author of *Wealth of Nations* laid the foundation and framework for a capitalism hierarchy during the birth of our nation, an ideology accepted not only by authors and economists, but by governments and organizations as well. The year 1776 should not only be known for the Declaration of Independence, but as a year capitalism, supply and demand, inflation and deflation started to really take shape from Smith's book *Wealth of Nations*. At the dawn of the Industrial Revolution and during the Age of Enlightenment,

Smith advocated a free market economy as more productive and more beneficial to society. "Every man is rich or poor according to the degree in which he can afford to enjoy the necessaries, conveniences, and amusements of human life." (http://en.wikipedia.org/wiki/The_Wealth_of_Nations) This book basically sowed the seeds for being judged according to one's materialistic wealth, and since then America has seemingly gone AWOL (military term for "Absent WithOut Leave") from being humble and modest.

America has become the land of immediate results. If an individual is too obese then they get gastric bypass surgery or liposuction to shed the weight instantaneously. If an individual doesn't like their stomach they buy an Ab Belt off the infomercials instead of putting in diligent work at the gym. If an individual doesn't like their appearance they go under the knife of Dr. 90210 to get elective cosmetic surgery, or get Botox injections, etc., all desperately trying to fit in to this image of perfection that our pretentious culture is breeding. Also, I've noticed an over-saturation of Extenze commercials. The excessive advertising for Extenze, a pill designed for male penis enlargement, is pumped into our subconscious minds, by showing these commercials over, and over, and over again, slowly brainwashing the consumer to purchase their product. The weak-minded are easy targets and quickly lured into their scheme with the use of glamorous girls, acting as decoys and promotion tools for Extenze. America, we need to stop and take a good look in the mirror to see the monster that has manifested within us, which is an America where instant gratification trumps any thought of long-term ramifications. This is why the Devil moved to America. God is certainly shaking his head at us as his goal for mankind was the antithesis of what we've recently created. We've become a narcissistic country, devoured by the quest for material wealth and to be rich, yet a majority not knowing how to fuse the pieces together to create that level of financial success shown on TV. This false reality, once realized, can be a leading cause for depression and criminal acts. Furthermore, watching TV can drive the mind to keep dreaming about possessions that appear to be essential for happiness. These are the illusions that many have bought in to. The human mind likes to emulate what it sees, which in turn it tends to believe. With America's current culture, which is amplified through TV broadcasts as well as unrelenting advertising and marketing campaigns, the promise that one day we'll become rich and happy is a mirage. As Tyler Durden from *Fight Club* states "Advertising has us chasing cars and clothes, working jobs we hate so we can buy shit we don't need. We've all been raised on television to believe that one day we'd all be millionaires, and movie gods, and rock stars. But we won't. And we're slowly learning that fact. And we're very, very pissed off." This quest to be rich is possible yet our culture makes it seem glorified where with riches comes great happiness. Often, one's imagination of becoming rich evolves into reality through age and maturing where one starts to see how becoming a millionaire is much easier said than done. Don't get me wrong, America has the most millionaires and billionaires in the world but we should not infuse our youth and population with dollar signs and greed. Happiness should be discovered and found within our human intangibles and imperfections that each and every one of us is born with.

Britney Spears, Paris Hilton, and Lindsay Lohan's whereabouts constantly litter the media forums. The gossip spreads like wildfire on MSN News, Yahoo News, as well as most major news broadcasts. Our culture's news headlines are polluted with garbage that only takes precious time away from real threatening issues of immediate concern (i.e., BP Gulf Oil Spill Disaster, Darfur, Famine, AIDS, etc.). Yet, for some reason our culture seems to care more about where these prima donnas and celebrities ate lunch or what club they went to that night, and with whom. The paparazzi aren't entirely to blame as their business is only fueled by our culture's demand for insight into these celebrities' lives. We must open our eyes to our future. Our future is still malleable but we are quickly running out of time. There are greater forces than we can possibly fathom that are at work in the universe that are about to shape our destiny. It's time to reverse the downward spiral, which has kept us in limbo for far too long. This effort is going to take each and every one of us to succeed, but through unification we will script a better coexistence. Helping a fellow man is profitable in every sense, both personally and bottom line.

Greed has many shapes, faces, and forms. It has no boundaries and must be stopped. Pharmaceutical companies, like oil tycoons, epitomize an exuberant greed and make billions in profit with the corrupted pyramid scheme of keeping the sick strung out on prescription pills and medications for their entire lives. How can this be? There is no money in the cure...period. Why would they cure our sicknesses and then not be able to profit off us? Once we're cured we won't need their prescription pills any longer. And, if we're cured and don't need pills then we'd be able to save our hard-earned money instead of shelling out big bucks for prescription medications. In their eyes, our health is much less important than their profits. They want to profit off the sick and sadly their souls will most likely burn in hell for all eternity. Frankly, I don't know how these individuals involved in such evil corruption can look at themselves in the mirror each morning without utter disgust.

However, special treatment is provided for the elite like the once-HIV-positive basketball superstar Magic Johnson. Remember most of us are taught that there is no cure for HIV and AIDS. So, if HIV and AIDS are supposedly incurable, how is Magic Johnson's sexually transmitted disease now untraceable? He may be a basketball icon but there are millions of HIV and AIDS infected people across the world, especially in Africa, that could use that 'Magic' antidote to cure their life-threatening sicknesses. Greed, one of the seven deadly sins, plagues our country daily and it's only getting worse. The Devil smiles as his swift entrance into our world will be welcomed with open arms. The Devil needs no bait on his fishing line to lure his human recruits. He doesn't fish with corn or worms, no lure, yet he casts his line into the stocked trout pond of America with a dollar bill on it and always hooks a dozen fish. The Devil has acquired his bait, his lure to recruit his army of henchmen to carry out his demonic will...money. Money is an illusion, a piece of paper with some numbers on it, created to blind the mind of men, a distraction and roadblock from reaching spiritual enlightenment. The Devil knows this and knows all too well that the minds of men are weak and easily swindled by money in all its shapes and forms. Lucifer chuckles at how easy the recruiting process has been in reaching his recruitment quota and heads to our world confident in his lure of temptation. He grabs his fishing pole, no HillBros can of worms, and with December 21, 2012 edging closer the world grows blinder to the grim reality. America we need open our eyes and wake up! We've invited Satan's top lieutenant, the Grimm Reaper, to sit down and dine with us!

The problem is that the Devil is such a skilled tactician that he is not perceived as harmful by many, yet completely the opposite. Satan's greatest trick was convincing man he didn't exist. Sadly, Satan's malevolent henchmen are getting raises and promotions as their deceitful and devious work brings rewards. We must open our eyes to let God into our lives and back into our culture. Our culture needs to gel with God and make Him "cool" instead of alienating Him from our lives. "Casting all your care upon Him, for He cares for you. Be sober, be vigilant; because your adversary the Devil walks about like a roaring lion, seeking whom he may devour." (1 Peter 5:7-8). Don't let the Devil devour you with a spirit-crushing blow. Life is a test, a battlefield we are born into. Earth is a tryst where good and evil merge and where forces collide in a paradox that our souls are caught in the middle of. We must not let the Devil confuse our eyes with misdirection and conjured magic. If you thought Criss Angel, David Copperfield, David Blaine, or Houdini were impressive magicians then know that the Devil has mastered this art, an art of deception and misdirection that can blind even the best trained eyes. Remember that Lucifer had God fooled, too, at one point as he was one of the highest-ranking angels before being cast away to Hell. We must open our eyes to see that a war for our souls has begun, and the duality of mankind is being recruited upon from both sides of the spectrum.

Be Grateful for Today

Open your eyes to live the short life you have been blessed to have. Being cynical but a realist, there are a million and one ways that a human can die, a million and one, as we are just fragile flesh and bone. If you're in good health be very grateful for today. Be grateful for the little things, the simple pleasures that this world offers. We have made improvements with our life expectancy in the US: 75 years for men and 81 years for women, (http://en.wikipedia. org/wiki/List_of_countries_by_life_expectancy) with statistics claiming women live longer than men. Nonetheless, death could appear at your doorstep at any moment, at any given time, without any warning (i.e., fatal accident, illness, etc.). Most tragic deaths happen without warning where that individual never would have believed that on that day they'd be taken by death. So, listen to your elders around you and truly understand that your health really is the most important personal thing to worry about and to be grateful for today. "Rejoice in thy youth." Your life span is a whisper, a flick in time's perspective, even if you live to be 100. Live for today, pray for tomorrow.

It's Often Wiser to Unlearn than to Learn

In our country, all but the extraordinarily rich (approximately 5 percent) of the 300 million+ residents that inhabit our 50 states are feeling some sort of anguish. Most of these well-to-do individuals voted for Senator John McCain in our nation's last election. Why? Money and greed will cloud even the best of minds and once money is earned it's extremely hard to give away, especially if your diligent work has been the yeast that's made your dough rise. Only the disciplined and mentally strong know how to effectively use excessive money for a greater cause without falling into the Devil's trap. Falling into the excessive-love-for-money-and-vanity trap that has crippled the United States happens too often. This plague was even addressed by the Pope who noticed on his recent trip to America in 2008 that we're becoming too overly involved and obsessed with our possessions and materialistic wealth, and that our spiritual connection is quickly vanishing. As Tyler Durden says in *Fight Club*, "The things you own end up owning you. You are not your job. You're not how much money you have in the bank. You're not the car you drive. You're not the contents of your wallet. You're not your fucking khakis." This materialistic and vain trend is often viewed by other cultures in the world as a poisonous, far from pure way of life. Take the beautiful Middle Eastern city of Tehran, Iran, for example. Their women dress in a way that's very modest and unrevealing to the contours of their bodies, which is the accepted and tolerated look with their Iranian culture. Many are not enveloped, driven, and distracted by the quest for designer-name brand icons, and in turn retain a high level of spirituality and faith.

On the flip side, American women dress in a fashion completely opposite that of Iranian women, completely driven by the world of Gucci, Louis Vuitton, Prada, Chanel, Dolce & Gabbana, Coach, and Burberry (the list goes on)—all accepted and tolerated in American culture. Many have lost their spiritual connection distracted by their excessive love for name brand possessions. We have to be careful as a country not to always think that our way is the right way, or the only way. America does help the world more than any other nation, but for the eight years under the Bush administration, we were the world's police, with an our-way-or-the-highway mentality, and many a times we impose our shallow, bleak ways on the world. This comes across as abrasive and very offensive to many cultures across the globe. What may be orthodox and tolerated in our culture may be unorthodox and intolerable in many other cultures, and vice versa. Sometimes it is often wiser to unlearn than to learn (i.e., imperialism, bigotry, greed, hate, racism, etc.). I strongly believe and advocate that this is a notion that needs to be adopted and incorporated into our American way of life.

So, how does one reconfigure and rewire a whole nation's brain to have them open their eyes to the bigger picture of God's intention for us all? How does one enhance a nation's vision to look beyond the surface of what they see to realize it's mostly just a facade? The nice cars, the nice house, the toys, the wardrobe, the bling, the quest for cash, the womanizing, etc., too often leads to instant gratification that ends in a downward spiral of emptiness, loneliness and depression. Understand that simplicity is elegance and often leads to peace, love, and harmony. We must open our eyes to see that spiritual balance comes without money. Know what success really means and like Warren Buffet claims, "I know people who have a lot of money and they get testimonial dinners and hospital wings named after them. But the truth is that nobody in the world loves them. When you get to my age, you'll measure your success in life by how many of the people you want to have love you actually do love you. That's the ultimate test of how you've lived your life." (*Parade* "10 Ways to Get Rich" September 7, 2008).

Despite his $62 billion net worth, Warren Buffet does not measure success in dollars and neither should we. Some may say, "Well that's easy for him to say since he's one of the richest men in the world," but what everyone needs to know is that in 2006 he selflessly pledged to give away almost his entire fortune to charities, primarily the Bill and Melinda Gates Foundation. The point that I'll make time and time again, along with Warren Buffet and others fighting the good fight, is to not only reap the prosperity from the seeds you sow, but most importantly, to give back to the world unconditionally and let your footprint and legacy resonate in a benevolent, proactive way. When tasting all the fruits of this Earth it is often a struggle and battle to find harmony and balance in one's life. If one tastes all of God's delectable fruits of the Earth, yet there is still an empty black hole in their soul, then that individual may want to wipe the slate clean and start from scratch, realizing that the problem starts at the source, at the beginning. Happiness is a state of mind and it's something that people struggle to find on a day-to-day basis.

Too often many individuals migrate towards the use of drugs and alcohol to cope with their mental altercations. Happiness can have a false reality when pollutants like drugs and alcohol are brought into the mix, thus increasing the downward spiral. And, once you've altered your brain, especially your serotonin and dopamine levels, your brain's equilibrium is bound to have an extremely difficult time finding its "happy place." Toiling with the dark side of drugs and alcohol will only make you suffer more in the long run through numerous symptoms, including depression, emptiness, withdrawal, and even suicide. The balance cannot be found pursuing this path. Having a few drinks or smoking a little weed is one thing but habitually snorting cocaine, smoking meth, cigarettes, crack, or shooting heroin, prescription pills, etc., will only distort reality. Furthermore, and to be completely honest, the user will nine out of ten times have a harsh time living in the real world after seeing the world of illusion that the drugs created. You have to look in the mirror while you're sober and make an honest and disciplined declaration to yourself about what you want out of life. If you don't lock that door and throw away the key, that drug, or whatever it is you're addicted to, is certain to come knocking at your door sooner or later. And, what may start as a light knocking will gradually become a loud pounding. Your brain can be a powerful deceiver and will conjure up a million excuses of why you need the drug but when you break it down, it's only because you were too mentally weak to say "no."

True freedom can only be found through the strength to release yourself from the tight grip and spell that the Devil has put on you, as well as millions of others. Once you're free of that negative entity, you'll see that happiness is found in the simple things in life and always better when shared with people you truly care about. Make no mistake, having enough money to never worry about financial stress is a blessing and should be cherished. However, "the world is full of rich men and women who are lost spiritually." (http://www.true-wealth. com/content/cpt2/ii_1.htm) Our culture has definitely placed money (and all it buys) before the love of God and that train must come to a halt. Whatever religion binds you, make a point "to minister the love of God unencumbered by the distractions of possessions. The bottom line is that money, like technology, is spiritually neutral. It can be used for good or evil. God always deals with the heart and the motives of the use of money. If the motives are pure then the fruit can be very, very good. Let's stop loving things and love people. That is the measure of true wealth." (http://www.true-wealth.com/content/cpt2/ii_1.htm)

Can you live without the items you adamantly swear you need to have? Of course you can! Sometimes removing yourself from poisonous environments can bring about self-actualization; you start to see clearly and begin to live free of gross materialism. Recently on CNN's *Planet in Peril*, they showed the indigenous people of Rwanda living in beautiful harmony. These people are simple and don't have much money or any assets, and yet everyone displayed a huge smile across their face and came across as such authentic, real human beings fused together by the power and love of family and friends. These are the intangibles that we as Americans need to reiterate and rediscover. According to America's standard living conditions they are living in an archaic, caveman-era, third world country. Think about this. When you're in a nightclub or a bar and you see so many fake, shallow, drugged-out zombies, and you start to see that it might be Satan's lair, then you're starting to open your eyes to see the light. Sometimes wisdom comes with age, maturity and experience, but it's at that exact moment where you have an epiphany and can break free from your binding chains and shackles to see the world in another dimension. You open your eyes and suddenly discover the benevolent, divine force that some have talked of but few ever felt. You feel enlightened, rejuvenated, reborn, and alive. The blindfold has been taken off and all of a sudden you are walking down that same trail you've always hiked but this time you go off the beaten path, unhindered like a bronco just released from his stable of captivity. We'd like to assume and pretend that everything is going to be hunky dory, but the truth is out there and you deserve to know. Using CNN *Planet in Peril* as a reference once again, it is sickening that because some individuals have to have ivory in their jewelry, elephants in Uganda are being hunted down and killed only for their ivory tusks. America is one of the top importers of ivory and this commodity that our culture craves kills one of the largest and smartest animals that walks the surface of planet Earth. Most purchasers of ivory don't even stop for a second to think about the aftermath or what it took to initially get what they're now wearing around their neck as a necklace. Every time you purchase ivory that's all the more reason for the hunters and poachers to kill, and chances are the largest land mammal on Earth was murdered for your taste in vanity. A similar example can be found in the movie *Dances With Wolves* starring, Kevin Costner, who plays Lieutenant John Dunbar, a post Civil War Union soldier. There is an appalling scene in the movie where the Sioux Indians and Kevin Costner's character, Lieutenant Dunbar who eventually goes rogue from the Union Army, both track a massive herd of buffalo only to find that the white hunters had already found the gigantic buffalo herd and ruthlessly slaughtered them, only to take their hides and tongues. "It becomes painfully obvious who the real savages are when the Indian's reverence for life is countered with the wanton destruction of the white hunter." (www. ahafilm.info/movies/moviereviews.phtml?fid=6006). In this dramatic, heart-wrenching scene, the field was littered with the skinned corpses of hundreds of dead buffaloes that were killed only for the value of their hides and tongues. Even worse, the white hunters didn't even take the buffalo meat as they left the buffalo carcasses to rot in the baking sun only to die in vain. The spiritually connected Indians were heartbroken as the buffalo had such a great spiritual value to them as well as provided them with most of their everyday essentials. The buffalo hide was used for their tee-pees and clothes, the buffalo meat was used to feed the Sioux tribes, and the buffalo bones were used for tools and weapons. Every piece of the buffalo played an integral part in Sioux life. However, Lt. Dunbar's personal encounter with the white hunter's dehumanizing greed was his breaking point. This eye-opening epiphany for Lt. Dunbar led him to respect the Sioux Indian way of life, and he would eventually become an adopted member of the Sioux tribe. His flip-flopping was seen as treason that eventually got him into trouble with the Union Army accusing him of turning sides. Worldwide commercial fishing boats cast hundreds of fishing lines into the sea and slice off the fins of approximately one hundred million sharks per year. That's a staggering number: 100,000,000 sharks. We can't just harvest these predators from the sea without serious risk to the balance of the ocean's ecosystem. Even worse, and just like the white hunters slaughtering the buffaloes only for their tongues and hides, or the elephants being killed solely for their ivory, the sharks are only killed by for their fins for the delicacy of shark fin soup. The commercial fishing boats catch the sharks only to cut their fins off, and once they've sliced off the fins, they throw them back into the ocean while they're still alive so that they drown. It's the same dismal scenario once again in Africa with the slaughtering of gorillas in the Congo and Rwanda, especially with the prized male Silverback gorillas. The same situation applies with whales, wolves, polar bears, and a plethora of other species, but I think you get the point by now at the destructive impact that our human greed entails.

Why would humankind do such a thing? How could humankind act with such blatant and arrogant disregard for Earth's beautiful creatures? The answer: money. Our unnecessary superficial wants are killing endangered species. Something is terribly wrong with our way of thinking and we need to radically change our mentalities as soon as possible. This reckless greed must be stopped. We just can't keep taking, and taking, and taking and raping the Earth of all her habitants and resources without consciousness. We need a mass enlightening to address and confront head on the havoc that we as a human species are wreaking upon Mother Earth. This bubble that many live in is about to pop. We must unlearn our destructive and violent ways. We must learn as a collective whole to walk gently upon the face of the Earth. From the animals' perspective, it would be much better if our destructive human race was on the endangered species list. However, this is far from the case. As said on *Planet Earth*, "100 years ago the human population was 1.5 billion whereas now in 2010 our human species has multiplied to 6+ billion." Mother Earth cannot feed our appetite much longer.

CHAPTER 8: THE TANGLED KNOT FROM HELL LEFT BY THE BUSH ADMINISTRATION

WAR PROFITEERING AND THE BUSH ADMINISTRATION

Our country was put under the George W. Bush spell in the year 2000. We let Bush and his cronies take us for lemons, only to get squeezed for eight years. They turned us into delectable lemonade that they enjoyed for those hellacious two presidential terms from 2000-2008. War profiteering is the main idea here, as its treachery knows no bounds and must be addressed. Can you say "Halliburton"? While the war profiteers' (defense contractors, oil tycoons, special interest groups, etc.) financial positions grew exponentially, the rest of the nation, unfortunately, became the squeezed cream of their Oreo cookie. We became stuck in the middle of the war profiteers' appetite for destruction sandwich. These atrocities should not go unpunished.

Our government is supposedly playing on our team, but with the Bush Administration, it seemed like they traded teams to work with, not against, Osama Bin Laden. The Bush cronies figured out early on that if they killed Osama Bin Laden, their war game would be over quickly and the US military industrial-complex would come to a screeching halt. Bush, Cheney, Rumsfeld, and the rest of his crooked organization figured out early on that if they kept Osama Bin Laden alive, they kept the war alive. Their strategy was simple to decipher: Make the America people fearful of another attack by the use of precision scare tactics and propagandist campaigns reinforced by 9/11. The Bush Administration knew all too well that the American people would be more in favor to staying at war with Osama Bin Laden still alive with the threat of another "imminent" attack. Furthermore, in their eyes, a longer war made for more profits with the cost being American blood. We've seen this war-mongering monster before, with Vietnam, and this out-of-control, all-too-powerful military-industrial complex. Former President Eisenhower warned us about this. Ron Kovic says in *Born the Fourth of July*, "Refusing to learn from our experiences in Vietnam, our government continues to pursue a policy of deception, distortion, manipulation, and denial, doing everything it can to hide from the American people their true intentions and agenda in Iraq. The flag-draped caskets of our dead begin their long and sorrowful journeys home hidden from public view, while the Iraqi casualties are not even considered worth counting—some estimate as many as 100,000 have been killed so far."

During a special Memorial Day service, U.S. Marine Corps infantry equipment comprised of helmets, rifles, boots, and personal ID tags, or "dog tags," stand in a ceremonial formation on the ship's flight deck to honor 23 Marines KIA. The memorial remembers the 23 Marines assigned to 2d Marine Expeditionary Brigade (2d MEB) who paid the ultimate sacrifice during combat missions in support of Operation Iraqi Freedom.

Osama Bin Laden, however, played the Bush administration perfectly and is receiving a standing ovation from his terrorist colleagues for bleeding our country into financial turmoil. As of October 16, 2009, America's deficit has tripled from a year ago and has surged to an all-time high of $1.42 trillion, the highest since WWII. (www.msnbc.msn. com/id/33348615/ns/politics-more_politics) These cronies misplaced their loyalty in the American people by letting money and greed deceive and blind them. I smell high treason in the air against the America people. Oh, what we could've done on the homefront of America with the trillion plus dollars this war will cost by the time it's over. For $1,000,000,000,000 we could have repaired all of the deteriorating infrastructure (bridges, roads, highways, etc.) throughout our country. For a trillion dollars we could've fixed the health care crisis, we could've lowered the 10% unemployment rate, we could've revamped the entire educational system by making teaching a more prestigious job and by paying teachers a higher salary. We could've brought an end to the drug and gang wars that have plagued our nation, and we could have tightened our US/Mexico border security. We could've brought the housing and foreclosure crisis to greener pastures. But in the eyes of these cronies none of these items were ever on their priority to-do lists. They may have talked tough on camera to misdirect the public but talking the talk is much different than walking the walk. To them 9/11 equaled war, and war is big business. A war economy has billions of dollars at stake. We must open our eyes to ask the bigger questions like, "Who benefits from war?" Tomahawk Cruise missiles are made by General Dynamics and are shipped to the US Navy. During a war, demand for these missiles skyrockets. Think about all the companies that make the parts and components, not just General Dynamics, that benefit from the Tomahawk's increased production. Or, take the defense contractor Lockheed Martin and the $65 billion F-22 Raptor program, for example. You create a war and you need more planes. Well, those F-22 planes cost $140 million each and are connected to 95,000 jobs at 1,000 companies like Pratt & Whitney Engines (http://news.yahoo.com/s/ap/20090326/ap_on_bi_ge/f22_crash). Lockheed Martin is also the defense contracting company that is tinkering with the Astra TR-3B, the "black" top secret stealth aircraft that we discussed in previous chapters. Billions of tax dollars are required to fund these types of programs. The same principle applies with the defense contractor Northrop Grumman Corporation. Northrop Grumman Corporation, in a nutshell, is a global defense and technology company whose 120,000 employees provide innovative systems, products, and solutions in information and services, electronics, aerospace and shipbuilding to government and commercial customers worldwide. This is the defense contractor that is currently building the unmanned autonomous helicopter, the Fire Scout UAV (Unmanned Aerial Vehicle) MQ-8B. These UAV helicopter drones are armed with laser-guided missiles can take off from anywhere to provide close air support. They can fly to a ceiling of 20,000 feet in altitude, searching for enemy combatants, and are equipped with state-of-the-art infrared sensors that relay pictures in real time to command centers. These Fire Scout UAVs helicopter drones have no pilot, no joystick, and no ground support team. The UAV is self-governed and flies by itself with a preflight loaded and programmed mission. The Fire Scout MQ-8B is capable of providing direct action reconnaissance, re-supply, and direct combat as a smart weapon.

Northrop Grumman's autonomous UAV RQ-8A Fire Scout on patrol. Notice no pilot governing this drone. Humans have been relinquishing too much control to the machines. These self-governing smart machines do not feel fatigue, do not need coffee, and can process the amount of information that a human brain processes in a year within a split second. They can perform calculations thousands of times faster, workout logical computations without error and store memory at incredible speeds with flawless accuracy. Renowned writer, producer, and director James Cameron might have been on to something when he delivered the Terminator movies to theaters which depicted a nuclear war against the machines aka "Judgment Day." We should never allow these autonomous machines to have control over our nuclear weapon systems.

The fact that our government has hired defense contractors to build these weapons is indicative that there is no end in sight for war. This war economy has billions at stake and it's obvious that our welfare and well-being on the homefront are superseded by the big business of war. Without war and a massive war-time defense budget these companies would not be building weapon delivery systems that can only bring destruction to the world. Even more disturbing is the fact that these machines are, in a sense, thinking on their own and taking over, relinquishing the human control of sophisticated armaments. Director and writer James Cameron may have been on to something when he delivered the *Terminator* movies to the world. With smart machines taking over we are getting terrifyingly close to calling these *Terminator* movies reality. Let's just pray that these autonomous machines never become self-aware and turn against the inferior species, the human race. We've got enough to worry about as it is, thanks to the Bush administration's sinister plot to keep this war and Osama Bin Laden alive and well. Barack Obama and his all-star administration may not want to completely shut down the engines of the military-industrial complex, because that is a concept that could get him assassinated—just like JFK when he tried to pull the plug on Vietnam. They may just want to lower the speed and RPMs at which the military-industrial complex engine is currently running at. We must open our eyes to see the imbalance in power between the government and its people. At this moment in 2010 the military industrial complex wields too much power over the American people.

If we gravitate towards a mentality of pacifism and philanthropy we will clearly see that if you can find billions of dollars in killing people then you can find billions of dollars in helping people. Impossible some may say. Well, "Impossible is a word only to be found in the dictionary of fools." The greatest discovery one can make is that nothing is impossible.

THE INCONVENIENT TRUTH

Our country is going in the wrong direction. Does anyone else see the correlation between former President George H.W. Bush, a former CIA Director, to Jeb Bush, the Governor of Florida during the presidential recount of 2000? Jeb Bush, son of George H.W. and brother to George W., played a huge role in helping his brother steal the 2000 presidential election away from Al Gore. Florida, as most of us know, is the state of the infamous recount vote of 2000, during which George W. Bush won the presidency over Al Gore. Was it a plausible coincidence or was it a premeditated Bush vision to empower the "black hand" to get its way to put another Bush at the helm of the ship? I believe it to be the latter of the two, and here's why. When your father used to work as the Director of the Central Intelligence Agency, anything is conceivable and obtainable. When you're the Director of the CIA you have carte blanche and your forte is knowing how to pull strings. You know the right people and you have the power, muscle, and clout to implement your will. However, imagine the flip side and where our country would be by now in 2010 if Al Gore, a Nobel Peace Prize Winner, had taken the presidency in 2000. Former President George H.W. Bush served as former President Gerald Ford's Director of Central Intelligence (DCI) from November 1975 to January 1977 (www.famoustexans. com/georgebush.htm) and Director of the CIA from January 1976 to January 1977 (www.nndb.com/gov/234/000043105/). With his powerful title, George H.W. Bush was answerable to only one man, President Ford. Ironically, Dick Cheney and Donald Rumsfeld were President Ford's two key appointees. President Ford appointed Donald Rumsfeld as his Chief of Staff when he took office after Nixon's resignation in 1974. The next year, President Ford made the 42-year-old Rumsfeld the youngest Secretary of Defense in the nation's history, and he also named the nation's youngest ever Chief of Staff, 34-year-old Dick Cheney. The legacy of Gerald Ford is gone but lives on vicariously through the Bush family, Donald Rumsfeld and Dick Cheney. President Ford planted the Bush seed that would root and grow. The members of George H.W. Bush's gang ran the White House during the turbulent 2000-2008 Bush Administration. President George W. Bush acted as the main puppet at the helm of the ship, while Dick Cheney served as Vice President, and Donald Rumsfeld as the US Secretary of Defense (www.thenation.com/blogs/notion/151567)

Former President Gerald Ford chats with Chief of Staff Donald Rumsfeld and Rumsfeld's assistant Dick Cheney in the Oval Office on April 28, 1975. The seeds of war mongering had been planted long before former President George W. Bush cultivated the current Iraq war.

Former Secretary of Defense Donald Rumsfeld, former President George W. Bush, and former Vice President Dick Cheney are guilty of treason against the American people for summoning the military industrial complex and war machine based off of lies. Do you remember the fabricated claims that Osama Bin Laden and Saddam Hussein were both responsible for 9/11? Do you remember the false allegations that Iraq was stockpiling weapons of mass destruction (WMDs)? All of these scare tactics were used to mislead and deceive the American people into an illegal war which has squeezed our nation to the brink of depression. The Sept. 11 commission reported that it found no "collaborative relationship" between Iraq and al Qaeda, challenging one of the Bush administration's main justifications for the war in Iraq. We must always question authority.

The first Bush, George H.W., was supposedly the first CIA "outsider" to hold the agency's top position. During his tenure as DCI he maintained a policy of disinformation and secrecy, despite a public show of cooperation with congressional investigations of CIA abuses such as assassination plots using Mafia hit men. (www.famoustexans. com/georgebush.htm) Do you know how much clout you need to have to be selected as the Director of the Central Intelligence Agency?

Once entrusted and in power, do you know how much authority one man wields in the power of his hand? You don't get into that position without knowing how to sidestep a few land mines. The Director of the CIA is capable of moving the world chess pieces in a position according to his premeditated intentions. Most "black operations" are orchestrated and conducted in the dark corners of the CIA, a world of secret agents, double agents, and top-secret covert operations where ghost reconnaissance is a way of life. This is a world that specifically operates in the shadows and in the darkness.

Now that you know the tip of the iceberg about the first President George H.W. Bush and his former days with the CIA, couldn't it be fathomable that he would manipulate the system in favor of his son to becoming the next president? Within the CIA, the saying is "once CIA, always CIA" because you never get out of the agency and are always affiliated. It's just like a gang or the mafia where you swear to uphold a certain creed and the only way out is in a body bag. The inconvenient truth of the situation that should of reached every American's door by now is that Al Gore was robbed of his presidency by the Bush "black arts" magic spell. This would've been a great time to rise up as a people and question authority, but we were inoculated with poison and did nothing but accept the Bush and Cheney clan with open arms. If only we could take a time machine back to the year 2000 and do it right. And, so you're up to speed on the specifics, the Florida election recount of 2000 occurred following the unclear results of the 2000 United States presidential election between George W. Bush and Al Gore, in Florida where Jeb Bush was governor. The election was ultimately settled in favor of George W. Bush when the Supreme Court stopped the recount and Bush got a majority of the electoral votes. (http://en.wikipedia.org/wiki/Florida_election_recount) If we were smart we'd open not only our eyes, but our ears to hear the shocking blow that former President Jimmy Carter delivered in a speech at an American University Panel in Washington. He told the crowd he was certain that Al Gore won the 2000 presidential election. There is "no doubt in my mind that Gore won the election" the President declared, saying that the 2000 election process "failed abysmally." He also snubbed the Supreme Court for getting involved, saying it was "highly partisan" to the Bush family. (http://rawstory. com/news/2005/Carter_says_Gore_won_2000_el_0922.html)

We must always question authority and challenge those we empower and are supposed to answer to. If we're raised to follow authority figures, then what does it say when they blatantly lie to us, the American people? What kind of examples are they setting for the American people and the world? After an eight-year nightmare with crooks in power, hopefully we've learned a timeless lesson that power doesn't always get used for good, something we as a people should have learned from world history. And, most importantly, we know we can't afford to make the same mistakes again or our country and all its founding principles will be lost forever. We must stay extremely sharp and vigilant when questioning authority figures. We must take affirmative action, like what we witnessed in this past presidential election in 2008. The people rose up in mass numbers and let the votes do the talking with a blowout victory and knockout punch with President-elect Obama triumphing over McCain. The landslide victory in votes shut the door for any possibly manipulated recount. If it was close the "black world" may have played that card but it wasn't able to be played. Not even close. We must remember and keep our eyes opened to the fact that we elect and put those appointed officials in power and we must never forget that greed can grow from having too much power. We must hearken to the call of justice and liberty and always challenge those with excessive power and those with their fingers on the strings playing the public like a puppet. The top tiers of the hierarchy are at the pinnacle of the pyramid of power. If greed is planted at the director's position, a rogue ideology will grow. These rogue elements of the upper hierarchy of the government are the ones that manufactured a rigged Florida recount, had ties with the Supreme Court siding favorably to the Bush family, and blinded and misdirected the public eye with their media circus. Initial reports claim that Al Gore wins, but wait? A recount? In Florida? Jeb Bush's state? George W. Bush's younger brother's governed state? Their father was in the CIA and DCI as the director. Their father was a member of the Yale University Skull and Bones Secret Club. The Supreme Court was partisan to the Bush family. Recount underway...News Media platforms provide Breaking News: GEORGE BUSH WINS 2000 Presidential Election in Florida Recount. This is the point in time where we had the Bush blindfold pulled over our eyes. We failed to realize that American presidents come and go, like George H.W. Bush, but intelligence agencies last forever. (http://www.mail-archive.com/balkannews@yahoogroups.com/msg01988.html)

What gets me heated is that we didn't even rattle the halls of power. The Bush administration and its henchmen inoculated the public with malignant propaganda and, in a sense, put the people of America in a submission choke-hold. What a revitalized nation we would have grown to by now with Al Gore leading the charge. A visionary and pioneer on global warming as well as an icon of going green, Gore was the catalyst and spark we needed to become more conscious of our future well-being. As a selfless, philanthropist concerned with the welfare of our species and our planet he had the right vision and humanitarian ideology that never reached fruition and never bloomed because of the tainted Florida recount. Just like that, his proactive dream for our country withered away and died. Our chance to detach our species from our addiction to oil fell short.

Now we're left in this 2010 quagmire, blindfolded with our hands tied behind our backs, and we never really brought the word impeachment into the limelight during the Bush years. Some may have whispered it but we should have been yelling it in masses. They wouldn't have been able to ignore a 20 million man march on the White House and the halls of Congress. Nonetheless what's done is done. We have spent close to a trillion dollars on this war in Iraq and it's deflating our way of life by bleeding the homefront. Wake up and open your eyes people! This is our money people and our government judgment makers are pissing into the wind! Our tax dollars are being thrown into a black hole where even light itself that travels at 186,000 miles per second cannot escape. What do we do when we're being walked around on a leash with a choke collar around our necks? Do we submit and stay passive when the wrong decisions are being made time and time again? We must never give up hope, ever, as it is one of those rare qualities you should be willing to die for.

Actor Mel Gibson portrays William Wallace, a Scottish patriot, defiant against English tyranny, in the movie *Braveheart*. In the final moments of the movie, which is based on a true story, a defiant Wallace screams out "FREEDOM!" while being tortured to death in front of a large watching mob. This compelling and dramatic scene symbolizes the raw power of hope. Never stop believing and never stop fighting for true freedom and for true liberty. William Wallace was beheaded for high treason against the King of England but his actions were not forgotten. His legacy created a chain reaction and Scotland eventually became a sovereign country, free from being a satellite owned and controlled by English rule. Wallace's life touched the lives of so many fellow Scottish patriots and in turn inspired and mobilized an entire movement to stand up and question English authority.

Someone in today world needs to stand up like William Wallace and lead a movement of epic proportions. In the movie, Wallace said "Every man dies, not every man really lives." This motivated a submissive Scottish nation to embark on an uphill journey to challenge the nobles and eventually severe ties with the entire English rule. In the film, Robert the Bruce, who idolizes Wallace's passion, states, "lands, titles, men, power, nothing...I have nothing," as he begins to understand why so many Scottish patriots are willing to devote and sacrifice their lives for the opportunity of fighting alongside Wallace. What we need in America 2010 is a synergistic movement that energizes and creates a spark of hope where you can feel the electricity in the air. An electric, decadent movement that mobilizes an array of people and ethnic cultures—black, white, brown, yellow, green, young, old, male, female—a diverse spectrum of Americans uniting for the cause of hope, freedom and liberty. As Kevin Spacey said in *Seven* if we want change, "we can't just tap the government on the shoulder, more likely we'll have to hit them with a sledgehammer to get their attention." For far too long "we the people" have been ignored. We should march, as patriots, with American flags in hand, on the Capitol Building, the White House, and the Halls of Congress, chanting, "I pledge allegiance to the flag of the United States of America and to the republic for which it stands: One nation under God, indivisible with liberty and justice for all." If we really want change we're going to have to fight and die for it. We're going to have to earn it like William Wallace did in *Braveheart*. We need to retake our country. Our republic, the land of the free, and our way of life was earned by our founding fathers' loyalty to something greater than themselves. That principle, just like in *Braveheart*, was the idea of freedom and all it stands for.

Our forefathers would be shaking their heads at the direction our ship is sailing in 2010, a country headed into hurricane-prone seas. We have so many brilliant, innovative minds in this country that just need a chance to shine. They need to be pushed to the next level but it seems as if during the past eight years with the Bush administration we have gone in reverse and become uglier as a nation. We've become a nation losing its sense of purpose with a rapidly depreciating dollar value. We need a boisterous wake-up call that registers in every American's brain. It will probably take Obama his entire first four year term to reverse and amend the policies that he inherited from the Bush and Cheney administration. People already want to point the finger and blame Obama when they should be pointing their fingers at former President George Bush and former Vice-President Dick Cheney. We need to give President Obama and his administration ample time to untangle the knot from hell that the past Bush administration left tangled for us and for Obama. Former President Bush had eight years to bring our country to its knees, so let's at least give Obama a four year term to stand our country on its feet again. Let's give President Obama and his team of perennial all-stars a chance to shine.

A FORGOTTEN NATION

What once was lost may now be found. If you couldn't tell by now, yes, I wanted Barack Obama to win in the last election. With John McCain's old age, plus the insurmountable number of nation-threatening issues to tackle, and the abundant amount of stress that he'd encounter, I'd put my money on a heart attack from his first presidential term in office. Barack Obama's biological father Barrack Obama, Sr., was Kenyan and his biological mother Ann Dunham was from Kansas. He is a mutt just like the majority of Americans. Furthermore, after his biological mother and father divorced, Ann Dunham married Lolo Soetoro from Indonesia, which is where Barrack lived from ages six to ten, and at ten years of age Barrack moved to Hawaii to live with his white grandparents. His background is the true American dream. He is the quintessential American. He has achieved the American dream from the ground up since birth and now has an all-star cast backing his every presidential decision.

A younger Barack Obama accompanies his grandparents from his mother's side. If America is The Land of Immigrants, Barack Obama is the perfect President...half white, half black...a true American mutt,

just like most of us. Before pointing the finger and blaming President Obama, we must realize the knot from hell (left by the eight-year Bush administration) that he must untangle before real change can be made.

When I, as well as millions of other like-minded Americans listened to John McCain speak at his rallies in 2008, we actually felt dumber for listening to the words that came out of his mouth. Many of us actually felt sorry for his ideology on what direction was needed for America. Who was writing his speeches anyway? The plain and simple truth was that McCain and his campaign team just didn't get it. He couldn't relate to the people of this forgotten nation like Obama could. Many, like myself, got a headache just listening to McCain speak, but found it even harder to comprehend how there were so many people standing behind him cheering and yelling "Use your brain vote McCain!" The question I've always wanted to ask was, "Were these people hired actors and actresses paid to support McCain's archaic ideology?" If not, it truly shows the vast contrast in partisan ideologies from all across this great nation. McCain's crippling unoriginality, like with Bush, and non-progressive, slash-and-burn politics were so trite and WWII-old-school that you'd think more voters would see through his bunk transparency.

Regardless, Obama won the election by a landslide and now spearheads the charge, uphill mind you, to revamp the system as we know it. Don't forget, the remnants of the Bush and Cheney administration still resonate today with the current recession as their past failures have been passed along to the Obama administration to correct. The fallout from this recession has caused hard-working Americans to feel gut-wrenching pain ranging from Los Angeles to New York City, and all the cities and towns in between. Mothers and fathers who've lost their jobs and are now unable to care for those dearest to them, and are having trouble even providing the bare necessities for survival. Their baby is hungry but there's no food. Food costs money and they've been laid off or are unemployed with no income. Their child or baby is sick and needs medical attention but there's no doctor. Doctors cost money and money comes from work. The grim reality is that unemployment in America is reaching the 10 percent mark with one in 10 American's grinding it out in the unemployment line. More people than ever before are relying on governmental assistance like unemployment benefits, Medicaid, Medicare, and food stamps just to get by. Another heart wrenching situation plaguing many American families is that the children are left at home in an absentee-dad situation where their mother works all day and night. Since the mother works all day and night to make ends meet, the oldest sibling has to watch over the younger siblings and babies all night long. Now the child heads off to school without eating breakfast and sleeps in school all day, completely malnourished and exhausted.

These anti-educational environments are common all across America. So next time you confront a bleak situation try and shed some sunlight on the darkness. We all must open our eyes and hearts to lend a helping hand to our neighbors and fellow Americans instead of turning our heads the other way, only to forget and walk away. "You shall love your neighbor as yourself" (Matthew 22:39) and maybe, just maybe if we heed to the Bible's advice we can start uniting as sincere and genuine human beings. Our President, Barack Obama, is the closest thing to an authentic human being of all the presidents to date, and his past proves he's somewhat of a saint. We're blessed as a nation to have an individual who embodies a blend of different heritages and ethnic backgrounds as our president in office at this crucial juncture in time.

As a torn nation at a crossroads, our fate and our future hangs in the balance. Is Obama the catalyst that's going to turn this nation around? Is he the solution? Only in retrospect will our nation's future reveal itself. Yet, Obama, like JFK, inspires us to get off our couch and to be what we dream we can be. For better or worse, something is now in motion that cannot be undone. The chemistry and sparks that Obama has with the nation is really something special. With his presidential debonair style, Obama rubs off as a regular guy that you could easily walk up to and talk to, or better yet, call by his first name—Barack. Words aren't just words anymore when you get up off your couch and start applauding during one of his speeches—and you're the only one in the room.

The power to motivate one enough to change their life is a very powerful tool that knows no bounds, and it can be used for benevolent or malevolent purposes. Adolf Hitler used his voice and powerful tone, charisma, and strong body language to captivate his audience and put them in a trance to build an army of darkness. The world has seen his evil brainwash not only German adults, but little German kids with swastika armbands saluting their Fuhrer, many of whom bought in to Hitler's venomous propaganda and willingly subjected themselves into Hitler's youth programs. If used for benevolent purposes—like we pray it is with Barack Obama—it can be a proactive catalyst that creates a spark of extraordinary positive change. We were a forgotten nation from 2000 to 2008 under the Bush regime, so let's embrace change, embrace hope, embrace Obama, and most importantly, embrace our neighbors.

The poisoned Hitler youth of Nazi Germany during WWII bought into Hitler's venomous propaganda. Evil is very real and can brainwash even the strongest of minds. If you want to see what evil is capable of then visit Auschwitz, Krakow, or Dachau concentration/death camps. We must never forget what happened during WWII. "Whoever saves one life saves the world entire."—Oscar Schindler

THE DAY AMERICA DIED

As you can probably tell by now I'm a strong advocate for Barack Obama and John F. Kennedy, and this passion brings us to our next eye-opening topic: the JFK assassination on Elm Street in Dallas, Texas on November 22, 1963, the day our country was murdered. What transpired on this day shaped America today and in retrospect, we see it was the day the military-industrial complex took control over the American people, silencing our founding motto "and that government of the people, by the people, for the people, shall not perish from the Earth." (Abraham Lincoln, *Gettysburg Address)* I must allocate a chapter to this sensitive topic as it is a vital piece needed to make this book sing to you. The unveiling of how these clandestine government agencies have mastered their black-craft-playbook and quarterbacked the "art of misdirection play" to summon the military industrial-complex with JFK's death is long overdue. We cannot trust our government because they've betrayed us far too many times to be forgiven. The black world felt no remorse and getting away with presidential murder only emboldened and empowered these clandestine government agencies.

This war-mongering demon was born on November 22, 1963, long before the tyrannical Bush-war machine misdirected our eyes and tax dollars to the Iraq war that we are still currently involved with in 2010. The war in Iraq will have bled the taxpayers over a trillion plus dollars by its end. Similarly, the Vietnam War cost $220 billion with 5,000 helicopters lost and 6.5 million tons of bombs dropped, and that was back in the '60s and '70s. The defense contracting company, Bell, was rolling Huey helicopters off their assembly lines and business was great—just like with the F-111 fighter planes rolling off the assembly lines at General Dynamics in Ft. Worth, Texas. In addition, business was very lucrative for a multitude of other defense contracting companies that prospered from the Vietnam War. JFK's death was orchestrated in the "black world," and it was his death that revved-up the engines for the military industrial-complex to move full steam ahead and into a country 12,000 miles away.

People want to know who killed JFK, but the more important question to ask is, "Why was he killed?" It wasn't the mafia who killed JFK and it wasn't Fidel Castro who killed JFK, it was our own government who removed JFK because he was a threat to the military-industrial complex. JFK wasn't killed by the mob for his younger brother's US Attorney General Robert F. Kennedy crackdown on organized crime. He wasn't killed by communists for the Bay of Pigs disaster in Cuba or the Fidel Castro assassination attempt, and most of all, JFK wasn't killed by the alleged assassin Lee Harvey Oswald. JFK was killed by the CIA. No one, except agencies like the CIA, have the absolute power and authority to change protocol and alter the presidential motorcade parade route. No one, except agencies like the CIA, have the authority to remove secret servicemen and security from the Dallas streets on the day of the assassination. And no one, except agencies like the CIA, have the authority to remove the protective bubbletop from JFK's presidential limousine. Furthermore, and to quote the movie *JFK*, "Security was waived off, the entire cabinet was in the far East, a third of a combat division returning from Germany was in the air above the U.S. at the time of the shooting. At 12:34 PM the Washington telephone system went out for an hour. On the plane back to Washington word was radioed from the Situations Room to Lyndon Johnson that there was one assassin. Sound like a bunch of coincidences to you? The cabinet was out of the country to get their perceptions out of the way. Troops were in the air for possible riot control, telephones didn't work to get the wrong stories from spreading if anything went wrong with the plan. Nothing was left to chance...he could not be allowed to escape alive."

Fidel Castro couldn't do it and wouldn't want to do it for reasons that would endanger Cuba. The mafia didn't pull the trigger on JFK, but they may have played a minor role in the cover-up. The mafia's involvement in the JFK assassination may have been at a low level with mob-affiliated nightclub owner Jack Ruby killing Oswald. However, Ruby was just one spoke of many on the JFK conspiracy wheel. The major players within the upper levels of the CIA were the ones with their hands on the strings. They were the directors orchestrating the show. These were the traitors that wielded more than enough power to carry out such an intricate and elaborate plot. In the Oliver Stone film *JFK* David Ferrie, played by Joe Pesci, is asked who killed JFK and he frantically states, "Who did the president, who killed Kennedy, fuck man! It's a mystery! It's a mystery wrapped in a riddle inside an enigma! The fuckin' shooters don't even know! Don't you get it?"

Do we as a people really believe the government and Warren Commission's story that Lee Harvey Oswald was the lone gunman that killed JFK? Or, have we learned through the course of *Open Your*

Eyes: To 2012 and Beyond to always question authority and ask the bigger question. Could Lee Oswald really have been telling the truth when he stated "I'm just a patsy?" Many, like myself, do not subscribe to the notion that Oswald killed JFK and do not believe he even pulled the trigger from the sniper's nest on the 6th floor of the Texas School Book Depository. Oswald was a foot soldier following orders and got played like a fiddle. I personally know as a former rifleman for the US Marine Corps Infantry YOU ARE NOT ALLOWED TO QUESTION ORDERS WITHOUT RANK...PERIOD. You take orders and you give orders based on a chain of command, and whether right or wrong, if a superior officer gives an order, you follow it without question. It's very similar to the lessons that Daniel Larusso learned from Mr. Miyagi in the 1984 movie *Karate Kid*. "No such thing as bad student, only bad teacher. Teacher say, student do."

Oswald was a student to the intelligence game, not a teacher, and he was not allowed to question instructions. He was the pawn that they moved into position just as they envisioned to be the fall-guy and scapegoat. After the police ambushed Oswald in the Texas Theatre, after he supposedly shot Officer Tippet, the swarm of police officers brought Oswald out of the theater to the angry mob. At this point, the American public wanted to blame and convict someone, so it was very easy to point the finger at Oswald after the corrupt Dallas police beat him up to make him look like the bad guy. And once they dragged him outside to the lion's den of awaiting media, press, and bystanders he was immediately eaten alive and sized-up and stereotyped as the perpetrator. Negative public perspective, not in favor to Oswald, was immediately infused into the mainstream public by heavy propaganda. The media forums and relentless misinformation campaigns buried Oswald in the public's eye, with no trial. Furthermore, *Life* Magazine sealed Lee Harvey Oswald's fate by printing a picture of Oswald holding a rifle, which Oswald denied to be a genuine photo. He claimed the *Life* photo to be a fake, a superimposed shot. The shadows on Oswald's nose fall in a straight line, but this is impossible. Because shadows are always diagonal and reflections are always up and down. Oswald stated calmly in the heat of all of this commotion, "I don't know what I am charged with, but I emphatically deny these charges."

The problem is that these CIA and black world operatives are good, I mean really good. Their game is basically flawless. Even former FBI Director J. Edgar Hoover had his hand in the cookie jar and played a role in the coup d'état. There was a tree that blocked part of the motorcade view from the sixth floor Texas School Book Depository towards Elm Street that was famously cut down by J. Edgar Hoover's FBI right after the JFK murder. The tree outside the window of the sixth floor Texas School Book Depository was an obstacle interfering in the line of fire to JFK's motorcade on Elm Street. So the tree was immediately removed.

However, even the best players in the intelligence game have off days every blue moon, and on November 22, 1963, a revelatory piece of evidence slipped through their net— the picture-says-a thousand-words-5.6-second-long Abraham Zapruder film. The Zapruder film provides a frame-by-frame sequence of JFK's motorcade slowly rolling down Elm Street, and most importantly, proves without a doubt that there was a shot from the picket fence from the grassy knoll. The Zapruder film adds further validity to more than fifty credible sources who claimed to have seen and smelled gun smoke from behind the picket fence. In addition, videos revealed that the witnesses moved in a pattern that leads and points towards the grassy knoll. Behavioral patterns and body language all react towards a shot from the knoll. While Oliver Stone was researching for his film he interviewed rock-solid military witnesses, two to three veterans from WWII who had been near JFK's motorcade on Elm Street that day and described the rifle fire as coming definitely from the fence. According to the Warren Commission report they "found no evidence of a conspiracy foreign or domestic" to suggest that the shots were fired from anywhere other than the book depository. In 1965, JFK researchers went through the Commission volumes and found that out of 121 witnesses surveyed, 38 gave no opinion as to where the shots came from, 32 thought they

214 | DREW R. MARAS

came from the book depository, and 51 witnesses felt that the shots came from the grassy knoll area. The Zapruder film doesn't just point out conspiracy, it screams it. It clearly shows the shot to President JFK's head, the fatal shot that tore his head "back and to the left, back and to the left, back and to the left." (*JFK*) Now, when I was in the Marine Corps Infantry trained as an 0311 (rifleman), we trained for combat and to kill or be killed. We were meticulously disciplined and trained to watch and observe the direction that our fellow Marine's body fell to the ground if shot. Snipers attached to our Echo Company specifically told us that you could determine the angle that the shot was fired from by watching how the body reacts to the impact from the bullet. For example, if a fellow Marine's body fell straight back then the shot came from the front, which is the direction that our weaponry would zero-in on. We were trained to pay extremely close attention because in urban warfare, enemy snipers are everywhere and can destroy the morale of your unit. You may never know where that enemy sniper is positioned until he kills one of your fellow Marines and brother-in-arms. Sometimes that is the only way to ascertain where a sniper is concealed. In addition, we were instructed by the Marine Corps snipers that if a Marines body falls forward the shot came from behind, if the Marine's body falls to the left the shot came from the right, and if the Marine's body falls back and to the left, like with JFK, then the shot came from the front right. The ballistics don't lie. The Zapruder film speaks volumes and is the only piece of evidence that we needed to solidify the conspiracy charges. What these hired, cold-blooded assassins were banking on was a triangulated crossfire, with JFK in the center of the turkey shoot.

If Lee Harvey Oswald, who also served in the US Marine Corps, killed JFK, then why would he take the more difficult shot on Elm Street? The History Channel claims that in his Marine Corps shooting tests Oswald scored well and could have done the shooting, but I believe this to be a black world power play of misdirection directly out of their black world field manual and playbook. Intelligence and black world agencies have had 46 years to doctor up and fabricate a shooting range score book, giving Oswald high marks to feed to the gullible American public. Yet, and contradictory to the History Channel's explanation, according to some of his old Marine Corps buddies, who didn't see it necessary to trample on a dead man's grave, testified that Oswald wasn't really that great of a shot. Oswald was a fair shot, he wasn't a bad shot and he wasn't a great shot, he was a fair shot. So, if he was a fair shot with a military calibrated rifle he must have been a horrendous shot with the Italian WWII rifle that was jokingly called the "humanitarian rifle" or "humane weapon" for being so inaccurate in hitting a target. This is the rifle that was found in the sixth floor of the Texas School Book Depository. When the Italian rifle was put to the test, none of the FBI experts could match the shooting with the ineffective rifle.

Why would Lee Oswald have this rifle sent to a blatant P.O. Box address that could easily be traced back to him? He wouldn't. Why wouldn't Lee Oswald just go into any Texas gun store and purchase the $12.88 rifle without any paper trail? The rifle matching up to Oswald's P.O. Box address, along with the rifle superimposed into the picture in *Life* Magazine was critical in pinning the assassination on Oswald. These two elements were paramount in convicting Oswald within the public's eye. Whatever the case, and further proving a conspiracy and disproving Oswald's guilt, the easiest shot on JFK in his motorcade would have been on Houston Street where the presidential limousine drove directly towards the Texas School Book Depository, not away from it like on Elm Street. This, however, was not the case. The premeditated plan of attack was to set up the slow-moving, 10 mile per hour presidential motorcade on Elm Street for a triangulated crossfire, with cross-hairs zeroed in on JFK from multiple directions. The military refers to this Vietnam-style tactic as the L-shaped ambush, which is a perfect ambush of triangulated crossfire that puts the target in the middle.

The hit on the president was carried out by two to three professional assassin teams working in tandem. Two to three teams of patient assassins that dressed and acted the part, enough to get Oscars for their award winning performances. One tool, of many, in the black world's toolbox is misdirection. Part of the art of misdirection is to completely blend in to your surrounding environment, as to not raise any eyebrows, and this is exactly what these professional assassin teams did. They dressed as construction and railroad workers by the grassy knoll. They dressed as mechanics and maintenance workers blending in to the ongoing maintenance crews at the Texas School Book Depository. They dressed as Dallas policemen and even secret servicemen to blend in to the streets—all part of the CIA and black world's elaborately conceived misdirection plan to draw the public's eye to Lee Oswald as the sole assassin. According to *JFK* director Oliver Stone, "They have patsies that are ready to go, or close to going. Somebody got Harvey Oswald the job in the bookstore, somebody decided the bookstore would be a hit ground, and somebody, who's smart, who's military, who's precise, rigged it so that the car would have to come that way and it would slow down. And, there would be a patsy in the window because it was the easiest window to access and see. As a military person, it's just my natural instinct," claims the twice-wounded-Vietnam-veteran turned director (Oliver Stone was awarded the Purple Heart and a Bronze Star). So, besides revving up the engines of the military-industrial complex to profit from the war in Vietnam for over a decade, why else would the CIA want to assassinate JFK?

In late April 1961, over 1,400 members of the Cuban Expeditionary Forces landed at the Bay of Pigs in Cuba. Their mission was to overthrow the communist regime of Cuban President Fidel Castro. The mission was a striking failure. Almost immediately it became known that the American Central Intelligence Agency (CIA) trained the "freedom fighters"—Cubans trained by the CIA to overthrow the Castro regime. President John F. Kennedy had approved the mission based on the CIA's intelligence and, soon after the failure, spoke at a meeting of the American Association of Newspaper Editors and assumed all blame for the failed invasion. His staff then began leaking information to reporters, blaming the failure on anyone except the administration. President Kennedy was quoted as saying, "How could I have been so stupid?" to trust those who were advising him, the CIA and the Joint Chiefs of Staff (JCS). Bitter tensions and resentment began to grow. Even more damning to the CIA, and what helped fuel their motive to kill, was an alleged quote by President Kennedy that he wanted to "splinter the CIA into a thousand pieces and scatter it into the winds." Eventually, he did with classified and top-secret National Security Action Memos 55, 56, and 57, thus ending the reign of the CIA. Two and a half years after Kennedy uttered these words he was gunned down along the motorcade route in Dallas, Texas. The official government story is that a lone gunman, Lee Harvey Oswald, killed Kennedy. Many, like myself, are not satisfied with the official version supported by the bogus 26 volume Warren Commission fictitious report where witnesses statements and testimonials were manipulated and altered from start to finish.

A popular conspiracy theory claims that because Kennedy was planning on dismantling the intelligence infrastructure, the CIA had Kennedy killed, and then later covered up the assassination plot. It is conceivable that "splintering the CIA into a thousand pieces" caused the CIA to wonder whether Kennedy was good for the CIA in particular and the entire country in general. (http://mcadams.posc. mu.edu/jfk_cia.htm) A line from the movie *JFK* stands out, "the strongest motive to kill somebody is self defense and JFK endangered and posed a threat to the military-industrial complex. Kennedy was too far ahead of his time and was killed for it." Insiders were already calling JFK soft on communism for his demeanor towards Soviet Premier Nikita Khrushchev and the 1962 offensive nuclear missiles placed in Cuba by communist USSR. Regardless of critics towards Kennedy's so-called soft demeanor toward communism, he was a saint who viewed the world without nuclear war. A man who said: "Mankind must put an end to war, or war will put an end to mankind."

"The only thing necessary for the triumph of evil is for good men to do nothing," said Edmund Burke. President Kennedy, a good man, was the people's president and many Americans place him within the top three on the America's best presidents list.

Nonetheless, evil men exist in parallel to good men and inside the eyes of the assassination plotters JFK was a threat to the military-industrial complex. Texas oil tycoons with ties to defense contracts networked to the military-industrial complex could have funded the JFK hit men in accordance and synchronized with the CIA. Many Texas oil tycoons harbored deep resentment towards the Kennedys, especially JFK, and wanted to engage in an all-out war in order to prosper off the addiction to oil needed to fuel our military convoys. They even distributed JFK "Wanted for Treason," cowboy-and-outlaw era look-alike leaflets across America to get their message across. It is conceivable and very plausible that certain oil tycoons were the financiers of the black operation assassination hit on JFK. With JFK in office, a long-term war in Vietnam could not exist, but with him removed from office little could prevent the commitment of American troops and personnel to Vietnam. The CIA and the black world had to work fast though to remove the threat to their agenda because JFK had signed the monumental Memorandum 263. Memorandum 263 was signed October 11, 1963, and was an order to have the first 1,000 US troops home by that Christmas of 1963, with all US troops and personnel out of Vietnam by 1965. Memorandum 263, along with the statement to "splinter the CIA into 1,000 pieces" sent shock waves throughout Washington and the corridors of power. However, four days after JFK's death, newly sworn in President Lyndon B. Johnson, who did not share JFK's vision, signed Memorandum 273 and reversed JFK's efforts 180 degrees to push America's chips all-in on Vietnam. Shortly after Memorandum 273, and in March of 1964, LBJ put Memorandum 288 into effect, which began attacks on North Vietnam and escalated America's participation in the war. With such a drastic 180-degree change in direction with America's involvement in Vietnam, it's fair to say that a coup d'état occurred. When JFK was pulling out of Vietnam, the statistics read: September 2, 1963; 16,200 US troops in Vietnam; 82 US troops killed. Twelve years later the damage was done and the stats read: 1975; 58,000 US troops KIA and over two million Vietnamese dead. The perpetrators of the CIA and black world quarterbacked a coup and evil prevailed. They managed not to get caught and had all the blame fall on their patsy, Lee Harvey Oswald. Their successfully played coup only strengthened their belief to know that they could get away with not only a coup, but presidential murder.

If we were smart, we'd look at the similarities between what happened in 1963 and what's happening now. Barack Obama's blowout presidential victory over John McCain has, like JFK, changed the political landscape. With Obama's move into the White House, a house cleaning is bound to happen and hopefully excessive power-wielding directors are going to lose their elite jobs. Obama has kept his word and, within his first week of being president, ordered the CIA to close down all secret "black site" prisons, as well as for the Pentagon to close down the Guantanamo, Cuba, prison within a year (www.msnbc.msn.com/id/28788175). I worry about another coup d'état in the near future.

Obama must be very cautious of those individuals who do not want to have the base closed. War is big business and people get killed over business, especially when there are billions at stake. JFK advocated budget cuts called for in March of 1963 by the closing of 52 military installations, both foreign and domestic, and look what happened to him. Back in the Kennedy era, sacred cows from the World War II generation were the ones in the director's chair with the intelligence agencies. Kennedy had General Charles Cabell, the Deputy Director of the CIA fired in 1961 for the Bay of Pigs fiasco. Kennedy also fired another WWII sacred cow, Allen Dulles, for the Bay of Pigs disaster, who had been the head of the CIA since 1953. Fired CIA Director Allen Dulles had plenty of motives to kill JFK. He, and many others who had "itchy trigger fingers" and who wanted America to get in bed with war against communist Cuba and the Soviet Union, felt betrayed because JFK did not provide direct air power or support, leaving the right-winged exiles to be crushed by the

Cuban army. Ironically, and far from coincidence, fired CIA Director Allen Dulles was a key commissioner on the Warren Commission and the strongest advocate of its theory that Oswald acted alone. General Charles Cabell was also Dulles's deputy of the CIA for nine years. Both men called Kennedy a traitor for his soft approach towards communism. However, what they called soft on communism, I and many other like-minded Americans consider the traits and qualities of a true humanitarian, philanthropist, and pacifist.

Then, of course, there's the CIA Director Richard Helms, who was at the time of the Kennedy assassination Director of Plans for the CIA. This is the top CIA position responsible for covert actions, like organizing coups and political assassinations. Helms served in that capacity until 1966 when he was made CIA director. All of these directors knew that their business was a nasty business and everything was highly sanitized with information continually being covered up. For example, when planning, coordinating, arming, training and financing repressive military coups—as the CIA has done so many times before—their henchmen and dark riders carry out mass arrests, mass torture and mass murder. Open your eyes to see what these guys are seeing, which is a world chess board that they are trying to control. For them, political assassinations are a valuable weapon in their covert operatives toolbox, but is one tool amongst many at their disposal, where the end result is a successful regime change that not only removes the dragon's head, but replaces the body politic.

These individuals that play the black hand, like with CIA Directors, specialize in the black arts where nothing is what it seems on the surface. Directors and playmakers at the top of these powerful intelligence agencies are the crème de la crème which is why they were appointed to their position in the first place. The pedigree of these individuals are best in breed at what they do. They've been programmed to win by attrition by whatever means necessary. They color outside of the lines. They've been trained to pass lie detector tests without pupil dilation, without an elevated heartbeat, without flinching, and to react without hesitation. They are cold blooded masterminds of the black worlds 'black arts'. So, and just like JFK did with his sacred cow intelligence directors, President Obama should be very careful when relinquishing directors of their commanding positions. To these types of individuals that would be considered an act of surrendering their position, which is one thing they haven't been programmed for, which is to lose. The word "lose" isn't in their vocabulary.

The CIA has been orchestrating regime changes and coup d'états for the last 50 years and have removed many entities and governments that are unhealthy to US corporate interests. Once the dragon's head has been removed, its head grows back engineered to their desires, with regimes that are more conducive to obliging and cooperating with the economic and geopolitical desires of the US corporate elite. The CIA has even attacked its own county to get what they want accomplished. A great example of this is when the CIA removed JFK from office, permanently, to get Vietnam accomplished. They cut off the head of the American dragon and it grew back as Lyndon B. Johnson who was obviously compliant with their wishes to "get boots on the ground" in Vietnam. This is what we, and President Obama, need to be extremely aware of: war is the biggest business not only in America, but in the world.

If you take anything away from this chapter, what you need and what we all need to remember is that "the organizing principle of any society is for war. The authority of the state over its people resides in its war powers." (*JFK*) This authority and this power is something we all need to open our eyes to. The day America died was only 47 years ago, let's not relive it with Obama.

AMERICA DIES WITH ONE BULLET

Why do our country's greatest and most humanitarian, visionary leaders seem to end up on the black world's hit list? And, once the target has been removed from power why do we always stand idly by and do nothing in the wake of such deliberate assassinations? If we don't stand up for our beliefs then we've conditioned and set ourselves up to endure another coup d'état. Don't let them triumph and kill our dreams for peace, love and hope. Don't let them deceive us and kill our perennial all-star Americans like John 'Jack' Fitzgerald Kennedy, Robert 'Bobby' Francis Kennedy, Abraham Lincoln, Martin Luther King, Jr, or Malcolm X. Don't think for a second that Barack Obama couldn't end up on that list. Navigate through history and remember that kings are killed and that ten to twelve senators (mostly Cassius and Brutus) conspired to kill Caesar behind closed doors and were successful. We must learn from our past history, stay vigilant to never let our guard down, and never let them drag our hopes and dreams to the gutter.

We must beware and open our eyes to recent headlines like MSN. com's "Obama Positioned to Reverse Bush Actions" because this is going to aggravate the powers that are benefiting and profiteering from the policies the Bush administration put into effect. The article states "transition advisers to President-elect Barack Obama have compiled a list of about 200 Bush administration actions and executive orders that could be swiftly undone to reverse White House policies on climate change, stem cell research, reproductive rights and other issues, according to congressional Democrats, campaign aides and experts working with the transition team" (http://www.msnbc.msn.com/id/27628719). Now, for the Bush administration profiteers and benefiting agencies this audacious move comes across like Obama's administration taking a long drag off a cigarette and blowing it directly into their faces without apology. I believe President Obama has the right idea but he needs to understand the giant establishment he's going up against. All I'm saying is that kings and presidents are killed and he must be extremely careful with his life and his family's. One lone bullet could shatter the optimistic and hopeful vision that he has brought to the table for America.

Barack should always be behind bulletproof glass because as a country imploding from weathering an economy draining recession we're not capable of enduring another JFK. The aftermath of another assassination equivalent to that of JFK would shatter the hearts, minds and souls of the American citizens. If the black world ordered a professional assassin to push a button on Obama, his death could mobilize a revolution. With so much economic hardship, all hopes hang by a thread. Americans have been battered on many fronts, including the raging health care debate to rising joblessness and the housing slump.

America's real estate and foreclosure nightmare can be felt in almost every city and town.

Many are taking their unhappiness public and protesting on the streets. This country is not ready to see a casket filled with a dead President. When JFK was murdered, in less than a second America died, and when his younger brother Robert 'Bobby' Kennedy went to honor JFK's death at the Democratic National Convention, the audience gave a standing ovation and applauded for 22 minutes straight. Try and fathom 22 minutes of straight non-stop applause to honor JFK and all that he stood for. The cherished chemistry that JFK shared with the American people was unparalleled until Barack Obama became president. Saints, like JFK, RFK, and Abraham Lincoln, have the unique ability of touching our lives individually. Barack Obama has the traits of a saint we cannot afford to lose. Obama is our last real chance for hope and our last line of defense to reclaim America for what she is. We must support Obama to uphold the following words that Abraham Lincoln spoke to a Civil War-torn nation in Gettysburg, Pennsylvania in 1863. Excerpts from Lincoln's 1863 Gettysburg Address state, "Four score and seven years ago our fathers brought forth on this continent, a new nation, conceived in Liberty, and dedicated to the proposition that all men are created equal...that from these honored dead we take increased devotion to that cause for which they gave the last full measure of devotion—that we here highly resolve that these dead shall not have died in vain—that this nation, under God, shall have a new birth of freedom—and that government of the people, by the people, for the people, shall not perish from the Earth." Old Abe is shaking his head in disbelief from the heavens above right now at the direction our government has taken this nation. Somewhere along the way, we the people were left behind.

AMERICA WILL REAP WHAT IT SOWS

Thank God America is guarded by the Pacific Ocean and the Atlantic Ocean. America, especially under the Bush administration, has, for better or worse, been the world's police. Many countries with radical elements hate the fact that we can attack them but they can't attack us on our home front. Our country's ideal location protects us by two vast oceans and our neighboring countries—Mexico and Canada—don't pose a hostile military threat. Ironically, this may hurt us more in the long run for the following reason: we are the world's police and often do much more good than harm, but collateral damage is a real touchy subject that breeds anti-American sentiment. Collateral damage encompasses the innocent men, women, and children who die from our attacks aimed against rogue terrorist groups. Sure, we use sophisticated high-tech GPS precision weaponry, laser-guided bombs lased by reconnaissance teams on the ground, and unmanned drones such as the Raven, Reaper, Predator, and Fire Scout. Once the suspect is lased or targeted he or she is most likely going to be terminated, but it's usually not that cut and dry. Innocent civilians frequently die from American operations dubbed "precision strikes." Civilian noncombatant casualties have been a huge source of friction between the US and the countries where our troops are in action.

Developed by General Atomics Aeronautical Systems for use by the U.S. Air Force and Navy, the MQ-9 Reaper is the Air Force's and Navy's first purpose-designed hunter-killer UAV designed for long endurance. We are launching cross border raids into sovereign nations, without permission mind you, with these unmanned drones and have killed many innocent civilians. We must put ourselves in their shoes...how would we feel if an aggressor nation was attacking terrorists on our soil, killing our innocent men, women and children?

Now, think about Vietnam and how many illegal black operations ran into the neighboring countries, especially Cambodia and Laos. It's the same thing right now in Iraq and Afghanistan. We are using those countries that we've occupied to launch cross-border raids, without permission, to attack neighboring countries like Syria, Iran, and Pakistan.

This is really going to stir the shit-storm of anti-American sentiment in the Middle East and across the globe. But it's the countries we are occupying who are feeling the wrath of devastating collateral damage. On November 5, 2008, Afghan President Hamid Karzai said that an air strike by coalition forces killed some 40 civilians and wounded about 28 in the Kandahar province. A Reuters witness saw three children with shrapnel wounds and seven wounded women in the hospital. To top it off, there have been scores of Afghans killed in US air strikes this year with totals in the thousands. We must open our eyes to what's going on over there.

The problem is that most Americans can't really relate to what's happening over in Iraq and Afghanistan. Most Americans don't feel their pain and heartbreak from the scores of innocent civilians that our bombs "accidentally" kill. Think about how we'd feel if some other aggressor world power nation were accidentally killing scores of our civilians and then saying, "oops, sorry...it was an accident." We'd be absolutely infuriated! Put yourselves in their shoes. It's been going on for far too long. This system and this US government has torn families apart from Afghanistan to the United States. What if it was our innocent men, women, and children who were killed and burned alive from a stray bomb? Our wives and girlfriends, our sons and daughters slain while eating or studying for school in the living room from a missile or bomb off target, only to read about a foreign commander stating something similar to what US forces Commander Jeff Bender stated in the recent civilian attack in Afghanistan that killed 40: "If innocent people were killed in this operation, we apologize and express our condolences to the families and the people of Afghanistan." I don't think that's going to calm the victims' families down and make everything better, and honestly, how many Americans gave their sincere condolences to the horrific war atrocities that have gone unchecked and unpunished from the US war machine? Not many. Either not many Americans even knew about it since Paris Hilton, Lindsay Lohan, or some other celebrity's whereabouts pollute and litter the headline news with irrelevant garbage.

Those who did read or hear about it probably didn't sincerely care; they do not live differently because of what happened. It's out of sight, out of mind. But it's through this ignorance that we are sowing the seeds to our own demise. This behavioral pattern of turning our heads until the problem is staring us in the face is a serious reoccurring mistake that we never seem to learn. This is a problem that many in this country need to open their eyes to see. America will reap what it sows; karma will always come back full circle. So, when a bomb blows up in a city and kills dozens, hundreds, or thousands of US innocent civilians from a terrorist who became a terrorist because a US air strike killed his or her family, don't be surprised one bit when you're pointing your finger at him calling him the bad guy. Yes, in a sense he is the bad guy, but there's a reason behind the creation of that malice. Instead, try to understand his mentality and why he would undertake such an act. It's only because he has lived through the nightmare of our US air strikes and attacks and seen our war machine inflicting collateral damage on his families and friends. His wife, his sons and daughters have been burned alive or killed in accidental missile strikes gone astray. Not ours. The ramifications of these actions would obviously lead to resentment against the aggressors' presence. Afghanistan President Hamid Karzai stated recently, "The main problem, which has become a matter of tension [with the United States], is civilian casualties. Civilian casualties should completely stop. The war in the villages of Afghanistan will never give fruit." (http://news.yahoo.com/s/nm/20081105/ts_nm/us_afghan_violence)

Barack Obama needs to bring an end to the Bush, cowboy-era style of violence that we've inflicted upon the indigenous peoples of lands we're occupying, the Holy Land of Babylonia and Mesopotamia. We need to lead by example. America is supposed to be a symbol and pillar of peace, freedom, liberty and justice. We have become victims of our own hypocrisy. As of April 2009, and according to the Associated Press (AP), "Iraq's government has recorded 87,215 of its citizens killed since 2005 in violence ranging from catastrophic bombings to execution-style slayings. Combined with tallies based on hospital sources and media reports since the beginning of the war and an in-depth review of available evidence by the Associated Press, the figures show that more than 110,600 Iraqis have died in the violence since the 2003 U.S.-led invasion. Yet, many estimated the actual number of deaths at ten to twenty percent higher because of thousands who are still missing and civilians who were buried or lost in the chaos of war without official records. The numbers show just how traumatic the war has been for Iraq. In a nation of 29 million people, the deaths represent 0.38 percent of the population. Proportionately, that would be the equivalent to the United States losing 1.2 million to violence in a four-year period. (http://news.yahoo.com/s/ap/20090424/ap_on_re_mi_ea/ml_iraq_death_toll)

Open your eyes to see that throughout the entire Vietnam War America lost approximately 58,000 US servicemen KIA over a 15-year period. So, in a short period to lose 110,000 civilians is a staggering number. There are serious consequences of our military actions. Look to our own roots to see what we did to the American Indians, whose land was once where you and I live. Our Union Army and cavalry slaughtered the indigenous peoples of the land you and I now call home. They didn't want to share the land, they selfishly wanted all the land. The standard United States schooling system and institution teaches our students that Christopher Columbus discovered the New World America in 1492, or that the Viking Leif Erikson discovered the New World 500 years before Columbus in 1001 A.D. Regardless, the real truth is that the American Indians had called America home for many, many moons, long before Erikson and Columbus were even born. We better open our eyes to see that we need to walk softly and gently upon the face of the Earth or it just may be our country that gets a serious wake up call.

If we plant the seeds of war mongering, then what will grow from that can only be hate. We need to incorporate a new growing formula to fertilize our seeds with, in order to harvest peace, love and harmony across the globe. The butterfly effect works both ways, for good or bad, so we must change our un-American policing ethics and morals, and we must change before the end is upon us.

WHY THE EXTREMISTS CALL US INFIDELS AND IMPERIALISTS

We must understand the mentality of our enemy and their devotion to their creed if we are going to create authentic change. These people are praying on their hands and knees several times during the day, every day 24/7/365, religiously engaged with their God. How many times do you honestly worship your God or higher power? Once a day? Once a week? Or are you a "two timer" that attends church only on Christmas and Easter? Religion for this selfless culture is the backbone for how they live their lives, and as we previously discussed in earlier chapters, America has become more and more spiritually distant. The extremist's patience not to pounce, but to sit and wait, and bleed our economy a slow, painful death is their most effective weapon. These holy warriors, or jihadists, know our pressure points and know how to play the psychological warfare mind game all too well. Time is on their side. These jihadists are starting to see, like the Soviets from the 1980s, that the US is unable to sustain a long, financially draining fight against them. These extremists will try to strike America at our weakest point, when we're most vulnerable to being breached. How are they going to attack? Think about it. Our authorities and enforcement personnel are looking for suspicious Arab and Muslim-looking individuals fitting the terrorist profile, so to evade our enforcement agencies they will most likely be training white terrorists, with European descent, who appear clean cut and polished, intelligent, but most of all inconspicuous so as to not raise any alarms. This is what Osama Bin Laden and his top lieutenants are banking on, a white-skinned trained terrorist to deliver a crippling blow to our economy.

They say we only monitor five percent of the cargo coming in from our ports, which leaves a terrifying ninety-five percent of the cargo unchecked, unmonitored. With so much wiggle room, a dirty bomb, or a biological or chemical weapon could easily be loaded from a US port onto a train where the train track goes right through a major city, or cities for that matter, releasing airborne biological entities at each stop. Make sure you understand what a chemical weapon is and the havoc it's capable of. As a former grunt in the Marine Corps infantry, I trained for nuclear, biological, and chemical warfare attacks, and believe me, it is one of those things I wish we could disinvent, such as the atomic bomb. If you're thinking about bombs being dropped on American soil, such as on Pearl Harbor December 7, 1941, this is most likely not going to happen today since we're fortunately guarded by the far-stretching Pacific and Atlantic Oceans, as well as guarded by sophisticated radar systems employed at bases like NORAD (The North American Aerospace Defense Command) in Colorado Springs, Colorado. No, the next attack on our country will most likely be absolutely horrific. What will do the killing will have no face, no visible shape or form to counterattack. "Among these weapons of mass destruction, biological weapons are more destructive than chemical weapons, including nerve gas. In certain circumstances, biological weapons can be as devastating as nuclear ones—a few kilograms of anthrax can kill as many people as a Hiroshima-size nuclear weapon." The death tolls of the atomic bombings of Hiroshima and Nagasaki, Japan, are staggering, and this was only for one bomb deployed per city. On August 6, and August 9, 1945, the bombs named "Little Boy" and "Fat Man" killed as many as 140,000 in Hiroshima and 80,000 in Nagasaki. Tens of thousands have perished from injury and illness attributed to the aftermath of radiation fallout. (http://en.wikipedia.org/wiki/Atomic_bombings_of_Hiroshima_and_Nagasaki) The bombs were ordered to be dropped by President Harry S. Truman. An invasion of Japan would have been too much of a challenge. Our servicemen would have had to combat 13 divisions of Japanese soldiers on their home court, nearly 500,000 men equipped with a fight-to-the-last-man approach. (http://www.milnet.com/nukeweap/hiroshima/hiroshima.htm) Whether it was morally right to drop the bombs is up to you, but know that thousands and thousands of our boys would have died invading imperial Japan, and quite possibly your grandfather or your father wouldn't have come home.

The word that first comes to mind is pandemonium. It's something that our young country has fortunately not seen on the home front. I pray that we will not see these horrors of the world but with so much room for error it seems inevitable. Make no mistake, and do not forget while you're living the good life, that these radical elements have declared "Jihad" on America. Now, understand that some of these extremists under these regimes believe us to be the infidel, and it's hard to blame them some of the time with the direction that our country is heading lately.

When they look at America many of them see a money-hungry, capitalistic, "I-want-to-be-rich-when-I-grow-up" country that has lost itself spiritually. A country that puts money before God. They see Americans obsessively chasing materialistic needs and wants, with most not even noticing they're toiling with lust, gluttony, greed, sloth, wrath, envy, and pride on a daily basis.

Sin acts as a detour and distracts us from reaching new heights with spiritual enlightenment. The cycle of superficialities never ends until that individual has an epiphany and wakes up one day and realizes that the simple things in life lead down the righteous and pure path. However, greed is driving the monster in our culture to keep growing. Most of these materialistic possessions are bought and purchased with credit cards and money that most consumers don't have, and it's especially hard to work for money you've already spent for something you didn't need. Why in America must we acquire these objects to feel validated in our image-driven society? Didn't anyone ever tell these people that the simple things in life lead to true happiness, peace, love and harmony?

So, by shunning spirituality and befriending the Devil and his sinful temptations, there is a reason the terrorists call us infidels and imperialists. Many Americans have lost all sense of spiritual priority and the fact that we put God second, and materialism first, is one of the reasons why the extremists call us the infidels and imperialists. They see a country that puts money, a piece of green paper with some numbers on it, in front of God. Once you're stripped away of your petty material things only then can you have your eyes opened to who you truly are and what your identity truly is. Your spiritual connection should make you feel complete, and that connection is more pure and self-fulfilling than any materialistic thing one can buy. So please, put yourself in the extremist's shoes for a moment and look at America through their eyes. What do you see? It might not be the America you thought you'd see.

ALWAYS QUESTION AUTHORITY

We need to seek more spiritual freedom as humans. Not all, but many people are living a life moving along in their metal coffins, inching along on the traffic-clogged freeways in the concrete, urban jungle of congested cities. Like marching ants living in a mundane, cookie-cutter world completely oblivious, where the future in their minds is all "peaches-n-cream-I'll-be-getting-my-retirement-and-401K-at-age 60"—they're completely blind to the truth of what's to come. The truth, it's a funny thing what people perceive to be the truth. TV, newspapers, advertisements, magazines, the media, are not always wrong but most of the time, they are withholding the bona fide truth. Don't let the media have control over your brain and don't ever believe what you read to be the exact truth.

We must always question authority otherwise we are just blind cattle being herded by a shepherd in the wrong direction unable to see greener pastures. The sheep (American citizens) are herded into position and are always fearful of the bite from the looming wolf (the government). I remember a time not so long ago when we were herded into position and convinced by the Bush Administration that Osama Bin Laden and Saddam Hussein were working together and responsible for 9/11. We were also told that there were weapons of mass destruction in Iraq. Obviously now we see clearly that we were strong-armed by fear tactics into believing those fallacies to be the infallible truth. People tend to believe government officials and bureaucrats know what they're talking about and believe they will make the right decisions. Too many people take their word at face value without questioning authority and realizing that "one may smile, and smile, and be a villain" (Shakespeare). Donald Rumsfeld and Dick Cheney couldn't have a war in Iraq without 9/11, or a defense budget for tyrannical world conquests. The cronies of our government disguised the truth to start the engines of the US military-industrial complex—something that former President Dwight D. Eisenhower (a.k.a. "Ike") warned us about. In Eisenhower's farewell address to the nation on January 17, 1961, he stated, "In the councils of government, we must guard against the acquisition of unwarranted influence, whether sought or unsought, by the military-industrial complex. The potential for the disastrous rise of misplaced power exists and will persist. We must never let the weight of this combination endanger our liberties or democratic processes. We should take nothing for granted. Only an alert and knowledgeable citizenry can compel the proper meshing of the huge industrial and military machinery of defense with our peaceful methods and goals, so that security and liberty can prosper together." (http://mcadams.posc.mu.edu/ike.htm) Ike warned us about the military-industrial complex endangering our liberties and democratic processes, yet the unyielding actions from the Bush administration triggered what we see in 2010 to be the great powers of the world already moving their pieces on the Middle Eastern chess board for a future clash (World War III). The key element and paramount ingredient for the Bush administration to getting their war in the ancient Babylonian and Mesopotamian holy lands, current day Iraq and Iran, was to summon the American public behind them using lies and the art of misinformation. Without this essential ingredient the recipe for war wouldn't exist.

The government had their motive, their story, and the majority of US taxpayers backing them, vital to launching the US military-industrial complex engine full steam ahead into Iraq. Regardless of the fact that this sacred holy land was home to the Garden of Eden and once called the cradle of civilization, the US war machine had a new, all-in destination in its sights: Iraq. The Bush Administration played the cards perfectly to get their war. Lobbyists for special interest groups

benefited, defense contractors profiteered, and agencies you've heard of
and 'black world' agencies you've never heard of grew in power from
the increased war budget. Agencies like the CIA (Central Intelligence
Agency), NSA (National Security Agency, which is at least seven times
bigger than the CIA), the ATF (Bureau of Alcohol, Tobacco, Firearms,
and Explosives), the DEA (Drug Enforcement Agency), the DOD
(Department of Defense), the FBI (Federal Bureau of Investigation),
the NRO (National Reconnaissance Office), the DIA (Defense
Intelligence Agency), the DNI (Director of National Intelligence), the
USDI (Under Secretary of Defense for Intelligence), S.E.T.I (Search for
Extra-Terrestrial Intelligence), the DOE (Department of Energy) (www.
intelligence.gov/1-members.shtml), the DELTA Group (responsible for
security of all alien connected people). (www.abovetopsecret.com/forum/
thread61316/pg1) These agencies, many of which are clandestine, harness
more power, more clout, and more muscle than your average citizen can
possibly fathom. These government players operate in absolute secrecy
never making the front page of your morning newspaper. They do not
exist publicly and are ghosts in a sense. They are merely shadows in the
darkness never unveiled to the light of the normal 8 AM to 5 PM world.
Yet, they maintain absolute control of the 8 AM to 5 PM world and
make it work in the fashion they planned behind closed doors, without
an incriminating paper trail, and without palpable evidence (i.e., signed
documents, top-secret memos, classified memos, etc.).

Look at Halliburton's stock value when the Iraq war started until
now and open your eyes to see how much its shareholders profited
from this warmongering, especially Dick Cheney. Many of these
governmental agencies that were listed and not listed above collaborate
with defense contractors and special interest groups to capitalize on
war. Their wish is America's command as they quarterback play-by-play
our country's next move. Nonetheless, every bad play is strenuously
felt throughout the wallets and purses of every US citizen. How much
blood can be squeezed from a stone? At the moment in 2010, plenty of
blood is being squeezed from the American people for war profiteering
and a multi-front war.

CHAPTER 9: AMERICA, THE CONFUSED

WE'RE ALL AMERICANS...WHERE'S YOUR FLAG?

I know what it really means to love my country. I enlisted and served in the US Marine Corps Infantry right out of high school at the naïve age of 17. I volunteered to be thrown into a thirteen-week, well-structured and extremely disciplined nightmare called Marine Corps boot camp, enforced by fanatical, pit-bull drill instructors at MCRD (Marine Corp Recruit Depot) in San Diego. I went in as an underdeveloped boy and I came out a man who'd learned real humility. Both of my grandfathers were US Air Force pilots in World War II, and my family lost a cousin in the Vietnam War, all of which inspired me to grasp what our flag really stands for: the red, white, and blue. God and country were everything back in the day for the patrons of this great land, so when and where did we fall off our horse? Look around in your neighborhood and on your block, how many of your neighbors are sporting an American flag outside their house? Not many. If we forget what it truly means to salute and pay homage to our flag then we've lost ourselves. Pay tribute and show your respect to those who died for the freedoms and liberties we take for granted. Pay tribute to all those who made your freedoms a reality through the ultimate sacrifice of their lives. God and country should be our number one and two priorities but lately it seems like that concept is outdated and too cumbersome for most. We must not only re-connect with our spirituality but we must also re-connect with our country.

In my opinion, the removal of the 'Pledge of Allegiance' in our schools only contradicts and deteriorates our country's foundation and creed that it was built on. I love this country and would honestly give my life for her, but make no mistake, I completely understand why I along with millions of other Americans do not subscribe to dying for George Bush's "blood-for-oil" war that President Obama is now trying to mend. Why grow beautiful children only to have them farmed and slaughtered for this type of war? Comedian Katt Williams said, "I am allergic to stupid shit." This mesmerizing, putrid odyssey that the Bush administration has taken us on must come to a screeching halt. It's indicative that we as a nation need to rekindle our love for the stars and stripes and never let our young country suffer because of personal animosity towards the Bush regime. We were fooled and conned into entering a war that we didn't need to be involved with and that's our mistake and our fault.

Do not let your love for the stars and stripes be tarnished by the actions of our last president, George W. Bush. The Bush administration is now finally out of office and our flag is still standing. Through thick and thin, throughout good and bad presidencies, our flag will still be standing blowing in the wind as long as we all do our part to remember to never let her fall and to always carry and represent her colors proudly. And I don't just mean on her birthday July 4. We must reiterate and truly take to heart the words of Abraham Lincoln's first inaugural address from Monday, March 1, 1861:

> "We are not enemies, but friends. We must not
> be enemies. Though passion may have strained
> it must not break our bonds of affection. The
> mystic chords of memory, stretching from
> every battlefield and patriot grave to every

living heart and hearthstone all over this broad
land, will yet swell the chorus of the Union,
when again touched, as surely they will be, by
the better angels of our nature" (www.bartleby.
com/124/pres31.html).

My advice to all of you is to get involved and advocate the truth.
So, open your eyes, buy yourself a flag and let American pride shine
from house to house throughout your neighborhood. We owe her and
those patriots who bled and fought for her that much. Put America
on a pedestal and stop taking her for granted. Take to heart the blood
that has soaked into the roots and soil of this land and great country.
"Liberty, in case you've forgotten, is the soul's right to breathe" (*Good
Will Hunting*).

LOVE & RELATIONSHIPS

Let's talk about love and fidelity for a minute. I have been in love
twice in my life and know that it can make everything in life more
enjoyable and more beautiful. Do you know the saying "happiness
is better when shared?" Well, it's true. Both times I've been in love
I've been blindsided by cupid's arrow. "Love, it's like God sent me an
Angel from Heaven that saved me from the depths of hell" (*Good Will
Hunting*). Music sounded better, the air smelled better, and the world
was simply more beautiful. The love was so powerfully euphoric that
I'd stick up for and defend my girlfriend even when she was wrong.
Love is something that everyone should experience; however, this is
not always the case. Growing up it's often just bred into your mind
that you will fall in love, get married, and have kids. This is usually
more of a fantasy, fairy tale, storybook tale, and is far from the truth
as our culture has manifested into an, to use an *Almost Famous* line,
"entire generation of Cinderella's and there's no glass slipper coming."
Love isn't guaranteed. One of the saddest things in the world to
witness is when you see a lonely, elderly person who never found his

or her soulmate and now they're drifting through the latter years of their life alone.

The problem is that people are often not content with what they have. Well, they are at first, but then move on to find what I call the BBD, or the "Bigger Better Deal." The BBD is one of the reasons for the fifty-five to sixty percent divorce rate in this country. The BBD is also a leading factor in why couples do not want to work through their problems together and weather the storm. Any long-term married couple will tell you that marriage isn't easy and it takes work. The puppy-love stage doesn't last forever, and as that new love feeling fades you will be tested from time to time. These tests show how strong the relationship or marriage really is. There are going to be ups and downs, trials and tribulations, triumphs and downfalls.

Today, couples run for the hills and link up with a new partner before even really trying to work through their problems. Marriages last because the two individuals are fully committed—mind, body and soul to one another and are willing to evolve through thick and thin. A smooth sea never made a skillful sailor and the best captains who've earned their stripes are the ones who know how to navigate through the roughest, most turbulent seas. If you get knocked down to the mat then you lift yourself up and carry on with your head raised proudly. Marriage is a death-do-us-part mutual agreement. Too many people get married impulsively, without knowing enough about their so-called soulmate.

The ugliness often appears shortly after impetuously tying the knot…So if you rush to get married and don't know enough about your partner, then you're probably inviting a catastrophic Category 5 Hurricane Katrina to dine with you for dinner. Know thyself and know thy partner. You can't just love the white bread of your partner. You have to love the crust of your partner. You've got to love the burnt crumbs at the bottom of the toaster tray of your partner. Then, and only then, will you know what real love entails. If you truly do love the ugliness (burnt crumbs), and beauty, of your partner, you just may have found yourself true love and someone to grow old with.

Our culture needs to be repaired so let's sow the seeds of love so that what grows from that is an America with a divorce rate other countries admire. If we cultivate love the harvest will be exponential.

BOYCOTT FAKE HOLIDAYS

This country's calendar is plastered with fake holidays. The other day was the nation's "Sweetest Day" and I couldn't help but shake my head at another fake capitalism-at-its-worst Hallmark holiday, conceived by erroneous marketers, advertisers and retailers. As Hyde says on "That 70s Show," "Romance was created by corporations to prey on losers who think buying nice things will make someone love them. Advertisers spend billions to make you think I'm a jerk if I don't buy you anything." Real, genuine holidays have significant meaning, such as Christmas, Easter, Thanksgiving, the Fourth of July, Veteran's Day, Memorial Day, or even Halloween. Oh no, not this one; this was supposedly the nation's "Sweetest Day." People, please don't buy into this as it's just a money-making scheme engineered to make you open your wallets and purses to shell out your hard-earned dollars, and with the economic recession every dollar saved helps. According to MSN. com, in 2008 fifty percent of Americans made $30,000 per year or less and many of these individuals have families to take care of. My point, most people struggling to get by on an airtight budget don't have the money or mindset to celebrate these luxurious made-up Hallmark holidays. I assure you that it is not the "Sweetest Day" for them. A word of advice: keep your money in the bank. The same applies for Valentine's Day, which I'd recommend not subscribing to. I have nothing against romance, sex, love, or an excuse to eat chocolates, but when a celebration that once aspired to have true meaning turns into a deformed, trashy, materialistic extravaganza, it's time to put my foot down and kick this nonsense to the curb. These fake hallmark holidays tend to scar individuals rather than help them. Think of the people who get nothing on these days and then think of the people who do get gifts on these days. Why must we buy into these holidays only to fork over money for love and acceptance? We must not believe that we need to buy things for one another to feel loved and validated on a specific day. There's 365 days in the year for that so go prove that lovin' feeling and show you care in your own unique way. 'I love you' doesn't need to be expressed monetarily by Valentine's Day's big business of predetermined displays of romance. The same principle applies for Earth Day. Open your eyes to see that one day a year doesn't count. The proactive idea is there but we need to take care of Mother Earth on a full-time basis to really make a difference. It's what you do when no one's looking on the 364 other days of the year that really counts. There are genuine holidays and there are counterfeit made up holidays that have no merit. I recommend subscribing to those holidays that were founded on truth and dismiss those fraudulent holidays that were conceived on greed. Save your money for the genuine ones, we're in a recession.

COLLEGE IN 2010? WHY? AMERICA IS "NOT HIRING"

Let's talk about being "trapped" in financial debt forever. Here's the old paradigm, the way the system worked for our baby boomer parents. They finished high school, went to college, graduated, then entered the "Now-Hiring" job market where they got a great, paying, stable job with security and benefits, met their spouse, had kids, raised the family in a storybook cookie-cutter house with the white picket fence, and lived happily ever after—the American dream. Right now, in this recession-plagued over-saturated American job market, the paradigm looks like this: you graduate high school and listen to your parents and go to college to get your degree to supposedly start your career and get that promised high-paying job. Now you've gone to college for four years. You've studied hard, got good grades, and spent $100,000 on tuition getting that degree which is now framed and hanging on your wall. You did what you were told by your parents and by the environment around you coasting along on that conveyor belt of conformity heading to college, which was all deemed as normal. Many parents stress that their children need to go to college to get the same opportunities they did. The difference is that those baby boomers, who are now parents, had lucrative jobs awaiting them out of college. That was then. This is now and that time is long gone. What the baby boomers went through entailed a completely different set of circumstances and those rules do not apply today. News flash people, that high-paying job is most likely going to be MIA when you finally do graduate from college.

Here's what they didn't tell you and what we all need to open our eyes to. You're most likely going to be flushed out of college into a sour, recession-dampened job market. You've got your hard-earned degree and you're applying to all these great positions that call for your specific degree, and you go to sleep feeling well-qualified for the job you're going after. But, the days and nights go by and still no you're-hired call comes. Then the weeks go by and still no you're-hired call. Months go by and your life support savings bankroll has diminished, so now you find yourself at a temp agency working a temp job for $10 to $13 an hour. Reality can be cold and bitter to swallow especially when the concept of school seems so secure.

College in 2010 is a business to bribe you out of your money. Do yourself a favor and keep your money. Better yet, take your college tuition money and educate yourself on buying property, especially foreclosures, because as Donald Trump stated, "there will be more money made in the next two years than in the last ten years combined." If you're looking to get ahead in 2010, college may only set you far behind and in an unrecoverable amount of debt. College is not the only way to succeed. The traditional baby boomer era way of doing things is defunct. You're being taken for a fool, a fool who's being misled down the wrong path. You'll be trying to pay back your student loans for the next 10 years making the minimum payments. This is my definition of "trapped." Now you're 30 years old and bald from stress, and with a third to a half of your life gone spent in debt you're stuck wondering why you gave that university all of your money that you were supposedly promised back through a great paying job.

This is not a hypothetical situation since it is happening everywhere and is all too real for the recent graduating classes today. The simple truth once again is that college is an institution, a business. I will admit this, which is if you're going to become a doctor, lawyer, teacher or something of that nature, then college is imperative. Teaching needs to be a prized and celebrated job with a $100,000 salary, not a mediocre $30,000 salary that we see all across this great nation. Maybe then, more great minds will aspire to become educators and instill a knowledge-is-power mentality to our youth. However, if you are going to college and planning on leaving with a general business or communications degree then good luck standing in line with everyone else fighting for the same job. You better have an ace up your sleeve to differentiate yourself from the crowd because you need an edge in this world, not just a degree. A degree helps but I personally think who you know trumps your school accolades and will benefit you more in the long run.

I have seen too many high hopes dashed. We need to incorporate a systematic rule of job guarantee out of college. If you give a big university the kind of money they're asking for to educate you, then there better be a job waiting for you when you cross the finish line, $100,000-degree in hand. My sister's friend, Katie, just graduated with a 4.0 GPA from KU and this Jayhawk is working three jobs out of college just to stay afloat. I asked, "Well, that wasn't in the deal now was it? To go to college and get a 4.0 GPA only to come out into the work force and work three mediocre jobs? Something seems a little wrong here, don't you think, Katie?" She couldn't agree more and told me to address this problem in my book. Say you get that dream job after committing to college for four plus years and you're coasting along making a solid future for yourself. Then in the snap of a finger, you've been stripped of your seemingly secure job, your company car, your benefits and insurance, and your life as you knew it, vanished.

Basically, you're an expendable asset that can be jeopardized to benefit share prices or inflate the CEO's bankroll.

With the fragile 2010 economy and slim-pickings job market, it's a sickening feeling to lose a job you thought was stable through years of hard, diligent work. You were the yeast that made the company's dough rise yet they didn't see or remember that when they crunched the numbers on paper. Once President Obama and his all-star team untangle the knot from hell left by the Bush administration, we must put our American educational standards on a pedestal so that we can compete in a competitive global job market. It's time we give more attention to the most important area that will benefit ourselves and our children—education. But at the moment in 2010, the $100,000 college experience isn't paying dividends. Do you see any 'Now Hiring' signs?

CHAPTER 10: PREPARE FOR THE END OF LIFE AS WE KNOW IT

First off, I'd like to cordially thank you for your patronage. I am extremely grateful and feel privileged to be able to share my vision with you and the world I see from behind my eyes. I sincerely appreciate your interest in my book and these unorthodox subjects. Hopefully, *Open Your Eyes: To 2012 and Beyond* has sung to you with unique lyrics that touched your way of life and your psyche. Second, I'd like to dedicate *Open Your Eyes: To 2012 and Beyond* to my Grandfather, Daniel Maras, and to all of those truth-seeking crusaders who put their lives on the line for something greater than themselves. For attempting to go against the orthodox grain sailing through turbulent, uncharted waters in order to shed light on sensitive subjects like December 21, 2012. I could've made a career out of the US Marine Corps and gone into the intelligence communities but then I'd only be a victim of my own hypocrisy, assisting in concealing the truth instead of helping to reveal it.

I hope my book *Open Your Eyes: To 2012 and Beyond* has provided you with curing clairvoyance, helping you see through all of the heinous, force-fed propaganda and poisonous lies. I and a growing number of Americans are sick of choking on lies. "We don't believe the government is telling us the truth and they don't care that we don't believe it...that's the problem," wrote author Mark Lane in his book, *Plausible Denial*. My hope is that these words will be heard from an array of forums, reach vast audiences, and spark a movement uniting "We the People" to fight back against untamed, corrupted power.

Kent State anti-Vietnam war demonstrators challenged the war machine and the military-industrial complex and four students were shot down and killed by Ohio State National Guard. This time there will be no surrendering to martial law. This time we will come prepared with an army in the millions and make mass citizen arrests on government officials who are guilty of treason. We will not be intimidated by M-16s and military personnel. We will continue to march through the bullets and over the dead and bloody sacrificial lambs that died for a cause greater than themselves. We will reclaim America and set her free from tyrannical war-mongering and world conquests. We will emancipate her from enslavement. Another Ron Kovic quote applies here, from *Born on the Fourth of July*, "Sadly, the war on terror has become a war *of* terror." No more bombs dropped. No more innocent lives lost from war that never makes headline news. They have woken up the sleeping giant. Revolution is brewing and for just cause. We must come together, in this moment of glory before the end, and gel as human beings. A bond that we must rekindle through compassion and selflessness towards one another free from bigotry. We must coexist.

The Coexist bumper sticker really embodies the direction needed for our country. Can't we all just get along and put hate, bigotry, racism, and personal beliefs aside for the greater good of our species? Why must we

be so destructive towards one another? We've been taught to hate which is something we must learn to unlearn.

I ask those who read my words to unite past petty differences in order to carry the flag of truth uphill. The black world has banked on all of us to be dormant for far too long and for us to be the dancing bear that got accustomed to his cage. Remember, the truth usually poses a serious threat to those in power, so truth and fortitude need to be embedded into our brains as a philosophy of life, country, and community. After reading this book, I hope you will become an avid interpreter on how to peel off the candy-coated layer to see the real substance beneath, how to distinguish and decipher fact from fiction, and most importantly to see why and how most of the subjects covered in *Open Your Eyes: To 2012 and Beyond* integrate and come to fruition in 2012.

So, tune yourselves in to the frequency of 2012, be a better person, know and truly believe that all men are created equal because in the end of days all the money and all the materialistic possessions will mean nothing and won't save you. 2012 is right around the corner and with it comes the beginning of Judgment Day. When standing in front of God, the celestial prosecutor, the question will be asked and the answer will claim the fate of your soul. Have you failed or passed the grueling test of faith with life on Earth? Have you lived an unjust, sinful evil life or have you been benevolent and lived a just life? The once-every-25,800-year great galactic alignment will start on December 21, 2012 and with it comes the beginning of judgment on your soul. This will be a rare cosmic alignment, where science and religion emerge as one and the same. Do yourself a favor and repent now to your savior, whoever or whatever it may be, from whatever religion you believe. As a people we have a tendency to ignore all warning signs until something happens, so open your eyes now to see clearly what you and many others didn't see at all before.

Open your eyes, and get contacts if you need them. After all, how could you see something if you weren't looking for it? If you're not looking for something then you're probably not going to see it until it's too late. Remember, the Maya just didn't keep time, they were meticulously obsessed with time, and events in space and the Earth's natural rhythms, understanding them with an astonishing level of accuracy. Doomsday was anchored to their deep understanding of their calendar. Their four prior calendar cycles ended in a catastrophic disaster of Biblical proportions, with the fifth cycle set to end on December 21, 2012. Why would the ending of this next cycle be any different from the past four calendar cycles? Just like the Maya calendar, the Jewish lunisolar calendar, derived from the ancient Hebrew calendar, ascends to its pinnacle in 2012 (5772-5773). This is known by those who believe in the Torah and Jewish calendar as the "beginning of the tribulation period."

The Earth itself is in danger as the sun moves into the galactic center, aligning for the great galactic alignment of 2012. Polar shift will alter life on the surface of the planet as well as in the depths of the oceans, which is where the USOs reside and is why their activity has spiked in recent years. 2012 has stirred the hive. Polar shift will trigger rupturing earthquakes, which will trigger massive tsunamis flooding all coastal cities, which poses a serious problem since more than half the world's population lives within 60 kilometers of the shoreline. The earthquakes triggered by polar shift and the wobbling of the Earth will start an unfathomable chain reaction of volcanic eruptions worldwide emitting millions and millions of tons of sulfur dioxide into the stratosphere. Super volcanoes containing extreme geothermal energy—similar to Yellowstone in Wyoming—will bury most of the United States in feet of sulfuric ash and poisonous debris with the help of the fast moving jet stream. Worldwide water and air sources will become extremely hazardous to drink without purification. The copious amounts of sulfuric ash and volcanic debris spewed out by the volcanoes around the world will be more than enough to block out the sun's rays for months, if not years. The sulfate particles released by super volcanoes worldwide will reflect energy coming from the sun, thereby preventing the sun's rays from heating the Earth. This will throw the Earth and its inhabitants into a "Volcanic Winter" like witnesses in 1816 dubbed "the year without a summer" which manifested from the 1815 Tambora volcano eruption in Indonesia (www.atmos.umd.edu/~owen/CHPI/IMAGES/volceff.html). The grain belt of the Central and Midwest regions will shut down, instantaneously affecting famine and food supply on all seven continents.

Once the engine of life, the sun, is taken out of the equation and darkness binds us, all life forms on Earth's food chain will start to rapidly deteriorate collapsing in a domino effect, one after another. With the sun's energy veiled by an impenetrable layer of ash the Earth's natural synergies will be lost, and the metabolic processes for plant life will come to an abrupt halt. The Earth's temperature will change drastically and the atmosphere will be unfiltered and inhospitable to the point where you'll need a protective suit to not breathe in the poisonous, gaseous air or be exposed to the havocked conditions outside. Without ample plant life the animals of planet Earth will starve. Without animals and plants to consume, a majority of the human species will starve. Famine will take over.

All value will be in food by this point so your money will only assist you if you're using it at this current time to build an underground self-sustaining bunker complex or fallout shelter with a healthy stock of nonperishable foods and water. However, when push comes to shove we will see how primitive and animal-like human beings really are when pushed to the brink of starvation. The famished ones who have not prepared for the end of days will truly understand the meaning of becoming a savage and a barbarian. And because most will not be ready, supplies will in short supply but in extremely high demand. If you think this situation is impossible because we're invincible as humans with carte blanche on planet Earth then you're sorely mistaken and haven't opened your eyes to the greater forces at work in the universe.

We are fragile guests to planet Earth soon to be humbled by her upcoming, once-every-25,800-year temper tantrum. The end of a 25,800 year cycle is upon us which is exactly why we all must open our eyes to not only learn from the past but to prepare for the end of days before the insurmountable problem of 2012 is upon us. The Apocalypse, Armageddon, Judgment Day, Doomsday, cataclysmic disasters on a Biblical scale, the End of Days as we know it. Whatever happens, whether it be a nuclear holocaust, natural calamities from polar shift, biological pandemic, or a comet/asteroid hitting the restart button for life on our planet, like with the dinosaurs, we must unite past our petty differences if we are to survive. "You only find out who is swimming naked when the tide goes out," said Warren Buffet and with less than three years left till the tide goes out on December 21, 2012, there are far too many skinny-dippers who are going to be caught naked and unprepared.

Whether you choose to talk about the topics encapsulated in *Open Your Eyes* is your prerogative, but know this...whether you choose to listen to this warning, you will be talking about it in the near future as December 21, 2012, pushes you, me, and our entire species into a corner. With all the plays that have been quarterbacked out of the doomsday playbook, and everything that has been said in *Open Your Eyes: To 2012 and Beyond*, with all the pieces to the puzzle placed before your eyes, do you really believe this all to be just a coincidence? Or, have you opened your eyes to see the sobering reality, that this could be reality? It's said that everything is connected to everything... the butterfly effect...you drop a pebble into a pond and the ripples radiate outwards touching and affecting everything. 2012 is that pebble.

The end as we know it is near. What we all do from this point forward is all that matters.

one person can make a difference and every person should try.

– John F. Kennedy

ABOUT THE AUTHOR

An avid researcher and crusading advocate for peace, love, hope and—most importantly—truth, Drew R. Maras uses his unique vision and passionate writing style to bring you the world through his eyes. Trained by the United States Marines Corps infantry, Maras has a provocative view of the world revealed in *Open Your Eyes: To 2012 and Beyond.* He is regarded as an original thinker with an uncanny instinct to understand life beyond the headlines. A catalyst for sparking proactive change, the author brings genuine and sincere devotion to the cause of revealing truth in today's world and its future. In his free time he enjoys the good company of family and friends, as well as writing, traveling, and  spending time outdoors with his two dogs, Malibu and Jayden. For more information visit the website at www.openyoureyesto2012andbeyond. com.

CPSIA information can be obtained at www.ICGtesting.com
Printed in the USA
LVOW120330140112

263879LV00002B/16/P